MW00721584

LAUNDERING THE DRAGON

BLACK
RENMINBI

© 2021 John D'Eathe
Publisher: Adagio Media
Website: launderingthedragon.com

John D'Eathe asserts the moral right to be identified as the author of this work.

All rights reserved. This book or any portion thereof may not be reproduced or used in any manner whatsoever without the express written permission of the publisher except for the use of brief quotations in a book review.
Creator: D'Eathe, John, Vancouver, Author.
Publication editor: Kevin McDonald.
Title: Laundering the Dragon. Black Renminbi.

ISBN: 978-1-9994339-1-8
Subjects: Novel. Money laundering. Asian and Canadian crime, politics and commerce.
Cover design: Alexa Love and Jazmin Welch.

LAUNDERING THE DRAGON

BLACK RENMINBI

JOHN D'EATHE

Published by Adagio Media

Meet the Author

John D'Eathe was educated in the United Kingdom in law and urban land economics. After training in the City of London he set off blithely for an adventurous business life in Colonial Hong Kong and Asia. A decade later he returned to England but moved on to Canada, commencing a long career in major property investment and development throughout North America and in various parts of the world. He traveled extensively and witnessed the various cultural subtleties of getting things done. He and his wife Lane live in West Vancouver and enjoy visiting their widely located family and friends.

Main characters

in order of appearance

Detective Sgt. Pritam Singh, RCMP, a Canadian from Mumbai.

Wong Mai Fu, a Vancouver nightclub owner, born to peasant parents in Guangdong Province.

Ron Leyland, a Vancouver businessman from a prominent family.

Maisie Leyland, a businesswoman and activist. Born Wong Mai Xi (*Mai Zi*) in Guangdong. Wong's sister.

Olga Wong, a White Russian from Hong Kong born in Shanghai.

Zhang Man Lok, a businessman and Party member raised in Beijing.

Victor 'Hinks' Hinkenbothem, a British Colonialist solicitor in Hong Kong.

Assistant Commissioner Jack Jackman RCMP, a Canadian who once served in Hong Kong.

Ah-Cy (Arcie) Huang, daughter of the Revolutionary Party hero, the Patriarch Huang.

Dean Dr Poon Ping Kin, an academic from China managing a 'bank' in Macau.

Thomas Quincy Inglewood, 'Tommy Q' and his son, James Quincy Inglewood, Canadian bankers.

'Logger' Leyland, Ron's father, and wealthy chairman of the Leyland group.

Steven 'Stump' Stumpenberg, and **George Oikawa**, Vancouver lawyers.

Leone Lawrence, a lawyer in Barbados.

. . . and **Wanchow**, the guard dog.

Contents

*"Crony capitalists and crony communists
will one day fire up a Dragon."*
                           – Ancient Chinese proverb

Chapter 1

Baffled: A 'Chinese' job?

DETECTIVE Sergeant Singh, unusually in uniform and complete with back-up, had banged on their front door early on that hazy summer morning in 2019.

Without preamble he shouted, "Wong has disappeared. It looks like foul play and you are implicated. What happened?"

Ron and Maisie just stood in shock. After a pause Ron replied, "Calm down, Pritam. We have no idea what you are talking about."

"Ron, I have given you so many chances but this has gone too far. Wong has gone. His wife reported strange circumstances. We need a statement: now!"

When Ron just shook his head, the detective turned appealingly to Maisie for help. "Ms Leyland, Wong is your brother and we need a lead. What is going on?" but she just sighed and shrugged dismissively.

"Very well," he stormed, "Mr Leyland, we will be taking formal statements at Wong's residence tomorrow morning. Until then it is under lockdown. Be there." And at that he left abruptly.

Naturally, as soon as the police had gone Maisie called her sister-in-law Olga, although they were estranged and had barely spoken since she had fallen out with her brother. Maisie had nothing in common with her but expressed her concerns. However, she found her totally blasé about Wong's disappearance, with little to offer as an explanation.

She said without emotion, "I returned from a trip to find the house open and ablaze with light. The first sign something was wrong was no noisy welcome from Wanchow. A quick search revealed both the dog and Mai Fu were not in the house, likely I first thought, just away for their usual brief walk. Then I went into the dining room and was totally spooked to see his favourite Giorgio Armani suit weirdly sitting at the head of the table, stuffed with twenties and with a bundle of hundreds for a head. There was no note but I searched the house and found nothing unusual.

"You know he stored bales of cash in the basement, which always worried me but it had all gone. I found our housekeeper locked in her attic room, too frightened to come out. She said she knew nothing, having hidden herself away out of sight after hearing loud noises down below."

"What did you tell the police?" they asked.

Olga replied, "I decided to call them but to leave things as they were. They arrived very quickly. I just said honestly that I was feeling a bit scared but mystified. They asked about a lot of things including the broken lock on the basement storeroom door but I could only shrug in ignorance."

She cheerfully added, "They took all the cash in the dining room but they assured me it was only for evidence, and there seemed no reason why it would not be returned to me after their investigation. So that's another good thing!"

'MYSTERIOUS disappearance!' glared the headline of Ron's *Vancouver Sun* newspaper the next morning. He had rushed to get it as soon as he heard it thump down on the doorstep and anxiously scanned the report.

"Inside sources tell us that Mr Wong Mai Fu's suit was filled with cash when it was left sitting ominously at his crafted dining room table in his magnificent West Vancouver mansion, yesterday. It is being seen as some form of underworld warning.

"His wife confirms he is nowhere to be found and has not been seen since. It is reported that the prominent nightclub owner has many business interests and is the subject of a continuing police investigation.

"His cell phone was found, all his personal records were undisturbed, and his faithful guard dog Wanchow is also missing. There is a total lack of evidence, and early police reports are that his disappearance is suspicious and likely a professional hit.

"Mr Wong's sister is Ms Maisie Leyland, the well known activist wife of developer Mr Ronald Leyland, who are members of the prominent Vancouver business family."

"Damn it!" he shouted, growling aloud and sending the new maid scurrying out in alarm. Now it was all public and they were in real trouble.

RON arrived at Wong's mansion to find it a hive of police activity. He recognised a local municipal policeman who said, "It appears that Mr Wong is known to the Mounties and they have agreed to take over the investigation. Detective Sergeant Singh is in charge and actually just arrived."

Ron had come to know Pritam Singh well. A very imposing, bearded and turbaned gentleman, he had arrived from India twenty years earlier to be united with an extensive family in Surrey, British Columbia, reportedly bringing good senior police experience. His first set of family documents was fabricated and the second set highly exaggerated.

Ron saw him across the room meeting his allotted team and Pritam acknowledged his presence with a curt, unreassuringly nod.

The Sergeant was very conscious of his strong sub-continental English accent which sometimes made him difficult to understand. This morning he had again put on his uniform and an imposing tall blue turban to impress them and improve his status.

Speaking clearly, he tried to issue them precise instructions on how he wanted the investigation conducted. One sharp-eyed young corporal raised her hand and demanded, "There is a disconcerting rumour circulating that this was 'a Chinese job'. Isn't that racist and anyway too early an assumption?"

"You know the Force is absolutely not racist," he corrected her defensively, "and that rumour did not come from us. We were all immigrants at one time, however long ago. Our duty is to protect our jolly good citizens from any bad fellows who have slipped in."

"So, Chinese, Sarge?" she asked sarcastically.

"My goodness gracious no," he responded indignantly. "Bad guys may well have originated anywhere but that casts no aspersions upon our other people originally from that country. In this case we find it is socially complicated even to mention the word Chinese, so it is best to avoid using it at all."

"You are trying to say that a Canadian is a Canadian," she observed, clarifying pointedly for him.

He hastily responded, "This case does involve some undesirable people from China but rather than say that, which seems to confuse the do-gooders, our Commissioner has instructed we call them Black Renminbians for absolute clarity. That will ensure there can be no suggestion of racism. They call their money Renminbi and the gang we are after are laundering Black Renminbi! Our duty is to ride down those villainous hombres and bring them to justice."

Raising his voice he rallied them with his long-rehearsed rallying cry, "What is our politically acceptable slogan?"

They all shouted in response, "Mounties always get their person!"

He held his head proudly high and asserting his authority barked, "Is that very, very clear?" They all avoided his eyes, mumbled, "Yes, Sergeant", and made a quick exit.

When he was alone, Ron went over to him and asked, trying to smile sardonically, "This sure complicates things, Pritam. So you are not saying it's a Chinese job?"

Pritam however was all business. "Ron, you and Maisie are clearly implicated and there is no way I can protect you anymore. This is your last chance to come clean! Do you or your wife have anything to say about Wong's disappearance?"

Ron replied stiffly, "Absolutely not, Sergeant. We have no idea what has happened to him." Shrugging sadly and raising his hands in defeat he summoned his team. "Corporal," he instructed the young officer with the penetrating eyes, "take Mr Leyland's statement."

SHE seemed purposely to leave him stewing alone for a while and he waited, deep in thought.

Of course Ron was well aware it was a 'Chinese' job although he had no intention of agreeing to that. He knew that the local district's population was thought anyway to be at least twenty percent of Chinese background, by house name registration anyway, most being regular hockey-suffering Canadian folk.

He was acutely aware, being in the real estate business, that more additional owners were recently concealed behind trusts or companies anyway, so who really knew who owned what, or how the ethnic mix worked out; if anyone cared.

Ron had grown up with local people from all over who were just Canadian, getting on with their lives like everyone else. He was part of the new Canadian generation which, starting at school, genuinely all took their diverse friends at face value and shook their heads at any misspeaking Neanderthal elders.

That made his own personal conversational racist lapses so much more annoying to him such as:

"Are you worried about Hong Kong?" ... "Not quite sure where that is."

"Guess you are fond of sake?" ... "We have been here four generations. It wore off."

"Jo sun." ... "Sorry don't understand. My granddad was from the Philippines."

"You Japanese make great sushi." ... "Actually we were from Korea."

"How did you learn to play hockey like that?" ... "Fuck off, idiot. I'm from Moose Jaw."

"MR LEYLAND," she said sharply, interrupting Ron's thoughts, "is this indeed a 'Chinese' job?" She sat down opposite him. "You should know. Your wife is Chinese ethnically and we understand a lot of your company business is conducted with capital from China. We are on to you, you know."

He answered the police officer defensively. "I don't know what you are implying by 'Chinese.' Our immigration business did indeed bring assertive new people and investors here from a wide variety of cultures and beliefs coming from the far side of the Pacific, first Hong Kong and Taiwan, then from China itself. Some invested with us. Our family lumber business and my own real estate division have prospered enormously through connections with Asia but not from Mr Wong. We broke off business connections with him many years ago and my wife severed any personal relationship. We have no idea where he is."

"Is?" she questioned him sharply. "And why are you so defensive about the word Chinese anyway?"

He just shrugged. "My wife is of Chinese descent but as you probably know is actively involved with the protection of human rights. She is very critical of the Communist Party fellows running the mainland of China, because they are now the racists. Internationally they apply their aggressive rule that anyone with the right skin colour and defining epicanthic eye folds is forever only a citizen of their motherland. If you are in their territory and thus in their clutches forget any other paperwork: you are obviously Chinese!

"Here at Leyland we work with people of all races living peacefully together in Canada by choice. They prefer the personal freedom and assurance of our actual private enterprise democracy. So I have no idea what you mean by a 'Chinese' job."

The Corporal had listened impatiently to his rambling avoidance of the direct subject and knew that was the best she was going to get.

"OK, I take your point that communism is the problem in China and has nothing to do with Canadians of Chinese background. But would you agree that some immigrants may have come from anywhere with criminal intent and these have not proved to be exemplary citizens? We think Wong is one of those!"

"Poor Wong," he muttered rising to go; at least giving her that satisfaction.

THE report of Wong Mai Fu's disappearance had immediately reached the self assured senior government officials in their luxurious apartment office in guarded Chaoyang in downtown Beijing.
Zhang Man Lok, chairman of *The Six*, commented unfeelingly, "It is good news. Wong had become a problem to our move on Canada."
They all agreed, of course.

Chapter 2

Ron: Oriental adventure

RON and Maisie decided that the best thing to do was to carry on as normal. Normal to Ron meant developing and selling condos so it was back to the real estate office to try to sort out the latest tangle Wong's disappearance had landed them in.

There was still a lot to explain, so he sat moodily staring into his coffee and wondering how his beloved family, like Canada, had been so easily seduced by unethical foreign money and why they had become involved with the wrong people?

It had all started strangely with Leaky Condos in Vancouver! Not long out of college in the 1980s Ron had taken over Leyland's small real estate division.

Short-cutting developers, plus sleepy officials, had plunged the city into a Leaky Condo crisis by building dozens of beautiful Californian-style buildings, all presold at excessive prices, many to the new overseas Asian investor market.

It never stopped raining in Vancouver so they leaked like sieves, filled up with water and prevented occupation. The Canadian developers built and sold them legally through one-off companies and sensibly were long gone.

Ron, as the sale agent in Vancouver was served official notice by the

City to repair a defective, empty structure he was managing because the authorities could not find anyone who appeared to own it. All Ron knew was their lawyer in far away Hong Kong was a person called Hinkenbothem.

On request, the lawyer did send Ron an outdated register of ownership names. "I'm afraid, old chap, you will find this unhelpful. My clients keep this offshore registry for constantly flipping the condos off the record, tax free of course. It is not much help because it is all in indecipherable Chinese. Their problem seems to be that your incessant rain has washed away all the value, making my clients frantic, because they also lent funds to the buyers."

Ron advised Hinkenbothem, "Send me enough money and I will throw a plastic cover over the entire building, mop up the puddles, patch up the interior and re-clad the exterior sufficient at least to get an occupancy permit. Then I will progressively unload the units on unsuspecting local Canadian buyers. All for a big fee, naturally!"

Hinkenbothem came through with the cash and Ron dealt efficiently with the Leaky Condo problem. Ron received a fat payment and the now-friendly Hong Kong lawyer assured him, "I am passing on the thanks of my investor client Mr Zhang Man Lok and his communist buddies, from the mainland. They only invested privately in Vancouver because your government inadvertently ignored collecting capital gains taxes on foreigners' profit from condo flips. But it all went wrong anyway and they have learned their lesson."

He was to be proved very wrong!

RON kept in touch with Hinkenbothem but the next time he became involved with the Orient was when he went to the British Crown Colony several years later to cash in on the political changes which were seeing hundreds of thousands of worried Cantonese people move their skills and savings to Canada, mainly to Vancouver, ahead of the imminent take over by China.

He was looking into setting up an immigration agency in Canada to facilitate even more Hong Kong people, but particularly to attract wealthy clients through the Investor Immigration Program, skimming the maximum fees but also supplementing his real estate brokerage business.

The urgent, richer immigrants were able to use their wealth to jump the queue and avoid answering too many inconvenient questions.

He had gone to Hong Kong at the invitation of his now-chatty friend Victor Hinkenbothem, who was proposing a partnership with a local agency owner called Wong Mai Fu, who would apparently produce the Hong Kong immigrants.

"How does he find and vet the immigrants?" asked the still-naive Ronnie.

"Who cares?" replied Hinkenbothem in his polished English accent. "He finds the bodies and you manage your Vancouver agency to settle them in over there. You can pay for anything in Asia, so you tell me what you want and it will be provided. Never forget dear boy, '*Ning Po more far*'."

Hinkenbothem was at least smooth, even if he sometimes talked in Asian riddles, and they did an excellent vodka martini in his posh Hong Kong Club but Ronnie was already deciding this all sounded too dicey for him.

"Call me Hinks," had started an enlightening evening explaining how the deal might work. "I still represent Mr Zhang and his commie fellas from the mainland who hired this Wong man, a crude nightclub manager, with whom we are rather stuck."

"Wong is a real wanker," he insisted to Ron's puzzlement. "But this immigration stuff is just the beginning of business possibilities. Until recently China was still hiding behind their borders working political things out, and here in Hong Kong we were just an isolated last British colony. Then suddenly mainland guys with money started turning up at my office looking for personal overseas investments. Later, you will tell everyone you were one of the first to invest their converted Renminbi in Vancouver! Heaven knows how they make it but when

China really gets going you will be swamped by their cash."

Ron looked puzzled. "What's Renminbi?" he asked. Hinkenbothem shook his head, wondering where to start.

"We previously funded your Leaky Condos through Hong Kong dollars. The Chinese currency is generally called Renminbi, meaning 'The People's Money' but is not used internationally, only within China. Even China's trade with other countries is not yet settled in their own currency. But one day, watch out! More important in the long run the experience showed them that Canada is legally wide open and my clients have chosen it for their excess Renminbi."

He spilled what was left of his drink laughing uproariously at his own joke.

Then he appalled his correct Canadian guest by bellowing "Boy!" to summon refills from the barman, a wrinkled but apparently revered ancient Club retainer.

Dominant status still needed to be demonstrated in the waning empire in the customary imperialist and patronising manner. It apparently made Hinks feel superior. Behind his back, however, he was called a Gweilo, in Cantonese a ghostly man, with dismissive sighs and befitting sniggers.

WONG Wai Fu had been a different question. Ron only went to meet him out of respect to Hinks' request and was already booked on a flight back to Canada.

He had found the colonials tended to call their Chinese colleagues by their given name initials, because they could not bother to remember their actual names.

"You can call me WF but Wong will do. People just call me Wong," smirked his new prospective partner, baring his stained teeth in what he considered a smile.

"My English is OK and you are OK, Lonnie. We will go to get Chinese immigrants," he said.

"Not Lonnie, Ronnie," corrected Ronnie patiently as they walked towards Wong's small office on Des Voeux Road at the edge of Central. "Ronnie; like Ronald Reagan."

"Ah. Lonald Leagan." he was assured.

IT BECAME a Leyland family legend that it was there, 25 years previously, in Wong's nondescript office that their eyes met in that first wondrous glance.

Those eyes: sparkling with intelligence, deep lurking sardonic humour and seduction, set in her beautiful, high-cheeked face, all framed by lustrous black hair. When she rose to greet him, his own eyes impulsively ran down her shapely, long-legged body.

Ron never really knew if alluring Mai Xi was in on the original deal to recruit him. "Want to see Macau?" she asked innocently.

She had later made the first move in an admittedly secluded booth but very public Macau restaurant, guardedly baring her perky firm breasts to him, while moving her searching hand lower and moaning into his startled ear that she had always wanted to try a Gweilo.

Ronnie was actively rising to the occasion when their tall, obsequious and tuxedoed Shanghainese waiter had chosen the moment to arrive and with a flourish to serve the Lobster Thermidor.

The unexpected revelations in the booth had so startled the server that in his excitement he attracted the attention of the entire dining room by spilling broiled lobster over Mai Xi's now fully exposed bosom.

The event somewhat ruined their moment but delayed Ron's departure, launching them on a wild lifetime of intrigue together.

Chapter 3

Zhang: Raising zealots

WONG'S present day disappearance had caused a bulging file labelled 'Wong, Mai Fu', to be redelivered to the desk of RCMP Assistant Commissioner Jack Jackman in Ottawa. He did not open it immediately but leaned back and closed his eyes in recollection.

The teeming, exotic Hong Kong streets and timeless junk-filled harbour of his youthful posting swirled into his senses bringing a happy smile, until memories of Wong and thoughts of the criminal Zhang forced a frown.

"Black Renminbian bastards!" he muttered to himself, sighing as he reached for the file. "Call Singh," he bellowed to his inspector assistant. "We need to know more about that bugger Zhang."

THE well-known Chinese prayer, *'Preserve us from interesting times'*, never applied to Zhang Man Lok, whose upbringing in China under the imposed communist system had been very different from the peasant Wong's.

Zhang was born in Beijing in 1945 just before the occupying Japanese surrender, to a previously well-established family who were essentially architects over the years but reduced to abject poverty by the invasion.

Then came years of struggle, within the ultra-corrupt Kuomintang regime, until later that decade The Red Army emerged victorious, bringing a new form of oppression.

His father's practice had been dormant during the privation of the world war and invasion, then during the civil war, which brought added years of suffering upon the country. The final Red Army victory was the end for the Zhang family who were clearly bourgeoisie and property owners, although now struggling like everyone.

After the Japanese were finally defeated with the help of the Allied forces and were driven from the country his father had made a determined attempt to reopen his practice, refitting some of their almost derelict properties. This obviously involved the Kuomintang who were in power for a few years, requiring bribery as necessary to get reinstated.

When their local area was occupied forcefully by the Communists and reorganised under a Peoples' Committee, he was seen as a Kuomintang lackey, summoned before them, denounced as a property-owning enemy of the people and summarily executed.

Their house was seized, his wife being lucky just to be evicted with her own life and her children, although she was abused badly in the process.

One of little Man Lok's first memories was of days hiding in a basement with his mother and sisters feeling hungry and hearing explosions and commotion far outside. "Can you hear the guns?" whispered one of his older sisters. "They are shooting people."

Then he remembered the shock of doors banging open and all of them being thrown into the street with his kicking mother being dragged away by some laughing soldiers.

It was of course a time of complete confusion in his young mind and he next remembered living in a poor tenement with his mother and sisters, fatherless and in reduced slum circumstances. The brood cuddled together at night on a hard bamboo bed separated from their mother only by a thin screen.

From time to time she brought back a *zan zhu*, uncle, from her increasing evening visits to the bars. and the hushed older girls held their breath, nodding knowingly in time with the creaking; suppressing their mirth.

He asked them, "What is happening?" but it was years before one of them explained to him the mysterious adult ritual which was being performed. The repeated experience left little Zhang puzzled and with a lifelong quick anxious reflex in the process.

WHEN he was older, his mother took him aside one day and talked earnestly to him. "The only thing I can give you and your sisters is a good education and you must enrol and attend. The Communist Party recognises sensibly it must indoctrinate your generation but in the process you will get an education. You have to go to school and work hard."

She herself worked day and sometimes night to provide them with the time to study and the young Man Lok took advantage and did very well. His juvenile memories were of missing his constantly absent working *ma ma*; a fear of his shadowy dead *ba ba*; exclusion by his secretive, giggling and mutually clinging *jie jie*; and loneliness. Always he remembered deep loneliness.

AS HE grew, they all took on any work available to support the family. It was not until he was older he realised the sacrifice his pretty young mother had paid but now understanding from his lessons at school it had all been necessary for the common good, brought by the glorious communist revolution.

While China still laboured with about ten main language groups complicated by dialect sub-sets, long ago the Beijing dialect had been adopted in its Mandarin form as the national language, so he was fortunate from the start.

He became a proud little member of the local communist Young Pioneers, particularly excelled at his lessons, qualifying himself for admittance into the revered Peking University, which was still in operation despite all the purges they had learned never to question.

His formal university degree was in business administration, which he found also to be mainly political. He still excelled academically, acting politically correctly to suck up to the right professors who invited him into the Masters program.

IT WAS there he came to the attention of the gentle Huang Ah-Cy.

She was very conscious she was from the famous Huang family. For that reason she understood why her fellow students avoided her, knowing her father was a hero of the revolution, continuing as a senior power in the new order.

She recognised the ruling-class infighting was still deadly in the struggle for personal power, dictating that it was best for people not to become friendly or seen to align with the players.

They all reluctantly wore similar dark clothing as was the political proletarian requirement and she accepted that she was actually quite plain and muscular, and the severe customary haircut did not help.

She knew what attraction she had came from her poise and self-confidence, derived from her privileged upbringing but also from her bubbling sense of humour. Her striking feature, however, was her wide smile, emphasised by her startling white and even teeth, another clear giveaway of early medical privilege.

Even so, she expected to be avoided and sought no friends.

Zhang Man Lok was thrown into her life without choice, instructed to study politically selected Chinese philosophy. "Hello," he said to her in the library, tentatively, "like to look up some old proverbs?" He was startled by her wide smile of agreement and knew immediately he was on to a good thing.

They were soon debating ancient myths, leading to them laughing together at the improbable proverbs.

She was outspoken, due to her status, and surprised him with her open opinions. "We are a generation of children being brought up in ethical chaos, so can we look to the ancient world of philosophy, for guidance?"

He had learned not to express personal opinions but she continued, "Ancient Greek and Roman theories are now of little value, nor the Western world's long reliance on the obviously ridiculous and impossible Judeo/Christian and Muslim religions which are fading fast in their decadent materialist societies anyway."

She lectured to a surprisingly attentive Zhang, "Our civilisation has reached a critical point where the theoretical basic honesty, integrity and respect for others taught through the ancient Analects of Confucius as a basis of relationships, is proving impracticable. This is giving way to necessary enlightened central control and enforcement. This is all for the common good."

Ah-Cy chuckled, "Confucius said, '*When the wind blows the grass bends*'. That does not bode well for our professors!"

It was a new experience for her and when he moved close to her in a corner of the library and actually took her hand, she was overjoyed.

Holding hands, they vowed devotion together to Marxist-Leninism which obviously offered the solution, empowering their generation of students as its chosen instruments of adoption. He assured her, "I absolutely support women's equal status and increased responsibility," when he found it was one of her passions

It was this sense of political duty and his close attention to her, which induced her to select him for her first ever sexual experience. Her strong build suited his aggressive, non-romantic approach and she climaxed quickly and vocally, bursting triumphantly into the chorus of a popular revolutionary marching song in exaltation.

It developed into a brief but vigorous daily physical ritual, now always accompanied by her quick tempo, patriotic vocals.

They showed their political support by joining the students' committee which debated university issues. When they were elevated to the Masters programmes as seniors, the committee members tactically appointed Ah-Cy its chair with Zhang, her known boyfriend, as general secretary, but were also assuming generous political funding would follow; which she arranged.

In this way she cheerfully found herself in the thick of the Cultural Revolution.

Within months they were all delighted to be designated as Red Guards and before they knew it, the university students' committee wielded incredible power.

Ah-Cy told the committee, "We must believe totally in our political system and we have to ensure it is not challenged. Nor, should any other confusing method of government be taught. We have to ensure that any professor silly enough to break those rules disappears from the teaching scene."

She saw no need for a rule of law or independent courts, just a denunciation by someone in the establishment which correctly meant an assumption of guilt, from which there was no appeal. "Get things done!" she enthused.

Chair Ah-Cy and Secretary Zhang were overwhelmed by the sudden respect they were shown especially by the faculty that literally feared for their lives. They grew to enjoy their powerful mutual notoriety and she decided to consolidate their position.

"Like to move in with me?" she asked.

ZHANG was jubilant, of course, that cozying up to the vulnerable and lonely, if rather solid and unattractive, Ah-Cy Huang had paid off so well.

As general secretary of the students' committee, he also could not believe his financial good luck. He was solely responsible for establishing the budgets and paying bills!

With respect to political matters funding seemed totally open handed, so he padded or invented absolutely unchecked claims. Over a period this established a sum of personal money he carefully spread around a number of accounts, which he did not reveal to Ah-Cy.

His first ever opportunity to invest then presented itself.

In common with the majority of men in China, now being joined by a growing percentage of women, he smoked heavily but the quality of tobacco and cigarettes in China had fallen abysmally with communist rule.

One of his commerce graduate colleagues, whom he sort of trusted, approached him quietly one day. "I have an opportunity for us to go into business on our own, importing Western cigarettes through Hong Kong."

Of course this was totally illegal but he was assured, "This is a foolproof smuggling trail which has never failed. It offers at least a four times capital gain per trip, if you have some cash to invest."

He researched that before communist rule, the international tobacco companies enjoyed China as one of their largest markets but they had been evicted by the new government. He was assured they would do anything to get their product back in, giving his entrepreneurial pal the opportunity to provide one such service.

Subject to checking it out personally, Zhang said he had the capital available, so the adventurous couple set out on a private trip ostensibly to gamble in Macau, but actually to survey the smuggling set-up.

It was his first-experience of long-distance travel in China which took them several weeks to complete by train, road and boat.

They slipped illegally by water into the British Hong Kong harbour, seething with thousands of junks unloading from the anchored or docked mercantile vessels. Then from a separate craft they observed their own smuggling process underway.

Later, up the delta, the bales of cigarettes would be loaded onto a daai fei power boat for the night run up the river but for now Zhang had the exciting participatory process of paying off the junk operators for their part in the job, handing over a bulging plastic bag himself to the tough-looking kid who had paddled himself alongside.

The grinning young brigand tried to explain in local Cantonese, "I have the junk's chop available to stamp a receipt." He held out his hand eagerly for the bag of Black Renminbi, which they understood and he departed over the side.

Zhang's connection with the Guangdong Triad was made and he got his first taste for the compliant women they always had available and whom they had thoughtfully provided.

"*'The mountains are high and the Emperor and Empress are far away',*" he reasoned, to his smuggler pal, laughing at their audacity.

HIS acceptance into the Huang family by her father had been much easier than Ah-Cy expected, as her parents were so totally absorbed in political intrigues that they had no time available for her problems. She had grown up living her own life. Communism produced independents she reasoned!

Times were uncertain and they did not marry immediately, although inevitably as a result of their regular action, she had produced their own daughter. Then her father in a rare display of interest suggested, "You should get on with a second try for a boy, because my national policy group has recommended a one-baby policy for the country."

Ah-Cy was an intelligent woman and understood the nature of their relationship but after discussing it with her father, married Zhang, tactically assuming they might produce a boy well before the one-baby restriction came into effect.

Her father and mother had approved by attending their marriage ceremony but as was the general practice Ah-Cy retained the Huang name herself but also for her children.

She was found a cushy job in the Publicity Department which they all laughingly, but very privately, dubbed propaganda because it was so obviously doctrinaire. She debated with Zhang whether he should work directly in political administration or the military, or go into the expanding nationally owned company world?

She told him, "Commerce will be safer. My lifetime experience is that the state and regional ruling groups are tightly controlled by remarkably few, aggressive families. The higher you get, the more acute the danger. I have witnessed periodic changes at the top involving purges when my powerful friends have been denounced, disappearing overnight. Who needs that?"

Zhang shrugged. "I am concerned about commerce. It is totally disorganised with the state now running almost all industrial production badly."

She retorted, "They indeed run everything and totally unprofitably. Do you want to be in with those losers?" He shot back, grinning, "You are supposed to be in public relations!"

She knew personally about turncoat but sensible capitalists and company owners living at their level who had skipped the country, many to Hong Kong or Taipei, but had seen those who optimistically hung on just disappear, together with senior managers, professionals and really anyone who was successful.

That was all very well now their communist policy was totally in control except that they had eliminated all their managers, which Zhang saw as proving a real nuisance.

However, with her reluctant support he had finally decided upon going into commerce, and landed a senior management job in a struggling state corporation, through her father's 'recommendation', reminding her that, *'The fish you catch does not swim in clear waters'*.

Chapter 4

Wong: Ancient smugglers

THE peasant Wongs had produced Maisie's older brother Mai Fu in rural Guangdong, which the colonialists still called Canton, in the early 1960s. They spoke local, colloquial Cantonese, a dialect scarcely understood outside their province.

It would ordinarily have been a time for rejoicing but frankly those decades had not been happy times. The family were badly undernourished, living mainly off the small lot they had luckily retained. There was little food to welcome a new mouth to feed; even male.

Before, their families had lived quietly for centuries in their convivial village, all working hard but always employed by local landowners.

Then strange armies marched through from the new Communist form of government which had been announced, far away. Nothing happened for a while except that some uppity, pseudo intellectuals, school teachers or the like, started lecturing them about the strange policies, but before they knew it the military had arrived and all hell had broken lose.

Their farmer employers and landowners disappeared or were just trucked away never to be seen again. Then the reorganisation began. Now owned by the state the land was allocated to the previous workers, expecting them to cooperate as friendly patriots.

Of course that did not work so they attempted something else.

The whole countryside was then rearranged into extensive socialist collectives where larger-scale production was ordered and farmers were intended to be compensated, according to land allocation and labour provided.

When this was not functioning either, they had been devastated by the Great Leap Forward, another idea which ideally forced the farmers off the land into mass dormitories, fed them communally and moved labour where needed. Unwieldy, overambitious and impractical, plus bedevilled by poor weather, the system had collapsed leading to extensive famine causing tens of millions of deaths.

This was the unpropitious time that little Wong came into the world. However, his family were lucky ones whose collective still allowed them to retain a small self- production food lot.

The reason his parents had kept their piece of land to till was the mountainous region surrounding the Pearl River Delta. Tiny flat green plateaux of farmland were evident where every scrap of useful land had been farmed for centuries but now proved difficult for the collective to manage. The large-scale projects worked best on the flat extensive arable lands.

Little Mai Fu's early memories were all of being in their little paddy field already labouring with his folks in the water to plant rice.

Their modest lot was high enough for him to see the flow of the Pearl River, a day's walk away, and this was where his father made the deal. He was by then a strong peasant boy not yet into his teens when they told him they had arranged the ancient practice of selling him on contract to a junk owner as a deckhand. He cried and begged for days but they did not relent.

The decision had not been made without serious family debate but his father, also emotional, insisted it was in everyone's interest to conserve food, while also getting him out of the starving predicament they were all in.

He always recalled trying to appear brave but his father finally counted the money as his sobbing mother bid him farewell on the jetty. He fearfully clonked up the gang plank in his working clogs, onto the junk and into a new life.

THE Pearl River Delta had hardly changed in a thousand years. This particularly applied to the junks and fishing vessels which had never adapted to the finer sailing abilities clearly demonstrated by the Western craft when they had essentially taken over those main sea lanes centuries before. Now they had thumping diesel engines but resorted to the age-old sail for economy when the wind was cooperative.

China had closed itself off from the rest of the world. Chinese gunboats prevented access by foreigners and tried to control the illegal movement of people and goods.

This did not deter the traditional nefarious activities in the waterways where boats were for hire to the highest bidder, to transport any freight around the delta or beyond. That had always included their staple business, running opium and morphine, but heroin was taking over the market.

His rough junk-mates all spoke Hakka which he had to learn and called him Wong. Trying to be grown-up he joined the common practice of smoking tobacco all day long.

This escalated when a boat-mate ordered, "Dip the end of your cigarette into the heroin powder." The older fellows who Chased the Dragon to achieve a really good kick inhaled from the top of the bags they used to transport heroin, laughed uproariously when he tried, falling coughing and semiconscious to his knees.

Just now, he helped in smuggling people into Hong Kong or Macau at the mouth of the delta. Then they took contraband such as cigarettes back, always avoiding the rare Customs and Immigration or naval vessels, although the cat-and mouse game was more a sport in an attempt to avoid paying their bribes for passage.

Only on one occasion in the next few years were they were caught, and then taken back to a Chinese dock to wait out the tiresome process of paying off the local Customs adjudicator, while their wretched human cargo languished in jail.

The extensive delta provided thousands of waterways with hidden inlets teaming with water-based activity. One of his first moments of great excitement giving exposure to the modern world was the arrival alongside of a daai fei, one of the notorious high powered 'big flyer' smuggling boats manned by brigands even by their own low standards.

These were China-based, armour-protected, with the ability to way outrun any vessel in the delta. They had the advantage that the British authorities were reluctant to open fire on Chinese vessels, so far giving them a free run using the much smaller junks for warehousing, deliveries and as their warning system.

Wong, in his mid teens, saw them all as heroes and adventurers and dreamed of eventually joining them.

OTHERWISE, he grew up cruising the open sea, ferrying hundreds of hungry refugees, but particularly enjoyed life when they docked in Hong Kong at the large and teeming Aberdeen Harbour, with its gaudy floating restaurants and acres of moored junks, sampans and seagoing vessels, all active in a blaze of colour and noise, enhanced by pungent smells. Everything went into the harbour.

This is where, in his late teens, he was ordered ashore. He was handed over to a stranger who brusquely informed him, "You have been traded for a job on shore helping to manage our fleet of sampan girls." He found he belonged to the Triad.

These traditionally nasty businessmen were being squeezed out of the unforgiving China where the new regime believed only they may rule. They were totally serious and killed any Triad members they could get their hands on.

While the Kuomintang had willingly accommodated the Triads into their corrupt management they were now being hounded out of China, with Macau and Hong Kong their obvious new locations.

Highly popular and fully utilised, sampan girl fleets existed in all the Hong Kong harbours and pockets of moorings, as in the Chinese coastal towns, patronised mainly by the local Cantonese men but also by the occasionally intrepid tourist or furtive local Gweilo.

The 20-foot boats, which also served as family homes, were cleaned out and lined with fresh bamboo carpeting for their use by the young women who were employed to offer full sexual services. Almost enough privacy was provided by roll-down bamboo covers over the curved boat frames, but it was accompanied by gently lapping waves and jarring Cantonese radio music.

The enthusiastic young Wong called his girls together for instructions, now back in Cantonese.

"We have to encourage repeat business so I want you to get to know your customers for recall. I will supply wet towels and tea with small snacks for the end of the action which must always be physical and pleasant. I have decided to agree a fixed fee per client with you and you can keep anything extra so it will pay you to work hard."

All that was required of the exploited but well-treated women was that they performed well. He was personally inundated with offers of a try-out from the hundreds of readily available refugee woman streaming off the daily junk deliveries.

With such quick learning competition to his business, he decided to charge reasonably, offering a high-quality experience which catered to all types of demand. The Triad provided the boats, security and covered basic costs, and he became a valued employee.

Repeat performance became his mantra and behind his back his nickname, but this quickly proved good for business with his boats clearly out-earning competitors. The young fun women sniggered that the slogan also applied to him personally, considering the multiple times they each had to satisfy his managerial freebies whenever one of them had a brief pause in customers.

Chapter 5

Communism: Finding its way

BACK ON the mainland, Zhang had remained employed for only a few years after leaving the university. He had made a major change in 1972 following a rare dinner with Ah-Cy's still famous father, the Hero Huang.

They needed his support and had decided they would make their pitch honestly. Zhang risked saying, "I have to admit my concern at the incompetence I am experiencing within Chinese commerce. As a business graduate I consider it my duty to do something about it. I just don't know how to go about it. If we can turn things around I do recognise this as an enormous personal opportunity but only if we can improve the economy."

In a low voice, but in a startling indication that Zhang had been accepted into the family, father Huang advised, "Nothing will change while our first revered leader is alive. You will have to wait for change in the next administration, absolutely not this one. I know a group who were working very quietly on business reform plans so you should return to the university as a professor in commerce. I can arrange that and link you up with the right people for the future but you will have to keep your head down for a while."

THUS Zhang found himself back in the academic world.

As the old despot grew weaker Zhang saw the political manoeu-vring around him became viciously deadly. He and five companions in his university planning group had been assembled as professors by anonymous but obviously very influential people who were acting very cautiously. His father-in-law arranged to instruct them through indirect sources but regretted they would disavow any knowledge of them or their programme if necessary. Zhang knew he was being used but what choice did he have?

He told Ah-Cy, "Our first highly dangerous study will be to try to establish the depth of the problem in a controlled state where propaganda praises state industry as being highly successful and allows no criticism of current political policies. We will need your help."

Ah-Cy had risen to an influential officer rank in state public relations attending the enormous headquarters building daily. She had access to extensive public records, but she shook her head.

"Do you think I'm crazy? I am entirely sympathetic to your cause but my bureau is riddled with informers. Sorry, it would be suicide."

Now she had her son, he was acutely aware the intimate encounters he initiated were rare and no longer accompanied by bursts of triumphant song. He was of course seeking solace with other women elsewhere; perfectly reasonably, he thought.

He now understood the absolute desolation and real danger of the political life he had chosen for success. For a while at the beginning, with Ah-Cy, he had found a kindred spirit and thought he could defeat his incessant loneliness. But they had drifted apart and again he was always alone.

AT THE end of their first academic year – now under the code name of *The Six* – Zhang reported to their hidden mentors on behalf of his colleagues. "We are convinced China must get out into the world and be far less introspective. It is necessary to adopt those parts of capitalism that are required as necessary for Chinese communism to beat them at their own game. First, we must modernise industry and commerce; put decision power back in the companies where it belonged. We must send students overseas to learn from the capitalists. Interaction with the despicable capitalist world is unavoidable."

The second year they worked upon an extremely ambitious internal capital expansion plan. This time he reported, "We must build needed communications, factories, facilities, roads and railways. We have completed that draft plan." By the third, he was planning ambitious expansion throughout the world.

With time on his hands, Zhang's conviction that economic expansion depended upon better contact with the outside world, had led him to start learning English. Ah-Cy surprised him by joining.

"Good morning how are you today," Zhang greeted her in strained English. She replied, "I am fine thank you. How are you?" accompanied by her signature giggle he rather regretted he was hearing infrequently now.

They worked totally different schedules and lived in their own sections of the ageing residence the university provided. However, they kept their language interests very private.

The Six knew their proposals went against the most basic communist principles but they convinced themselves they were in practice not abandoning Marxism and Maoism as their basis but just adding a supporting rudimentary form of capitalism. Their exposure still simply meant execution.

The waiting was stressful but finally in 1976 Huang informed him authentically that the grand old fellow had died, and they gathered quietly to celebrate the future. There was still a lot of dangerous negotiation going on but Ah-Cy's father appeared to remain in the power group.

Even then, Zhang had a couple of frustrating years before their new leader finally consolidated his power. They then found themselves as one of the revered economic advisers to the new regime, still proudly going by their nickname, The Six.

They contributed especially to the ambitious 10-year economic plan adopted by the next national congress, imposing a high rate of growth in both industry and agriculture, extensively using foreign technology and promoting enormous capital expansion.

It was the start of the new, modern China. It was the emergence of Renminbi.

NOW into his thirties Zhang unexpectedly was in a more powerful position and able to express his opinion at family gatherings. He stated pompously, "This is a critical turning point in China's economic expansion from which we will realise our capability to eventually control the world. This time, the Chinese expansion program is working and I helped achieve it. Look at it now: gaining momentum at almost ten percent annually."

Ah-Cy suggested dryly, with her disparaging laugh, "Well, you sure have surprised yourselves and the world by stumbling upon the right choices!"

The Six were specifically instructed to assist in the reform or merger of the hundreds of thousands of state owned corporations. They took away direct political control in order to put some actual management back into the decision process; theirs.

Disguised as a need for more skilled business leadership, they insinuated themselves onto the boards of leading corporations, taking control of top board positions with enormous financial leverage which they milked to considerable personal advantage.

Zhang had always been the informal leader of The Six and he took on management of their growing hidden assets, pooled for mutual security and support.

But, *"Every step leaves a footprint,"* he warned his partners.

Chapter 6

Wanchai: Oldest profession

WONG had turned 21 and was a tall, skinny lad. He was still running his girls in Aberdeen Harbour when he was told to put on clean clothes to report at the Sea Palace, the largest of the gaudy floating restaurants.

There, at a corner table, looking out over the crowded harbour, he was politely offered tea by a senior local Triad member. "We are very pleased with your performance for us here and you did well with the sampan girl business. It is time for you to move on and we are sending you to manage a small hotel property in Wanchai. Have you been there?" Wong just shook his head.

"Wanchai is the busy Hong Kong bar district, and the hotel is owned by one of our Mainland contacts. I will give you the address. Report there in the morning."

Back on shore, at daily cash collection time, he called his favourite half a dozen best performing girls to meet on the largest boat for an announcement.

"This would be the last time you have to entertain me as your boss, because I am leaving tonight. I will give you each a goodbye bonus but first we will have a romp together so you can earn it."

They needed no further incentive, throwing off their skimpy shifts to leap into action, severely rocking the sampan to disturb the already noisy dockside with shrieks of laughter, as they attempted to outdo each other for that extra bonus.

They knew there would happily be no repeat performance. An exhausted Wong dragged himself back to his lodging to pack his few belongings for the new adventure.

THE next day he was greeted in the bar of the ageing hotel in bustling, noisy Wanchai, by a bent old barman called Au who said in Cantonese, "You were expected. Have a drink first and then I will show you your quarters. Sometime today you will meet our lawyer Hinkenbothem to be briefed."

Helpfully, Au produced a business card with the colonial gentleman's name reproduced in Chinese on the back.

They had a good laugh about the strange Gweilo names and Wong admitted, "I only really speak Cantonese or Hakka but I have picked up a little English at Aberdeen."

"Don't worry," Au told him "I will act as translator," which became his principal function in the coming years.

The strange man Hinkenbothem arrived in the afternoon.

After helping himself to a couple of brandies at the bar, he turned to Wong, speaking English, "Here is a management contract both in English and in Chinese for your signature, tying you to a three-year contract to run the hotel."

Wong had never seen anything like it and not quite knowing what had been said to him looked quizzically at Au.

"Doesn't he understand? How can he run the hotel?" demanded the exasperated lawyer. Au asked him to be patient and explained carefully to Wong that it was generous, allowing that he would receive a small percentage of earnings if the hotel did well. Accommodation with food was provided. Wong got the message he had absolutely landed on his feet.

Another shot of brandy seemed to pacify the haughty Englishman so he continued, "The owner is a chappie from China but has given business control to a new financial guru in Macau called Dr Poon, who will contact you. They decide whom they wish to hire, I'm just their solicitor."

One thing worrying Wong, which he asked Au to clarify with the lawyer, "Are the owners the Triad?"

Hinkenbothem laughed. "Assuredly absolutely they are not, dear fellow. They are businessmen from China who bought the building for redevelopment in the future as Hong Kong grows. But they obviously knew someone in the Triad otherwise you would not have been released, so you should probably behave yourself." Au translated.

"And learn English fast!" the lawyer added.

WONG was developing into a sharp businessman. He had already looked around the bar and decided he should stock it with his skilled girls from Aberdeen. With the news that the Triad were still influential, raiding Aberdeen was obviously out of the question but he thought cheerfully they must all have sisters and friends.

His 'quarters' turned out to be a haphazard collection of rooftop rooms, to him a palace, providing the luxury of a personal telephone for the first time in his life. He settled in happily learning how to succeed in an urban environment, reporting by his telephone to his new masters in Macau.

He found it strange to be dealing with the very odd Gweilos, evidently controlling everything in the city and who now formed a fair proportion of his customers.

The young Wong entered into the management of his busy hotel property with enthusiasm way beyond his education level but with confident belief in his ability He had been thrust into an unknown colonial Hong Kong, because up to that point his life had been totally Chinese.

He knew of course the Communists had taken over China but his world in Aberdeen Harbour had been controlled totally by local strongmen, dangerous Triads. Now, not only did he have the strange English language with which to contend but there were lawyers, accountants, a Governor, apparent personal freedoms, even independent courts of which he had never heard.

More immediately, he had to contend with the bar, the girls, renting rooms, all attracting a mixed bag of local Chinese fellows, American sailors, expatriate business or servicemen from the United Kingdom; people from around the unknown world out there.

All of this was a new, exciting experience. He had helpful Au in constant tow for advice or translation, but had yet to meet his immediate boss, the formidable sounding Dean Dr Poon Ping Kin from Macau.

Chapter 7

Banks: Modern smugglers

THE suave Dr Poon had started his career teaching finance a few years before in 1982 up the coast from Hong Kong at Huaqiao University, as the young head of the Commerce Department.

Then, he had the ability to act from the power of his politically sponsored education; although he did not flaunt that. In fact, he rather tended to keep it secret to avoid clashes with the strangely outspoken overseas Chinese students who made up most of his classes.

He was a proud officer in the United Front, an institution of the early communist foundation set up to infiltrate and exploit the vast Chinese diaspora. Chinese people settled in other countries consider themselves nationals of those countries but Dr Poon knew the People's Republic considered a Chinese anywhere forever to be a Chinese naturally loyal to the motherland.

They were being invited back as part of a re-education programme, to become part of the massive overseas network they were building to control the unsuspecting Western world.

He understood they had to get the kids young but these had not been indoctrinated from birth to understand the special nuances of the unique Chinese communist system which benefitted everyone. They had strange ideas about their personal rights, not realising that everyone had to be subjected to discipline by the system in the interests of all.

The idea that an individual could perceive his own rights and interests were greater than those of the state, as determined by the all-loving central policy makers, was obviously ludicrous.

A good example was Stephen Ji from Singapore. He had turned out to be a problem. and Poon had mistakenly signed him into Huaqiao. That was when the professor made his life-changing error.

"Stephen Ji from Singapore is such a pro-American asshole," he shouted. after far too many beers at a casual faculty meeting, unfortunately in English, showing off and trying to be funny.

A colleague, pointedly in Mandarin, shouted back, "We all have the same problem with Ji. He disrupts all the classes preaching about his ridiculous rule of law, the rights of the individuals and private enterprise systems."

Another shouted, "Yes, and the clever American-speaking Poon enrolled him," to generally derisive but sympathetic mirth.

Ji was taken away next day by two serious looking fellows in uniform.

That was the last the professor saw of him, which unexpectedly solved his political problem although he tried not to admit to himself it bothered his conscience. He very privately hoped, but doubted, Ji was safely back in Singapore.

Since everyone knew he had personally admitted Ji to the University he started to worry he would receive a similar summons. Then to his horror, the same two grim functionaries approached him.

But one tried hard to smile and just handed him an envelope. "Open it," was all he instructed. His concern eased to curiosity when it turned out to be a summons to attend an obscure nightclub the next evening.

THERE, he was directed to his host who was already set up in a discreet but large private room. Pushing a drink into his hand, he said, "I congratulate you on exposing the pro-American traitor. so I thought you would enjoy this patriotic girlie show. I have a modest investment in this club. so I wanted to tell the local Party committee I was promoting their anti-American creation."

He had arranged a private show which he understood ridiculed America and their decadent striptease. He asked, "I assume you are aware of the depravity there?" to which the professor replied guardedly, "A couple of years suffering for the Central Party in Boston at the MIT Sloan business school, acquainted me with their immature ways."

His host surprised him by commenting in English, "So you have their language for trading overseas. That is very good."

"Absolutely. Well American language!" Poon replied. "But you surprise me, sir, speaking it yourself."

"Just a little from many years in university," was his host's guarded reply.

The dancing troupe which marched in to loud, stirring patriotic music, was composed of scowling mature matrons, dressed revealingly but as tough revolutionary guards, apparently selected solely for their hirsute endowment.

They reached their triumphant finale by holding down the spread-eagled, melodramatic villainess, dressed as a despised but pretty George Town American patriot, with her own transgression clearly exposed.

Although women were not his inclination, Dr Poon applauded the serious patriots who were prancing their putdown of America, as was expected of him, nodding his enthusiastic agreement when his host shouted over the din that humbling America was their glorious revolution's prime objective towards achieving world domination.

When things had quietened down, his host asked, "What did you think of the show?" In a moment of unguarded honesty he said, "Honestly I found it rather crude. I prefer more subtle traditional entertainment." The pensive official looked at him re-appraisingly, retorting that he too was a fellow classicist, nodding seriously in agreement.

He quoted a proverb earnestly that, *"You must not choose the one you do not trust, but you must trust the one you choose!"*

SERIOUSLY, the host added, "In our selected political way of life we can trust no one, but must develop as trusting a relationship as possible. I think we could work well together. I am actually offering you a promotion."

He explained unnecessarily, that in real life he was of some importance in Beijing. "We have met like this because this is personal business and I will be placing a great deal of trust in you. If we move ahead we will first need to set up a trace-free system for communication. I represent a group originally in university together, who continue to call ourselves The Six although we are actually now Five because one got too greedy to share."

Poon took this as a not too subtle warning. If he were taken into their confidence, there would be no turning back.

He complimented Poon on having a reputation as one of the country's early computer experts having trained in the United States. "I want you to set up an international system which can transfer investment cash anywhere in the world without detection. But also develop the ability to extract information from any other systems or spy on others if need be. We will provide all the funds needed for hiring and operations, with you reporting only to me personally."

He chuckled to himself. "We have 'several fellows' in detention we can willingly supply, who appeared to be experts in hacking, or any computer crime, if you need them.

"Of course, the banking operation will be just a cover, your main responsibility being to manage our substantial personal funds. A Chinese promotion college is also needed in Macao anyway, and with your academic and political qualification you are perfect for the appointment.

"If you accepted, therefore, you will become sole director of the 'bank' you will establish in Macau and also found a China-sponsored business college of which you will be the Dean. Your income level will be substantially higher than now; probably double."

Dr Poon nodded. "I commend you on the strategy of locating out of China itself, and of mixing your own funds with other general business activity, one of the classic methods of money-laundering to creating confusion. Thank you for the opportunity which I readily accept."

Not that he perceived he was being given much choice but he had no family to disrupt. The two of them shook hands in agreement.

His new employer then named himself as Zhang Man Lok, advising that he could easily be found as a senior business manager in Beijing and Shanghai but that he and his associates must never be identified with their investments. He would only meet Poon when absolutely necessary, with confidential infrequent communication.

Poon was not sure what these new appointments would bring, but he was already trying our Dean Poon in his mind. It sounded good!

Chapter 8

Jackman: A Mountie rides in

IT TOOK young Wong a couple of years to learn the bar business and he had by then picked up rudimentary English. He had met Dr Poon several times and found him easy to get along with but thorough about the bookkeeping, which was still fortunately all recorded by Au.

He had made all the necessary business contacts, especially with the local police detachment which kept the streets safe for commerce but, even with the constant attempts at reform still demanded substantial 'tea money'.

Chatting animatedly in colloquial Cantonese with their sergeant, Wong naturally came to a quick agreement on how he had to operate and immediately started providing them special services at the hotel, as was normal.

The sergeant boasted to him, "A few years ago police corruption become so obvious the Governor had to declare a general amnesty and we promised to behave! So now we have to be careful." He laughed uproariously, putting out his hand for cumshaw in part jest. Wong had been a bit annoyed when his skinny little sister Mai Xi had first appeared on the scene but she was growing up and he hardly saw her as she stayed well out of his way.

His first big test threw him untried into the Gweilo community.

A noisy group of local young businessman, he observed mainly to be white, had taken over half the bar to bid a drunken farewell to one of their members who had been posted away to a branch in another country.

They were regulars, knowing the bar girls by name and when drunk calling, "Boy!" in a joking way for more beer. But they mainly used the bar to drink gallons of the local San Miguel in the hot and humid weather.

Therefore, in the early hours, they staggered from the bar, shouting " Goodnight Au," happily, finding the impressive little sports cars they had parked around the local streets, to roar off noisily in unison.

Unfortunately one of them had not gone too far before he crashed into a street-side food cart smashing it to pieces, pinning the vendor in the wreckage.

A half a dozen cars stopped in silence while a wailing ambulance arrived. The responders shook their heads sadly before taking away the covered victim.

The obviously shaken, now somewhat sober sports car drivers had returned to the bar to regroup, with Wong and Au inevitably being dragged into the recriminations. It turned out that the guilty driver, sitting with his head in his hands sobbing, was a makie learnie Canadian in the local branch of a big bank from that country.

One of the shaken young men confessed to Wong, "You don't realise how serious this is for us: he is Jimmy Q!"

Wong summoned Au to explain. "It appears that he is James Quincy Inglewood, the oldest son of a well-established Canadian banking family. who is given the honour of the second name Quincy, to facilitate the generations old custom of using Q. So he is respectfully called Jimmy Q to all in the bank."

When Au had finally explained all this strange Gweilo double-talk, they decided he must be very important! Wong saw a business opportunity; called his contact in the local police division, asking for an immediate meeting with the manager of the Canadian bank and within an hour had hammered out a deal.

By the middle of the next day Jimmy Q had left the colony, his expensive MG sports car had disappeared from the police compound and the vendor family had accepted an extremely generous payoff. The local police sergeant, Wong's drinking pal, had determined it was an unfortunate accident requiring no charges to be laid.

Wong had personally earned a large fee and everyone was satisfied, except of course the unfortunate street vendor.

Wong took the opportunity to report fully to Dr Poon pointing out he had avoided any embarrassment for the bar and that their remunerative popularity with the expatriates had grown due to his quick and sympathetic action. He was rewarded by the news their owner, Mr Zhang, was thinking about opening a nightclub in Central, where he might be involved.

WONG thought that was the end of the car incident but a week later he was visited by a burly young Canadian in sports clothes who asked, "May we have a private conversation?" His visitor was hesitant when Au was called but quickly continued when he understood Wong's lack of English.

"I am Officer Jack Jackman of the Royal Canadian Mounted Police and I am attached to the Canadian consulate. I have been briefed on your help with the Canadian Bank problem but I am not about to betray any confidences. I am new to the colony, serving in plainclothes. Very privately I am looking for contacts in the Hong Kong police force that are under the radar," he announced rather naively.

This caused translator Au total confusion and with Wong demanding suspiciously, "What this radar?" It all became so farcical trying to explain they just broke into laughter which called for another round of drinks.

"Where is this Canada?" Wong demanded, in English warming up to the idea and boasting to Officer Jack he knew just the people to introduce. It started an unlikely friendship but more important his discovery of a country called Canada.

WHEN he had first strolled around Hong Kong, it was several years before the 1997 handover to China, and Jack Jackman was experiencing total culture shock. It was the end of their summer but still with both temperature and humidity approaching a hundred. His shirt was soaked with sweat.

He had arrived by his first long-distance air trip straight from Calgary where they were experiencing one of their snap snowfalls, predicting a severe winter. Why he was selected from thousands was one of the continuing mysteries of the RCMP although he had been called to their academy in Regina for a two-week briefing on Canadian immigration law with allegations of strange goings-on at the consulate.

He found that most people in his office conducted their business in Cantonese, some in Mandarin but very few in English, other than visiting Canadians or locals who wanted to show off their bilingualism.

Thus he had an interpreter whom he often suspected to debate what he should be told. He had been instructed in Canada to keep his eyes open for any payoffs or strange behaviour but he actually found all their activity unusual. Since they were speaking a foreign language he had no idea what was going on.

However, the documentation was fairly straight forward often with agents conducting their business in English making it easier for him.

All the boring work, processing, dating or documentation, he left to the dozens of local clerks, not initially knowing that was where the money was to be made; where much of the fraud was practised.

WHEN he arrived he had never seen such enormous crowds, many in shabby peasant clothes, some loudly hawking to spit on the sidewalks. The green trams clanged; the heavy traffic belched smoke; the noise was deafening.

The cross-harbour Star ferries disgorged a continuous stream of people whose Cantonese language was so raucously loud that they all seemed to be arguing with each other.

The air of excitement came from the thousands of people pouring in from China looking for work and he quickly discovered many of the women had taken the easily available employment in the sex trade in Wanchai and Tsim Sha Tsui offering their services at what he saw as incredibly reasonable in Canadian terms.

"Get it out of your system," his sergeant had advised him. Having no friends, he needed little encouragement to spend his evenings exploring the exotic, noisy bar districts, with the Chinese music or clacking majong boards always subject to the background din emanating from the upper-floor crowded tenements.

He returned to bar girls whose company he enjoyed, getting their standard encouraging greeting, "Why you no come see me long time?"

He would then spend his night on the hard bamboo matting in her sparse one room refuge for a negotiated 'long time' session somewhere up among all the cacophony. He cheerfully accepted their giggling encouragement of the big, friendly but fumbling, stranger from a strange land.

This was the stage he was at when he had discovered Wong's comfortable bar with all its attractions. It immediately established a firm base for his future Wanchai activities, adding an unexpected contact with Hong Kong's seething but unseen underworld. Old man Au was already giving him a discount, added to which he only had to go upstairs rather than risking the chaos of the tenement buildings.

Wong's strange English was gradually improving and Jack was picking up some Cantonese, so they were even able to sit together to chat over a beer. That was when Jack first broached the question of Triads.

"An informant told me a strange story that their bitter enemy, the communist government in China, has approached them for a truce in Hong Kong. His tale was that China is intent upon setting up a coercion system to ensure that future politicians under the new

'One country; two systems' government do not uphold the promised democratic system.

"They apparently want the Triads to enforce future elected officials vote in the interest of China, giving them an edge in the management of the territory. It appears they were offering easy transportation of drugs as one of the inducements. Can you find out, without risk, if this far-fetched story is true?"

Wong had no idea what far-fetched meant but he got the general gist and said, "I will ask around."

He did not have to take any risks because the approach to the Triad by China was all the talk among his friends in the bars. There was indeed a rumoured negotiation underway by which they were looking forward to increased drug shipments.

With the sudden realisation young Wong was now running an establishment downtown, the drug dealers started falling over themselves to be his supplier. This was a totally new business but Wong gave the impression he was an established, experienced dealer making future supplier arrangements.

He was able to get the satisfaction of reporting to Jack as a policeman that the rumours were true but sensibly made no mention of his new business.

"I bring back a couple of pretty new girls. I will call them." They were summoned to the booth to meet Jack very puzzled at the strange language which they had never heard before today, but with the explicit words already dripped from their lips in the promotion of their trade.

BEER had always been the choice in the bars particularly because of the hot and humid weather but with the advent of air-conditioning hard liquor and cocktails had made their debut. Now with influence from around the world, and increasing tourism, the drug trade was thriving.

Wong spoke to his friends in the district police, very quickly understanding the terms under which his new business was to be conducted.

He had been aware there had been some trading in his bar but essentially he decided, sensibly, that he would only trade within his own premises, certainly not impinging upon other territories.

He also found that Au, who knew everything that happened, was already up on the business, able to take over the individual dealing. His suppliers from Aberdeen recognised this was just a part of their operation, with assured safe payment, so their dealing volume grew.

Wong however insisted upon simple rules prohibiting any drug use in the bar. He fired any of the girls who became addicted, just for practicality.

He settled down to an orderly life, just running the hotel.

Chapter 9

Immigrants: 'Your wealthy masses'

FOLLOWING his appointment as Dean at the Macau College in 1984, Dr Poon enjoyed his first years left alone quietly investing the money sent to him. He also set up the college, already operating with 500 students supported by a faculty gearing up for fast growth.

As instructed, Dr Poon had left the day-to-day management of the Hong Kong property to Wong but continued to carry out periodical financial audits when suggested by Hinks. So, it was an event to be summoned to Wanchai for a rare meeting with the owner.

He had contact occasionally with the very muscular young, smartly dressed assistant who delivered confidential documents from Mr Zhang in Beijing, unsmilingly admitting to being called just Lo. One day, Lo suggested briefly, "Spruce things up at the hotel and dress up the girls. Mr Zhang is coming."

THE fateful meeting took place in Wong's quickly touched-up Wanchai premises with Hinks trying to take notes. The fuss amused even the taciturn Zhang, because they all spoke at the same time in different languages and were besieged by a bar full of cheeky, competing girls out to impress the owner.

Both Hinks and Dr Poon had been surprised that the Beijing businessman and politician spoke such good English, when necessary, but the language changed according to the need.

He had women made freely available to him everywhere he travelled, as was the normal Asian business practice, but Zhang's attention was drawn to the pretty girl in her mid-teens wearing an intriguing school uniform, dutifully doing her homework in Au's work cubicle.

Seeing his interest, Wong recognised the advantage. "That is my sister Mai Xi, a lovely girl. I am sure she wants to meet you." But Au interjected immediately and surprisingly firmly. "No, she is far too young. We have several delectable, mature employees eager to entertain our illustrious owner."

Zhang just shrugged, indicating a couple of the other young women to their squealing great delight, but his eyes kept returning to the girl he had been denied, still sitting demurely in the background.

They escaped to a quieter small local restaurant where Zhang outlined his plans to open a nightclub in Hong Kong Central, to add to others he owned around the world.

"I am enough impressed with the reports on Wong's success with the hotel property to offer him management of this new similarly all-cash venture," he announced, obviously to Wong's great delight.

Hinks and Dr Poon, he obviously dismissed as functionaries, stressing this was a personal investment. "This is not included in the general business Dr Poon manages for me but he will act as my financial agent as is working well at the hotel."

The following day he had a very private meeting with Wong and to his surprise Au, who turned out to be Zhang's local informant on the drug scene. "Wong, get the usual drugs from your contacts at Aberdeen but Au will supply you the bennies, pot and meth that the rave culture is demanding. Get to work on it now."

MAI XI was indeed young when Zhang came to the hotel, an insignificant but watchful, maturing, uniformed schoolgirl sitting quietly in the background, with his hard face and demanding eyes impressed forever upon her memory.

WONG had heard neither of the rave culture nor indeed of disco itself but had the great good luck of tapping into the end of that popular phenomenon, giving the opening of the nightclub an outstanding business start.

They had enjoyed several years of success and by the time the 1990s came around Wong was an established downtown personality. This was when Ron Leyland had appeared on the Hong Kong scene sounding out the immigration business.

Everything that followed might never have happened had it not been for the Triad. Wong never needed to get involved in immigration at all, being fully occupied in his club activities.

It started with Jack Jackman now accustomed to being welcomed at his favourite nightclub corner table. "There is a very disturbing rumour circulating that several Triad leaders have managed to emigrate to Canada under cover of the flood of immigrants that we have approved. Can you find out if it is true?"

Again, it just took a couple of conversations in the bars with his friends. Wong reported with glee to Jack's discomfort, "You right. They all laugh about infamous crooked policeman, government officials and Triad leaders now living in great comfort. Canada welcome with open arms."

"These are all fanciful rumours," Jack protested, "because the Canadian entry requirements are very carefully policed. How do these stories get around? All rubbish. Maybe just one or two have slipped in?"

Wong's now established Aberdeen Triad dealers were reassured that he boasted such a cosy relationship with the RCMP. They were getting concerned about increased attention and pressured him to assist a steady flow of their members into Canada, to develop business in North America. Mr Zhang had nodded his enthusiastic approval.

He did not of course mention the Triad connection to Jack Jackman but when he said, "I have many good friends want to live in Canada. How do I help them?"

Jack suggested, "Set up a simple immigration agency. Make an application to me and I will smooth things along at the consulate."

On a later evening, Jack brought the papers in English but with Chinese translation, along to the nightclub for Hinks to peruse on Wong's behalf.

Jack then completed his section vouching Wong had been satisfactorily investigated, launching him into the highly trusted Canadian immigration business. Jack had earned several freebies but now with the impressive upper-class nightclub girls.

Wong still only had a vague notion about the very cold country called Canada except that it was up above the United States on the map, with herds of buffalo roaming about. Jack had proudly once shown him a portrait of him in a red coat with stiff cowboy hat, sitting on a horse, wearing puffy pants, holding what looked like a wooden lance. Surely they had cars and guns? This had confused him so much he confessed to lawyer Hinks he needed a contact in that strange country.

"I may just be corresponding with the right Canadian fella," responded the lawyer helpfully. That was how Ron came to visit Hong Kong and how his fateful meeting with Mai Xi had came about in the first place.

HINKENBOTHEM'S notion of getting Leyland involved in Wong's immigration business was not initially an easy sell. Ron informed him, "The great majority of immigrants arrive through the regular immigration program but I am only interested in the more lucrative investor program. All I want to do is meet the people with money to invest, but your proposal also involves me in providing general immigration services. No go, thanks."

Hinks did not give up. "Come to the colony for a pleasant trip anyway and we will kick around the possibilities and some other ideas I have over martinis at the Hong Kong Club. Then we can spend the weekend at the races at the jolly ol' Jockey Club!" This had tipped the balance.

SO RON flew to Hong Kong and indeed found a great new friend in Hinks.

To humour him, he went to check out his first immigrant interviews in Wong's small office downtown although honestly they were all in harsh Cantonese, giving him no clue what they were talking about.

He did not intend to stay long but his attention had been captivated by Mai Xi the moment their eyes had met.

She had been pointed out simply as Wong's sister working quietly at her desk but he thought her stunning. He was told Wong had arrived illegally from Canton some years before during the famine caused by the disastrously backward Great Leap Forward, apparently joined later by his little sister, Mai Xi.

Wong had no formal schooling, particularly in English, which was all too obvious but she had the advantage of the excellent colonial education system. She even had a recent Business Diploma.

Not only did she speak educated Cantonese, he was told, but also Mandarin and to his great relief English. She was later to say "Impeccable English, eh? " taunting him on his Canadian accent.

She apparently had her own business but for the moment she became his translator, sitting demurely by his side dressed in alarmingly short silk cheongsams. She worked seriously and was apparently oblivious of his acute awareness of her very up-thrusting, bra-free posture.

"Why you Canadians so dumb?" asked Wong, actually being serious for the moment. "The Americans are tough. They check everything."

He was laughing at their latest problem, with Hinkenbothem urgently needing a dubious client's police confirmation of no prior offences or convictions but which he boasted he would obtain for cash from a pal at the local station. "I can buy any paper," he assured positively.

When he returned triumphantly waving the required police assurance, obtained for "Just five thousand Hong Kong," Ron, that trusting Canadian, would not initially believe police anywhere did that sort of thing.

Mai Xi finally relaxing a little smiled politely and said quietly, "Ron, you are so naive." She also did not mention, at the time, that the police bribe would be charged by Wong to the client at tens of thousands, Canadian dollars, of course.

She explained patiently, "The vast majority of people emigrating to Canada are honest and their applications are straightforward. They just have to patiently await their turn. Wong makes his money around the dubious clients, who are often in a hurry, and whose papers need some 'massaging'."

Ronnie was, of course, only interested in the investor immigrants but Wong grunted that many of them were not really that wealthy. Ron insisted, "They have to document a high net worth, and invest a few hundred thousand in Canada, although granted most of it is returned a few years later. So they have to be well-off."

Wong shrugged. "My bank fellows will give any papers for a fee. Lawyers in Canada can get my clients loans with Canada banks. They are on the take. Leave money and Hong Kong to me, Lonnie," he insisted.

"Ronnie," said Ron, now automatically. He puzzled how a bank loan could provide the money in Canada while the government said the deal was to bring more capital into the country, but he was beginning to be bemused by this whole immigration deal.

Maisie who had been listening with amusement, chirped in, "Canadian expat officials are usually honest but *so* trusting. Their local staff can all be bought by Wong. He has special connections and claims he can get anyone accepted. For a bit more, ten thousand or, so he can move clients to the top of the pile."

This was just the beginning for Ronnie but already he was incredulous at the extent of naivety and corruption in the public systems he was learning about, which made some of the just dubious real estate goings on back in Canada look like child's play.

He had to admit to a lot of mounting trepidation. If it had not been for the prospect of getting to know the alluringly mysterious young Mai Xi, he would quickly have ditched the immigration business, returning to the safety of leaky condos in Vancouver.

Chapter 10

Macau: Losing face

MAINTAINING a professional distance but intrigued by her beauty and intelligence, and indeed her differences from her brother, Ron invited Mai Xi to a 'business' dinner at The Mandarin.

Mai Xi arrived wearing a stunning, slinky, long, red cheongsam which took his breath away. After seating her and ordering their wine, he tried to concentrate on what she was saying.

"Tell me more about Canada. Why are you so interested in Hong Kong and China?" she asked, rather to his disappointment, actually talking about business.

"We have a long history involving Chinese immigrants but you might know our ideological Canadian Christians played a part in establishing communism in China in those confused days just after the Second World War."

"Ah, of course; following Bethune," she broke in.

"Then China disappeared from our view, appearing briefly on the side of North Korea in 1950 during their ill-fated attempt to take the entire Korean peninsula communist, only to disappear again. Canada took its time to acknowledge the Communist government, although we were one of the first Western nations to recognise you in 1970, albeit with some weasel wording regarding Taiwan and lobbying from the notorious 'Mish Kids', left-wing offspring of those original communist supporting Canadian missionaries."

She broke in again but this time critically. "Not so free with the 'you' please. You are talking about The Chinese not Hongkongers."

Ron flushed slightly at the valid criticism and hurried on. "OK, I accept the rebuke and no, we do not condone communism. Our relationship is based upon trade, absolutely does not show an approval of their authoritarian, nasty form of government."

"Still," she mused, "it does seem to me that in your politics the lust for profit trumps tiresome ethics." Ron was realising he did not have a pushover on his hands and he planned his recovery while they ordered dinner.

"I personally started taking an optimistic view of the revival of China back at college when in 1980 they established their first open economic zone in Shenzhen providing a sign China was liberalising.

"Then we learned about the agreement that had been reached in 1984 between the British Government and China to return this territory before the end of the century but leave the system of government much as it is for another 50 years; 'One country: two systems'. I started to like China."

She jumped ahead of him. "But then the Tiananmen Square massacre shocked everyone. But it was followed closely by the positive sign of the opening of the Shanghai and Shenzhen stock exchanges in 1990 and so you conveniently forgot about it!"

Ron shook his head sadly. "How quickly Tiananmen has been ignored. However, it added to the concern and uncertainty in Hong Kong. As you know tens of thousands of talented and well off local Chinese citizens, worried about their future, took advantage of the Canadian Immigrant Investor Program introduced strategically. That's why I am here."

"Yes," Mai Xi agreed. "Canada is winning valuable new successful citizens from Hong Kong, whom the United Kingdom did not want nor invite."

Ron told her he was still puzzled. "Already, we are seeing many who had previously fled to Canada are returning to your temporary colony. Why?"

"Well, that's good for you in a way because it encourages many more to apply. We see Canadian citizenship as insurance. A lot of our wage-earning clients have returned here to their mistresses, but leaving their wives and kids to enjoy a pleasant life in Canada without them, Why not? You provide great education and a 'free' medical system."

"True," Ron admitted, "at least free to some of them because they earn nothing in the country and pay no Canadian income taxes. But many more stay in Canada; just settling down to new lives there. As a businessman I can clearly recognise a large market to be exploited."

They discussed business and politics impersonally the entire dinner with the sole exception at the end, when she looked him earnestly in the eye, putting her hand in an assuring gesture over his and saying, "I do hope we continue to do business together."

Well, it was apparently intended to be just an assuring gesture but the jolt of excitement that shot through them both at her touch, indicated differently.

Nevertheless, purely as a businessman he thanked her for the very edifying evening, assisted her with her long dress into her taxi and waved goodnight.

MUTTERING to himself incredulously Wong demanded, "Why are Americans so nasty. They tax world-wide earnings. Canada is good though, they only tax on earnings in Canada."

So Ronnie had to explain to his prospective clients through Mai Xi, "It is not quite that simple but, yes, just stay the required years to get the safeguarding citizenship, then come back to Hong Kong where you pay no Canadian tax."

What a profitable turn-over business this could be, thought Ronnie, still undecided and already a week overdue back in Vancouver.

"But I must pay Canadian tax on my world-wide earnings while

I am in Canada getting the citizenship?" asked a client. Wong cut in and yattered quickly in Cantonese. Ronnie asked Mai Xi what he was saying.

She summarised, "In theory, yes, some tax. But how will Canada check? Just pay enough to keep them happy and not asking questions."

Ronnie interjected, "They will have to be honest but I do agree the Canadian tax system works to a large extent on an honour system."

Now Wong was genuinely puzzled, "Honour system. What is that?" When they heard Mai Xi's translation of Ronnie's explanation they laughed uproariously, slapping each other on the back as though it were a crazy comedy show.

Ronnie was obviously beginning to skate on thin ice, a Canadian concept he well understood. Many of the things he was arranging and some of the people involved were proving dubious but he consoled himself that the money was peanuts.

They were mostly just ordinary Hong Kong folk, sufficiently familiar with the English language there to consider Canada, appreciating the personal protection its democracy offered, and fearing eventual communism, especially for their children.

So it was something of a relief, when the Mai Xi asked innocently, "Like to see Macau on the weekend?" which invitation changed his whole life's paradigm.

SHE had very correctly booked two rooms for them, admittedly connecting, of course at the magnificent Hotel Lisboa Macau and had reserved in the grand restaurant. They were about to enjoy their infamous lobster thermidor dinner together.

Perhaps it was the second bottle of Pol Roger but their pent-up emotions had got rather out of hand in the supposedly secluded booth. The oft-repeated Leyland family legend gleefully tells that the unexpected scene so surprised their waiter that he stumbled and spilled the lobster dish.

Her carefully selected, diaphanous silky blouse just happened to be wide open and slipped from her shoulders as she jumped up to ward off the falling culinary creation, leaving her breasts tastefully bathed in pink lobster sauce.

The startling spectacle attracted the entire room's attention including the Filipino orchestra, which lapsed into a stunned silence. He threw his jacket over her shoulders protectively, escorting the speechless Mai Xi from the totally silent but enthralled dining room.

They were mortified by the wildly appreciative, spontaneous burst of applause they heard behind them.

AFTER the lobster incident they had rushed to shower, following which he rejoined Mai Xi in the bar. Apparently her erotic mood had passed.

"Do you know what losing face means?" she asked, still clearly upset. "I am well known here. This could affect business relationships."

She however snuggled up to him, a few salty tears dampening his face. New top buttons had inexplicably come undone. From that moment he was hers.

Chapter 11

Mai Xi: Innocent beginnings

MAI XI'S familiarity with Macau had been earned from a tough life of experience.

Years before, Wong was initially disinterested when a poorly dressed strange man came into his bar in Wanchai, asked his name and left a dirty, skinny ragamuffin tyke of a girl with him. He knew kids could clean up to work and grow up into the profitable shapely bar girls.

When the stranger quickly departed, his interest changed to annoyance as he read the note stitched to her dirty cheap jacket and learned she was a sister sent from the starving Guangdong countryside by his mother. They were broke and desperate but pleaded they had taken this risk at least to give her a chance.

Her name was Mai Xi. The little wide-eyed peasant girl was in an apparent state of shock from her journey with total strangers into a foreign big city and it was days before she even spoke.

Several of the ancient Wanchai streets were being redeveloped with modern buildings which had prompted Zhang to buy the bar and hotel property as an investment, awaiting demolition. It had an old-style colourful and noisy bar on the ground floor, a few floors of short-time hotel rooms above and the manager's place on the grimy roof.

This is where Mai Xi was to spend her coming years living in a converted closet on the roof, scrounging food in the bar and essentially ignored by Wong. Although almost totally without any ethical concerns Wong did recognise traditional family responsibility and kept a grudging eye on his little sister. He thought vaguely she might be useful in the future. After all she was a female, although rather scrawny and mousy.

By the time she got into her teens all that was beginning to change. Mai Xi had become a very bright and self-assured young woman, loved by all the workers and bar girls in the hotel who advised and helped her in every way they could.

Her second father, in a way, had proved to be the sympathetic bar manager Au, who had taken her under his wing from the beginning and protected her totally from direct exposure to their openly expressed bar girl hotel activities.

He was a very tolerant bar manager whom the girls adored for his helpful gestures never followed by a payback backroom groping. The management objective was to maximise room rentals but Au turned a blind eye to a quick dollar they earned by discrete finger-dancing.

Lap-dancing was however too noisy even for him to overlook, rattling the beer glasses and distracting nearby quiet drinkers,.

MAI XI was from that young age nevertheless totally immersed nightly in the main physical nature of the hotel and learned how to look after herself and stay away from the action.

Au had insisted she attended the local public school which had been opened on the top floor of a new nearby tenement building and later guided her into high school education.

He also purchased one of the newly popular desktop computers and installed it in his kiosk at her request but he joked at the loss of his office.

At this stage Wong noticed that his little sister was now a tall, well-rounded and athletic teenager but more important that she was a top student, capable of useful administrative duties. She was provided with her own office space, complete with a computer and moved to a tiny but real bedroom on the roof which she adored and decorated happily.

When the nightclub was opened downtown, Mai Xi, now in her late teens, was promoted by Wong to a job in the office. She was quickly aware that the depth of criminal activity, drug use and nefarious dealings there, far exceeded the quiet alcohol consumption and harmless short-time sex upstairs at her much lower-class home hotel.

For the first time in her life she knew she was being dragged into something way out of her control. Her upbringing had left her totally competent to deal with the continuous male advances she received although she had selectively accepted a few and was far from a virgin, mainly from trying it out with safe school friends.

But the blatant, expensive prostitution, now also involved women brought in from other countries, markedly Eastern Europe and Australia.

The illegalities of Wong's new business activities served to send her home to her little hotel haven, now managed by Au, more concerned each night. Wong, involved with strange men coming and going from around the world, had also matured and moved to a smart apartment, on The Peak, of course.

She did not know it at the time, but Wong taking on the nightclub was in fact a critical turning point of her life.

The class, achievement level and sophistication of the people to whom she was exposed in the downtown business centre, mainly speaking English, changed her personal expectation which was quickly expressed in her stylish dress, high heels and confidence. In two years she had developed from a deprived, aimless refugee to a poised, stylish young woman.

Her main diversion during that period had been to attend Mandarin classes to improve on her high school courses. They were all aware, of course, of China's imminent takeover of Hong Kong and she thought knowing the main language better would be advantageous.

It became useful sooner than she thought when Wong announced,

"The auditor from Macau is returning to check affairs and he mainly speaks Mandarin. I need you to come and translate."

She had long known about Dr Poon Ping Kin who seemed young to be Dean of a business college in Macau but also to manage a bank in some way involved with the owner of the hotel and nightclub. As the dreary business evening dragged on Mai Xi realised that the Wong establishment was being dishonest with him and this added even more to her concerns.

The next day, having spent the morning over papers and accounts, she lunched with the Dean Poon and learned to her surprise he spoke clear English.

"College in America, at business school." he explained.

Carefully, and tactfully she replied, "So you must know you are not getting the full story of what is going on in the club? It disturbs me."

He was obviously very bright and just chuckled. "My team in Macau is sophisticated enough to know everything that was going on. Honestly, I don't want to know the sordid details of which I am sure the owner is aware. Thank you for your honesty, which I appreciate."

Finally having someone in whom to confide, she switched back to more confidential Mandarin unburdening herself about her worries and ending telling him the story of her life. She knew, obviously she was taking a chance but she instinctively felt drawn to asking advice of this rather sensitive man who had not come on to her at all as most others did these days. He smiled and just said, "Let me give it some thought."

A while went by without further contact with him but then Wong called her into his office.

"You remember that money-man from Macau? Well he says you must go to their school for a business diploma. You leave for Macau now."

Chapter 12

Proposal: Convincing seduction

THE morning after the lobster dinner debacle in Macau, a visibly
relaxed Mai Xi had taken Ron to lunch with her friend Dean
Poon Ping Kin. She introduced him as her dean from business school
but they were obviously close friends.

"Ron, meet Ping Kin, my saviour!" The professor humphed in
rebuttal.

"No, seriously; enrolling me in the business school and then after
graduation making me your office manager back in Hong Kong
changed my entire life. I am independent of my brother Wong and
have my own apartment on Garden Road. All your doing!"

Over their first glass of wine he explained in halting English,
"Outside my college duties I run our 'Macau bank' which is basically
a private merchant bank. I also have a separate team which provides
technical computer services. Mai Xi is our Hong Kong rep."

Then he gave up and asked Mai Xi to translate.

"His bank converts Renminbi into foreign currencies through their
agents, branches or other banks, for his clients to buy assets overseas.
They are well connected internationally with the tax havens, hedge
funds and money markets. Their skill is in knowing where to find
the various currencies to make deals. Admittedly it is called shadow

banking but in itself it is not illegal and has been around for hundreds of years. He invites you to become their contact in Canada if you like? They are looking at investing more there.

"He reckons this is just the beginning and you would be getting into the business at the right time. The Western world is totally unprepared for the economic expansion of China and you have no idea what is going to hit you. He says he has been absolutely staggered on his trips across Canada to find how easy it is to move money into your country and then to just have ownership disappear.

"His experience is that Canada provides the most perfect system for them to use with neither real estate nor corporate share ownership needing personal disclosure or registration, so nobody knows who owns what or who should be paying taxes. Your lawyers and banks can do absolutely anything they want without check."

Ping Kin broke in excitedly in English. "We are setting up hundreds of Mickey Mouse companies, trusts or organisations owning anything. Nobody cares as long as the money keeps coming. It's Fantasy Land!"

He was so pleased with his 'Mickey Mouse' illustration he did a little dance and chanted it several times, waving his hands in 'Mickey' gestures, obviously picked up from a visit to Disney.

"SO WHERE is the money coming from," asked a suspicious Ron, still laughing, "and why do you Chinese want to move it out of your country?"

He was answered by a shrug from the calming-down Ping Kin.

"Let's face it; China is partway between communism and capitalism producing a race of people who have to look after themselves because they get no individual protection from the state. Many in the new middle class who have done well are afraid and prefer the security of the Western world. There is also a thieving criminal underworld and politicians who have benefited one way or the other from their positions and all have accumulated enormous sums of hidden money.

"Sometimes people just walk in with a suitcase of yuan they probably have quite genuinely saved and want to move out of the country. Then we have the infamous local casinos depositing cash with us by the truck load for transfer overseas. It just becomes an enormous flow of money that is now accumulating to exit through Canada and some other countries like Australia because of your naive, easy-going cultural ways.

"We have the money and we have the process kindly provided by you to move it your way. Do you want it? In fact, we could help with the Immigration Fund I understand you are thinking of starting and maybe fund a condo development as well and see how it goes."

It had all started as innocently as that.

THAT evening, back in Hong Kong Central, she steered him off the Macau Ferry. They fought their way through the bedlam of traffic, trams and teaming shouting people, to his grand old hotel, where she left him, demurely going up on her toes to kiss his cheek, just murmuring, "Sleep well!" coquettishly.

When the uniformed lift boy slammed the metal door shut, he ascended alone in silence to the air-conditioned peace of the smart top floor hotel lounge.

He strolled out of the lift, back into the sanity of his orderly, upper-class world. Ron considered himself a standard, blue-eyed, sandy-haired, six foot two, ethnically ex-Brit.

A privileged Canadian upbringing, character forming rugby and hockey at the best boys' private school, an ethical university business education, marrying a very proper and pretty childhood girlfriend, then taking over one of the family's establishment businesses, had just not prepared him for all this.

He was frankly a little confused by an Asia which was totally devoid of recognisable ethics and morals, but which he found strangely challenging and exciting. But immediately meeting Mai Xi had saved him from the soul-searching encounters that Wong had been enthusiastically offering but it had clearly raised other major personal dilemma.

He was missing Mai Xi already and reached for the heavy room telephone to dial her number, which he knew by heart.

Chapter 13

Investors: Returning with the loot

R ON had found Ping Kin's business offer fascinating and, he was convincing himself, potentially financially rewarding. His 'couple of weeks in Hong Kong' kept extending due to 'important business'.

Ron learned Mai Xi was already into the process up to her pretty neck, explaining the work she did for Ping Kin's Macau 'bank' after graduating and representing them in Hong Kong.

"Do you know Macau has been Portuguese since the mid-1550s, a clear 300 years before Hong Kong was annexed by your trading British? It has now settled down into a unique region within China with a special administration maintaining a high degree of autonomy, run by secretariats and executives appointed locally and providing flexibility for any international business arrangements, especially in association with their notorious gambling casinos.

"Everyone knows, of course, that Macau is really ruled by the low-profile Macau 'mafia' running the casinos and controlled from China, so remember never to cross them!"

"Flexibility!" she giggled in emphasis.

"The mixed-race locals still call themselves Macanese, but were there long before the Scottish and English drug dealers took over the delta by force, grabbing Hong Kong as their distribution centre.

"Macau has always been sleazy and a recognised concentration of crime and corruption for both Europeans and Asians. Things have become worse or better depending upon your needs. It just modernised! It used to just be ho-hum gambling, drugs, booze and exotic Portuguese-style prostitution or even simple cigarette smuggling, but it has branched out to become an international money marketing centre. For the Chinese business elite it has become *the* Renminbi conduit but in practice they run much of the money on through Hong Kong institutions."

"GAAU je in Macau, gaau je ?" chanted Wong loudly at dim sum back in Hong Kong after one of their weekends away, for all in the restaurant to hear. He was always ready for ribald fun at Ron's expense. Even so, trying to be friendly Ron had set himself the task of learning a few Cantonese words daily.

"What was Wong shouting to us at dim sum?" Ron asked later. Mai Xi told him without a trace of a blush that her brother had been informing everyone in a very crude way they were intimate in Macau. She was holding his hand but in no way defensively.

By then she had somewhat forgiven if not forgotten her loss of face and honestly she just couldn't get enough of him. Apparently, contrary to Wong's derisive anatomical suggestions involving his waved and extended little finger, she found Gweilo equipment and performance highly satisfactory.

This became obvious to all, with his visit extended way too many weeks to explain, when Ronnie casually asked, "Wong, what's the Cantonese word for pregnant?"

RONNIE'S wife was not upset at the news when he finally returned to Canada, nor even particularly surprised. They had no children and a quick divorce was not difficult to arrange. They both readily agreed to irrevocable marriage breakdown and a fifty/fifty split; not that they had much to share, both being big spenders.

"Can you look after it?" he begged her. "Uncontested it will only take a few months." He was busy.

Now he had to set up the Canadian side of the immigration activity and document his arrangements with Wong and Ping Kin. Also, it was time for him to explain his long absence and new business arrangements to his father Logger Leyland. After all Logger was still chairman with controlling shares.

Everyone in town called him Logger Leyland, even Ron and his older engineer, 'outdoorsy' sister. Pretty but tough, she preferred the company of women. She had always been interested in replanting and forest preservation and was intent upon taking over the Leyland lumber business, much to city-man Ron's relief.

"I agree on the surface the immigration policy appears a bit dumb but Canada needs the bright Hong Kong immigrants or in honesty their children," Ron started out to Logger defensively

The out-of-date Logger retorted, "They will not be real Canadians until they live and sleep hockey, speak only English, or French in Quebec of course and stop constantly bitching or comparing things with 'back home'. "

Ron actually sighed at him and then insisted, "But it is also useful to get their money to develop commerce and produce jobs. That is the whole idea of the Investment Immigration Fund we have launched in Hong Kong.

"Each immigrant puts the prescribed hundreds of thousands of dollars into the pot to finance a commercial endeavour approved in Canada, in our case one of our real estate projects. The immigrants get almost no interest on their money and we cunning Canadians own the equity. Bingo!" Logger nodded in grudging approval.

"All we have to do is to complete the project, wait for the market and inflation to increase the value, then one day refinance to pay the immigrants back. Not so dumb, eh?"

Ron finessed his argument. "Everyone wins and even the government will eventually collected taxes. It is a little on my conscience not to pay more interest but hey, throw in the protection they are buying, education and a universal medical system and they are doing just fine."

Logger admitted he was convinced and went along with it!

IT TURNED out that the demand to emigrate from Hong Kong was brisk, taking them only a few months to accumulate enough in the fund to commit to his first commercial property. Somehow Mai Xi had come up with the cash herself and she was on his early list of prospective immigrant rabbits or rather clients, Ron reminded himself.

The very next day after the fund closed, Wong phoned to say he had a long-term tenant from Macau for the planned first building at the asking rent. Ron should have a good rest, snigger, snigger, because Mai Xi was on her way to Vancouver with the details.

IT WAS good advice from Wong. They were already tense with desire by the time they embraced and kissed deeply at the airport luggage carousel. "Why did you bring all this stuff?" Ron laughed with impatience, as he fought to load his Mini Cooper with her ton of luggage for the two-week visit.

They were not to emerge or even look at the urgent business papers, or anything else come to that, for several days. Finally, one morning she dumped her briefcase on the pillow and spread papers around the bed to discuss 'The Tenant'.

He shook his head. "These are just Macau numbered companies; they are not even registered in Canada yet. What sort of tenant is this?"

Mai Xi chuckled, purred would be more descriptive of her now physically relaxed compliant state. She dropped her voice and looking around furtively, whispered, "Chinese government fellows. Wong says ask them for whatever documents you need and our bank will also provide any financial guarantees."

"Don't worry, silly." she teased, raising her voice."These are investors vouched for by the bank and they will be represented by Wong who will sign anything without reading it."

Even in his relaxed condition this news raised a surge of concern. The money all seemed a bit too easy. She held him closer and his alarm was replaced by another rising urgency.

"Really no problem," she quipped disarmingly, mimicking Wong in his ear, "I will explain all, but first......." and the contracts were sent flying around the bed under the renewed action.

FINALLY exhausted for the moment, bringing a bottle of wine back to bed she snuggled up and told her story.

"As you know I attended the business diploma course at the new Chinese private college in Macau. Wong and the college dean were both employed by the same high officials in Beijing and were working together on several businesses. So I easily got accepted. I valued the civil liberties under the Hong Kong British way of life I was brought up in, so when the subject arose at lectures I was very outspoken criticizing the oppressive nearby communist system.

"Macau obviously was physically a part of China, although it had its own independent status, so I was a bit surprised anyone would bother over a 20-year-old girl's ranting and particularly when I was summoned before the principal, Dean Poon. When he came around his desk, spoke softly and almost begged me to tone down my political opinions I naturally assumed he was now finally coming on to me and told him pleasantly to piss off.

"But he just smiled, spoke frankly and kindly, pointing out I was now much closer to China in many ways and did not have the Hong Kong Court system to which I could run.

"Then he just said I should grow up and be realistic. He dismissed me with a wave of his hand, but with a worried frown on his face. I actually appreciated and followed his advice.

"It was not a big college so I saw him around, he gave some lectures and we passed the occasional pleasant word, all in Mandarin of course. Then a strange thing happened and I heard a rumour he was in trouble.

"Although it appeared anything went in Macau, a combination of the Portuguese Catholic tradition and prudish local leaders had produced a community biased strongly against homosexuality, which was actually illegal. There were rumours they were out to get the apparently gay newcomer, Dean Poon who had been a little too obvious and physically active.

"I owed him a great favour for extracting me from the risks of Wong's clutches in Hong Kong so I knocked on his study door, rounded his desk being careful not to get too close and proposed we become 'An Item'. He thought for a scant couple of minutes, before replying it was great tactical thinking which he accepted with pleasure.

"With finals a few months away a little insurance always helps but the arrangement was probably not necessary for me because I was already passing with honours. I liked Ping Kin a lot so I never told Wong the truth, but it also has made him a little wary of me which is useful and protective.

"Macau has still not legalised male stuff together so we kept the subterfuge going because we were having fun. Ping Kin has hired me ever since in the bank and I also work on the computer project. As you saw I help out my dumb-dumb brother, but Ping Kin remains my apparent lover but also my friendly boss. I like to think of him as my Pearl Delta, modern day, dashing gay pirate which he really is in practice."

"You are so romantic. Good thing he is gay or I would be sailing with my cutlass to your rescue," threatened Ron sternly.

"My hero," she laughed.

"Ah!" exclaimed her actual lover, "So the embarrassment at dinner in Macau was not just over lobstered boobs but more that you had been exposed out with another man."

She snuggled up close again. "Now you know all my secrets. When do I move to Vancouver?"

Chapter 14

Infatuation: All sinophiles now

MAI XI immigrated as soon as they could arrange it in 1993. They found a small, although very exclusive, house in Kitsilano near the beach, an easy drive from the Leyland family mansion in Shaughnessy.

She took her relationship with Ron and the move to Canada very seriously and announced, "I am now going to be Maisie Leyland!"

They were married in a quiet, non-religious, mid-morning ceremony on the beach, followed by a hilarious wedding lunch with the family and friends at The Yacht Club; hilarious because baby Cathie was almost due, stretching the skill of the Vera Wang designers who nevertheless produced a stunning wedding gown.

IT TOOK a couple of years for the first Immigration Fund to spend all the money from the Hong Kong clients and for the free-standing properties to be built. A reasonable time after Cathie was born Maisie moved into the office to co-manage the immigration business.

Ron always complained that Vancouver had one of the slowest and most onerous development approval processes in the world, actively restraining development and forcing up rents and the cost of property. However, working with Wong and Macau they had arranged a further three Immigration Funds, with proposed developments wending their way through that slow approval system.

At the beginning, in those early and simple days, they were happy dealing with Hong Kong dollar immigrants and setting up transfer systems. They earnestly set about bringing in their immigrants, smoothing their entry and spending hours on such mundane things as finding the easiest Canadian points of entry with the shortest procedural backups.

Demonstrating their uncertainty, over half a million Hongkongers had stayed in Canada but estimates suggested at least half that many had already returned.

Their customers transferring capital had a myriad of offered reasons for having the money and there were no restrictions. They just documented the amount, shared a fee with someone and dealt with the transfer.

Most of the people they were dealing with financially had been subscribers to their Immigrant Funds. They had all their records and there were no apparent restrictions so the money transfer business just sort of happened.

Ron was finding dealing with Hongkongers and Taiwanese very comfortable. They were accustomed to the similar Canadian democratic system of personal freedom and protection, with most basically prepared to deal reasonably fairly with the trusted authorities in return.

He soon found some going back and forth, frankly with many of them earning non-disclosed off-shore income which no one really bothered about or checked. "You said it is an honour system," Maisie reminded him.

THERE was still no sign of the promised tenant for the first building which was mainly a warehouse but all the Canadian documentation and registration had gone smoothly and without question.

Wong signed and sent all the papers and took over as the absent building manager. Although the tenant was a numbered company in

Macau, the lease had been covered by the bank and the rent was paid fully and on time.

MAISIE found it amusing that in relating to her Ron had become a Sinophile reading extensively about Chinese history, and insisting upon taking her on tours of that country when they were back over that way.

One of their early trips had been to Maisie's traditional, but deserted, family village in Guangdong to search of her family, from which she had never heard. She excitedly remembered a little gnarled man now sitting alone by a shack on the deserted street.

She happily recalled and translated his rural, colloquial Cantonese. "He says 'bad feng shui' took hold of the village and that my mother died along with many others during the great famine. My father disappeared with all the men to look for work in the big city a long time ago."

Ron was appalled. "What can we do to help him?" he asked.

But she replied with tears in her eyes, "I offered, of course, but he is too proud to accept charity."

She was heartbroken but when back in Hong Kong she tearfully relayed the story to Wong, he merely shrugged.

RON had been highly supportive when their new Prime Minister dashed to China as one of his first endeavours to perform abeyance to the great new business prospect.

All the Canadian politician's colleagues and especially business tycoons were pressing them for more political connections and within months of achieving office the Prime Minister was there in Beijing enthusiastically talking about his Pillars approach: economic development partnerships; sustainable development; good governance; the rule of law protecting human rights; and peace with security.

The massive delegation of naturally trusting Canadians genuinely believed China was heading in the right direction with all the human rights stuff but nevertheless tactfully avoided making it an issue as the hunt for profit prevailed. At that point Ron was as enthusiastic as they were.

Maisie just sighed as he was swept away by the confident belief that China would change towards a more liberal and humane system of government. He enthusiastically vowed he would play his part.

There were tough Canadian trade negotiations with the United States, going on as always, and he told Maisie, "This is finally Canada's opportunity to get some serious leverage against the US."

She told him that he was dreaming. "Canada is lucky to be a part of North America and the US totally defends Canada."

She chortled, "Your low defence budget helps pay for services like the extensive medical system because you can leave that all to America. Believe me, the comrades in China will never change and you had better keep on good terms with the States."

SHE was instructed in her new-comer classes that Canada integrates immigrants rather than assimilating them as expressed by their earlier flamboyant prime minister when he had introduced his multi-cultural policy.

"His general idea," Ron told her, "seemed to be to give the older folk a 'back home' atmosphere to see out their days grouped together in enclaves, arguing faraway politics in their original languages, while their younger people take to hockey and baseball, adopting our values and doing the integration bit in a Canadian language."

PRITAM Singh dwelt in one such new home from home district where he had been found and recruited by the Royal Canadian Mounted Police, who had learned of his apparently impressive police background in Mumbai before coming to Canada.

The intention was to keep an eye on the possible intrusion of foreign political activities in Canada but it was quickly decided that he was too obvious an appointment so he was diverted to commercial crime of which he knew absolutely nothing and where he was totally useless.

He learned he would be mainly undercover so he was assigned to a division vaguely associated with pipeline security. The subterfuge was cleverly chosen to confuse the public about their real lines of enquiry but they were rarely involved with the transporting of liquids, other than in their local pub.

As to be expected the name had been leaked and to gain entry to his new office he now had to fight his way through a hoard of placard-waving anti-oil fanatics. They all agreed their cover was perfect and laughed that a leak was to be expected.

Chapter 15

Conversion: Money is just money

IN THOSE early years Ron and Maisie travelled together period-ically back to Hong Kong and Macau setting up their business. Ping Kin had become a friend to Ron also and they could see how his increasing world travel was changing him.

He admitted to them one day, "When I first arrived in Macau way back in 1984, carrying out the secretive Zhang's instructions, I realised that even measured by Chinese standards the city was espe-cially corrupt, although admittedly efficient at it. Now, a decade later as the century draws to a close, China is doing well with the changes in policy direction, but it is still a second-rate power. We have no international currency and the yuan, the Renminbi, is only of use within our country."

Reassuring, Maisie suggested, "Well, the growing economic prog-ress of the state should please you. Production is on the rise despite some setbacks."

"My personal problem," he admitted, "comes from my exposure to the outside world. We are losing our traditional Chinese respect for authority. China is becoming an unhappy land of distrust and of secretive cartels, for which I work. The ruling group, military and police all work together with no political or legal system to keep them in check, allowing them to do absolutely anything they want. They are self-perpetuating, especially by family, and much of what they do is concealed from the people. No opposing person has a chance to express an opinion and even passive opposition is crushed, as had been clearly experienced in Tiananmen Square, and in many less publicised protests around the country."

He instinctively and dramatically glanced around to ensure no one was intruding on his thoughts, even though he was relatively safe in Macau, to their understanding amusement.

"Seriously though, my two years in America made me wonder if they had not taken open expression of opinion too far but I admit to feeling safer there."

"You are certainly becoming less doctrinaire these days," agreed Maisie. "What about fighting back to get revenge for the Opium Wars you used to teach?"

Wanting to add something to the discussion Ron offered, "Yes, but the Western world was only able to invade China because it had a long history of corruption and infighting which weakened the entire system. That is what worries me."

They both looked at Ron quizzically. "That is one way of looking at it," Ping Kin admitted.

"Or explains their need for communism," Maisie added thoughtfully. "But now you are conducting a reverse modern financial invasion, with hundreds of millions in funding and using your computerised network to move money from China instantly anywhere in the world, without question!"

"Well yes." Ping Kin agreed. "Thank you both for being concerned. All these professional things are going well, and I have become well established but I am not a happy man, personally. The rough dark sea at the head of the estuary outside the Macau harbour is my salvation from all this human nonsense. I sail my little boat straight out away from shore enjoying the solitude, for a short time feeling totally in control of my life."

"Don't be so dramatic!" Maisie joked punching him on the arm affectionately.

THE day came in 1997 when China officially took over nearby Hong Kong. Officials had made pompous speeches, the bands had played, the flags were run down and up. When things had quietened, and a few years went by, everything went on as normal but Hongkongers were now in two minds.

The general opinion was that China had changed their attitude to the outside world and were apparently moving towards a more open, freer system, to Hong Kong's long-term advantage.

Ping Kin supported this view. "This unique 'One country; two systems' has been set up for 50 years continuing the basic British arrangements to keep international business calm and flowing, so what is all the fuss about?"

"I disagree," Maisie, retorted. "The way they run things in Beijing, this agreement will only last while it still benefits China and gives convenient access to the Western world."

Ping Kin chided her back, "You have become too cynical since you converted yourself to 'Maisie'. Self-interest alone will make them preserve Hong Kong for many years."

The Hong Kong arrangement sounded good also to Macau which now had a similar deal with China for its own future.

With a prosperous Hong Kong and immediate fears there calmed, Ron indeed found the demand for Canadian citizenship cooling in the new century but in Vancouver their general immigration business was still expanding, producing a fair share of investors.

Their company growth came from Wong who had built up his network of agents extending now into China aiming at its increasing middle class and he was pushing would-be immigrants their way daily.

MAISIE shouted loudly at Ron, "I want to expand our immigration into Taiwan." The end of her message was however whipped away by a strong gust of facing wind. They were out on their comfortable Bayfield 40-footer sailing together on the blustery Vancouver English Bay.

Ron just shouted urgently in reply "Pay attention. Tack! Tack!"

Then he roughly grabbed the tiller from her, now bellowing, "Coming about!" he tacked expertly onto a new pounding tight course.

As they heeled over dramatically to her complete alarm she screamed wildly, "Let out the fucking main sheet!" to his great delight at her vastly improved English although he offered no relief of her terror.

Back at the Yacht Club bar when they were nursing a couple of Hot Toddies, he relented and asked politely, "I believe I heard you mention something about Taiwan?"

"Yes, you bugger," she responded, pleasing him even more, "that immigration market is opening up. We must jump in."

"We just got going on Hong Kong. Isn't that enough?" he asked.

"No," she insisted, "they are a democracy and think the way we do. Also they have become very prosperous and will bring lots of money into your precious real estate."

"OK," he conceded, "so long as you manage all the immigration yourself. And one deal breaker: no brother Wong involved."

"Are you kidding," she agreed. "I'll also make sure it doesn't worry Ping Kin politically and then I'll get right on it."

HEARING about all this heightened activity Ping Kin flew to Vancouver to propose the next immigrant step. "I want you to open up a Canadian Money Services Business, an MSB."

"Whatever is that?" puzzled Ron.

"Typical of you Canadians," laughed his new friend, "just another totally unregulated way of moving money. I have inherited the ancient craft of fei-chien, Chinese flying money. But we have evolved far beyond that ancient simple time of unrecorded, coded money transfers. Now we have offshore banking and international systems so complex they cannot be tracked, and now we deal literally in billions.

"Anyone, without any background check, can tie into all that in Canada by simply setting up an MSB quite openly, and deal in money without having to answer to any regulating authority. It's quite crazy! Your federal and provincial authorities that do exist seem more intent upon competing rather than cooperating. They do not even have computer programmes which allow exchange of information."

Ron concurred. "I well know Canada is the only major country in the world without national securities controls or land registration which leaves enormous gaps. But this is surely banking?"

"You, Ron, as a real estate person do not need to register to provide money services or have any specific rules applied to you." he assured.

"Nevertheless," responded Ron "if we do this, everything will have to be conducted legally," not sure they were listening. He worried as he heard Maisie and Ping Kin yattering together excitedly in Mandarin, making plans for the future like bosom buddies.

Maisie, seeing his frustration, translated quickly. "Essentially, he says they will just be placing or investing money through us. On the practical side, we will do everything using their computer programmes which I know well."

Ping Kin interjected enthusiastically that they had started communicating on *the internet*, causing Ron to raise his eyebrows quizzically. "Don't worry. I know this internet is new to you but it appears safe and we are now using it extensively."

They quickly hammered out a deal which would have Maisie running a small money services operation in Canada in conjunction with Ping Kin's Macau bank, mainly aimed at funnelling currency converted from Renminbi directly into Canada.

She explained, "Naturally his clients are extremely wealthy people, mostly men of course, who find it prudent to diversify capital overseas for all sorts of practical reasons as you can easily imagine.

"They think only the stupid controllable masses everywhere have embraced social media. The one percent know it is preferable that they are not personally identified and particularly that their wealth is never disclosed. Thus they see their bank's second duty is to obscure records so that beneficial ownership is always hidden. This is not illegal, just prudent and British Columbia offers a perfect system that encourages that obscurity.

"We will mainly deal with day-to-day smaller capital transfers but they also add up to big sums They come from identifiable individuals sending their annual $50,000 allowed overseas, groups funding investments, numbered companies, by suitcases of yuan, everything you could imagine."

Ping Kin broke in, speaking English. "This is where you come in. The economy in Canada and particularly British Columbia is taking off, providing a safe political place to park money. The West Coast is beautiful, with welcoming permanent increasingly Mandarin-speaking Chinese communities. In the foreseeable future it will obviously become a Chinese city.

"Hongkongers are coming over now but believe me when China starts booming you will see a flood of The Chinese you won't believe; all different from the people from Hong Kong and bearing lots of money!"

Ron insisted, "One thing: no money can be laundered or from Triads or criminal groups."

Ping Kin assured him, "Absolutely not, although I often received funds from companies and trusts that might have been laundered before it gets to me. I usually have no idea whether currency exchange permits have been received because the money just comes through banks or money agencies as money, often with numbered, corporate trusts or obscure owners.

"If I learn to the contrary later I will give you the opportunity to close out the account. Then I will re-invest elsewhere. Don't worry. Maisie will keep a serious eye on me."

THEY did not indeed have to register with anyone back in Canada, so all they had to do was open a 'money' office in their building, knock a hole through to the reception to provide a service counter, put up some signs in Chinese and backup English of course. Leyland Co. was in the money business.

Since they were joining Ping Kin's network, everything was already set up online, requiring a simple connection as the Canadian office of many. Their staff was Mandarin, Cantonese and English speaking, with the communication equipment all capable of operating in Chinese.

They advertised, offering to transfer funds between offices for clients, to help find any investments in Canada on demand, particularly real estate.

The full money services package they offered included exchanging currencies, cashing checks, transferring money for personal use, couriering cash, offering consumer credit, making payments by telecommunication or providing bill payment services, so they were quickly very busy.

With a fully operating plug-in system to join, within weeks their new endeavour was up and running, true to expectations generating a steady flow of money.

It broke naturally into two sections, one related to the immigration business where the clients preferred the anonymity of privately conducted transactions which was embraced by Maisie and her team. The other section concerned the popular investment in real estate, often involving partnerships with larger sums of money which diverted directly to Ron's side of the business.

"THE trick for us will be to set up a system which satisfies Canadian law and our own consciences but still attracts the Chinese Renminbi legally," Ron had instructed, but he need not have worried.

Overnight their Canadian company was into acquisitions or financing in a big way being referred seemingly straightforward investors. They set up a Real Estate Investment and Finance division, hiring new staff to look for deals across the country.

Leyland Co. received a fee for finding the investment; a fee for managing it; and a fee in the future for selling it or redeeming the mortgage.

Ron asked Ping Kin what returns his investors were expecting. He assured him, "They are mainly looking for the return *of* their money rather than a return *on* their money, which should allow you easily to out-bid your established Canadian investors. That will all push up values anyway. Security of capital in safe Canada is their key consideration."

Maisie was much more forthright. "I strongly suspect from Ping Kin's guarded comments much of this is cash skimmed by senior officials from state enterprises, being parked for safety outside China. Those fellows lead a precarious life so they all do it. Skimming in China is OK so long as colleagues share but don't get greedy. Getting their loot out of the country however needs the cooperation of the big banks or skilled operators like Ping Kin.

"Where that leaves us as Canadians I'm not sure."

Chapter 16

Prosperity: Expanding horizons

PROMOTED by now to Inspector, Jack Jackman had stayed in Hong Kong after the takeover by China. The territory was administering itself under the new arrangement but the Canadian immigration process continued essentially unchanged.

He had a good bachelor run, but on one of his leaves back to the endless horizons and silence of the Manitoba prairie, his widowed mother insisted upon him accompanying her to their Ukrainian Orthodox Church, as it turned out for the explicit purpose of a reunion with his childhood sweetheart.

The young woman quickly discovered, traditionally in the family barn, that he had developed a very acceptable mature approach to life, so she immediately married him enthusiastically and returned with him to Hong Kong. His visits to the bars were over.

In fact, he had not been to the Wanchai bar for years. To his credit he had learned Cantonese, but his friendship with Wong had steadily disintegrated as he became more aware of his involvement in large-scale drug dealing. He could personally overlook nightclub frolics but absolutely not the drugs.

There again, he was not dumb, knowing drugs were in all the bars and nightclubs, but when a report came across his desk implicating

Wong with the Triad in major drug movement, he realised how much he had been misled.

There had also been enquiries into corruption in their Canadian mission including alleged favoured immigration deals and widespread early approvals. Up to now Inspector Jackman had skated above it all, until the noise in Ottawa got so loud they were pushed into having a really serious investigation.

The only option he had was to come clean with a report back to his superiors in Canada. "I became imprudently friendly with someone who is now being seriously investigated but general enquiries totally clear me and my expatriate staff of wrong doing."

Being Canadian, they were very sympathetic to the plight of their young fellow officer, whom they had sent to a strange land, and promoted him as a Superintendent back to safe rural Alberta. The elevation was to show their confidence in him and was really to avoid the embarrassment of any investigation of a Mountie in far away Hong Kong.

He returned to Canada to his wife's great delight, still bitter at the deceit of his friend Wong Mai Fu. Those memories were quickly lost in his totally different new duties where his knowledge of Hong Kong, Chinese crime or even his skill with Cantonese was not put to use.

He resigned himself to a life of comfortable policing purgatory in the boondocks.

AT THAT same time, Ron was seeing their money transfer business increasing progressively as more new Canadians returned to prosperous Hong Kong.

These transfers were noticeably by wage-earning men, sending back regular money through Leyland to support their families left in Canada, but wanting no banking record. There was some reverse business, for example with Filipino women sending hard earned money back home, but little cash was involved and it all appeared straight forward.

Transacting his larger condo development financings he did wonder at the source of hundreds of thousands of dollars which were transferred by new business investors but he had no reason to suspect problems.

Wong was introducing new immigrants and Ron noticed a subtle change in their attitude, particularly those increasingly from China itself.

"I am getting out of my depth," he admitted freely to Maisie. "I sort of understand your special Hong Kong Cantonese culture as half-half. On the one hand they appreciate their personal freedom through the court system there, having protective laws upon which they can depend. But on the other hand everything in Hong Kong is material and they are all happy daily to pay kickbacks for special favours or bribe freely to get around the system. They tolerate the modest 15 percent flat income tax rate there but are damned if they will pay up to 45 percent in Canada! Some expect to continue to have it both ways when they come here."

Maisie laughed that it was because soft Canada put up with it. "Why pay for something if you don't have to?" she asked.

Ron's bigger problem was that as they moved into the new century much of the immigration business had become different to him. Their volumes were increasing and Wong was referring some clearly shady characters.

The large majority of clients they dealt with personally were decent cooperative families just looking for a better life in Canada. Maisie admitted, however, "Newcomers are sometimes furtive but clients from China can be very different because they seem guarded, and show mistrust of authority. This is all a recent process."

Way back in the 1970s a Canadian Prime Minister had visited China and publically welcomed family unification. This had started a steady trickle of people from China to Canada after decades of almost no emigration.

Now with increasing middle class prosperity in China, the number coming was growing quickly. "At least jarring Cantonese is being replaced by smooth Mandarin which is much more pleasant to the ear," Ron observed, "but fewer of our clients have previously been exposed to English."

However, Ron's personal work was in Canada. Wong produced the clients with Ping Kin looking after what went on in Macau. Nagging at the back of his mind was Maisie's deep involvement in the whole process fuelled by her continuous quiet business calls in Mandarin with Ping Kin. She knew exactly what was going on.

The deals and his concerns just kept getting bigger.

THEY were both dismayed and frankly taken aback when they were asked by Macau to rubber stamp the documentation of a totally non-existent condo development.

The approach, which came out of their Macau office was quite simple. A property had actually been purchased in Vancouver by an obscure numbered company with a Macau address but heavily financed in Canada by a local bank. Outline condo development plans had been submitted to the city.

From then on, so far as they could make out, the company had never started construction but had been issuing false invoices to Macau investors who had sent funds to Canada supposedly in payment for construction but really going straight into their Canadian account.

The laundering model was apparently working smoothly. The proposal from Macau, although not from Ping Kin personally, was that Leyland adopt this project to bring even more legitimacy to the programme.

Appalled, they together contacted Ping Kin who said apologetically, "It was just one of my keen young men who does not understand the difference between China and Canada, and assumed everyone everywhere is in the same 'beat the government' game. Those instructions should have gone only to Stumpenberg, who is conducting all that invoice-faking business through his trust accounts. We try not to become involved in that sort of thing but money movement is getting complicated. I certainly apologise. My fellows here are getting stressed."

PING Kin explained later, "Sorry. The pressure is on due to the enormous excess of Renminbi floating around here and demand for conversion. When I studied at MIT no one had heard of Renminbi or even of a yuan."

Reverting to being Professor Poon he lectured, "Then it became clear that China had finally stumbled upon a winning formula. With development visibly active throughout the country and exports being offered, China opened its doors, to the delight of the international market which finally discovered the existence of the yuan, although it was still only being used within our country.

"The People's Bank of China was one of the first things the Party established, replacing the several in use, and its early creation of 'Ren min bi', the 'People's Money' was its essential move. While it was indispensable internally, the currency was initially neither unknown nor needed outside the country. Now we are beginning to build a surplus in foreign currencies, especially the almighty American dollar, but conversions are also flowing out, mainly illegally, as enormous personal profits are being made. My clients are creating incredible personal wealth. They are each individually so busy now they are more than happy to leave their pooled personal investment problems with me, hence all the cash!"

"I assume," joked Maisie cheekily, "you are doing well personally out of all this embarrassment of riches?"

He sighed. "Believe me, Maisie, I have derived great wealth out of all this, but I envy you your life. Yes, I am a first-class jet-setter but I have a lonely life in Macau and as yet see no long-term way out. From your point of view, I am just one agent of many pouring currencies derived from Renminbi out upon an unsuspecting world with Canada an eager recipient."

"Sorry, chaps," he finished, in his quaint English.

Chapter 17

Allurement: Success of Titty Bars

LEYLAND had always been advised by straight-up Canadian law firms upon whom they relied to provide honest, totally legal advice. So Ron became shocked as it slowly dawned upon him that Steven Stumpenberg was totally crooked.

Steven came from a family line of distinguished Vancouver lawyers with whom they had dealt from time to time but Ron learned that he himself had struggled through law school. Unkind fellow students suggested he was pushed through because of the family name.

Whatever the reason, in view of his small cluttered walk-up office in a second rate building, far away from the family firm, it was apparent to all that he had not prospered.

Nothing could be further from the truth, because Stump was an exceedingly wealthy man. He owed it to excelling in the practice of obscurity, deception and frankly any dishonest illegal activity.

He had articled in the family firm but they were relieved when he opted to set up his own practice. During articles they had placed him where they thought he could do least damage, in charge of the practice's trust fund, based upon the one accounting course he had merely audited. For him it was a revelation.

There were now four aspects to his business: the obscuring or hiding of his client's identity; managing their money; running it through his trust fund; collecting his fee. He had become an expert at all of them.

He was a member of the fast-growing network of lawyers The Chinese were assembling internationally. As such he was directed to meet the newly arrived Mr Wong by his client from China, Mr Zhang, to the settle him in and look at the setting-up of a nightclub in Vancouver.

"May I call you Mai Fu?" he had asked warmly. "But that will be just between us. In fact, I will make you disappear."

Wong struggled to follow the new concepts but Stumpenberg explained slowly. "I use myself as your trustee, nominee, and sole director or in any position available. I can incorporate a variety of corporations, trusts or charities, in any array of combinations which you will find confusing. But trust me! As a result, I guarantee you personally will disappear in the confusion, becoming untraceable as our helpful Canadian registration system enthusiastically encourages.

"The second stage of my service will be to make all the money untraceable using my trust fund which can receive investments from any source, or send them to any recipient, without risk of discovery or even question."

Wong shook his head in wonder. "Yes," agreed the duplicitous lawyer. "I too find it difficult to believe law officers have been given this wonderful gift."

However, he did not take it for granted, purposely being extremely generous in his business dealings in order to keep clients totally happy.

He would bend over backwards to settle a dispute, literally giving away money, knowing that his only risk of exposure to the Law Society was through a stupid business dispute. Otherwise, everything was hidden, with the result that he was seen as a very helpful lawyer; a generous and wonderful partner.

His dubious business was growing by leaps and bounds.

UNAVOIDABLY arriving honestly as Wong Mai Fu, Wong had

decided the generous Canadian immigration offer was too good to miss, so he too brought his wife Olga and two children to Canada, a couple of years following China's takeover, to serve out the obligatory years of residency.

During which he of course would not be stupid enough unnecessarily to reveal his overseas earnings nor actually stay in the country. He had been advised by Mr Stumpenberg to declare some Canadian income, and that $30,000 a year would do it.

Mr Zhang also had new plans for him in Canada. Ronnie and Maisie had registered their home jointly in the usual way under their names, but Wong boasted his lawyer had set up a bare trust whose sole asset was the home.

He laughed that the title never really changed hands and Stump as trustee could even deal in the property for cash. In fact, he and Stump had a lucrative little side business going where they used the house to flip the title on behalf of clients seeking to 'legalise' cash deals. They shared the tax-free fees he earned. Very simple, they both agreed.

Wong settled the family in, with their debt-free mansion, country club membership and private schools. He commuted regularly to his Hong Kong apartment where he whispered to Ron he had "a cute little girlfriend" tucked away. That suited Olga and his children just fine!

CHINA eventually had been admitted as a member of The World Trade Organization in 2001, a big public relations coup. The following years had seen a swell of new state businesses with export companies forming every day. This obviously had improved Zhang and friends' rake off, because Ping Kin saw funds coming into Macau increase dramatically.

He phoned, "Maisie please encourage Ron to find larger real estate acquisitions and first mortgages. We have hundreds of millions available."

As she went into Ron's office with the good news, her brother Wong marched in proudly with an incredibly beautiful Eastern European blonde on his arm. She was at least a foot taller than he was, spectac-ularly way too busty but moving like a model. "Meet Katia who we brought in from Europe. She gets girls for the nightclub," he beamed.

Maisie just frowned and Ron quickly mumbled, "Hi", and diverted his riveted gaze back to the computer. He knew immediately the nightclub was out of bounds! But Wong had transferred money through them from his unidentified Macau investor to finance his plush suburban club.

They had both noticed the worrying '...*we*'. "Who were "*we*"?

"Why you not at grand opening?" he wondered. "All blue soft lights. Music. They are all beautiful blondes from Europe." He explained their shapes with his hands. "Just have tiny silky stuff on. Take off in private rooms but no quite touchy, touchy. Canada is no fun!" He went on to explain that this might just be an introduction; "Get it, get it?"

Ron rolled his eyes having decided just for himself this was off-limits, even more so when Wong boasted that it was essentially a cash business.

"They have trays of liqueurs. Fifty bucks a shot. Big bare titties. All cash. Sell like crazy" he whooped, "All night long."

"There is a special titty bar." Wong whispered to Ron, wiggled his fingers in anticipation. "We are very modern. Men too in tiny little pink jockstraps."

Later, chatting with Maisie, Ron shook his head in disbelief. "Can you believe this is going on in staid Vancouver? That we are a part of it?"

"I will kill you if you ever go there," she said but he shook his head. "Believe me, I'm going to stay far away."

"But you have not heard the worst. I passed money through to him today for a surveillance system they are putting in ...," she paused dramatically, "and for metal detectors!" They gloomily agreed never to be seen or certainly not taped there but knew their names were all over the paperwork.

OTHERWISE everything went beautifully, although America caused them uncertainty in 2003 by invading Iraq. The Chinese economy continued to expand unabated and money was still flowing in from there and from Hong Kong, plus increasingly from Taiwan, financing three more Leyland developments.

Then a furtive bearded fellow in scruffy jeans had slipped into his Gas Town pub booth while Ron was having a quiet contemplative beer on his own in the early sunshine, babbling something about, "Ammel, or animal or A-something".

He observed a lot of weird people around that part of town so he gave the fellow 10 bucks, patted him on the arm in a friendly way, telling him to "Sod off".

The intruder held up the bank note in surprise only to have it snatched away by the quick waitress and replaced with float of beer. Now Ron was stuck with his piercing eyes. Intently, he clarified, "Mr Leyland, I am Pritam Singh, a Mountie with CSIS working on AML," and took a long draft in relief.

Looking back, Ron could not believe that "AML" still then meant nothing to him until the turbaned beer drinker enunciated carefully, "Anti-Money-Laundering." Combined with the previous over-polite use of his name, Ronnie knew his world had suddenly become more complicated.

"Your brother-in-law, Mr Wong Mai Fu is well known as a high-roll gambler in the casinos." He looked around cautiously before continuing. "My inside informant tells me he arrives with bales of cash to buy gambling chips and he does not seem worried about always losing. This is very, very curious. Can you tell me what is going on?"

"If he is losing the money it does not mean he is money-laundering, it just means he is throwing it away and is being stupid. So what's your problem?" asked Ron.

The detective nervously wagged his head from side to side, in that curious sub-continental way and muttered partly to himself, "I know, I know, but there are other people doing it with cash. There has to be an angle!"

"I never go to casinos; I know nothing at all about gambling; I know even less about Wong's doings; I never even thought about money-laundering until you brought the subject up. Sorry, can't help," Ron assured him.

Concerned but struggling to follow his companion's continuing tirade, he said, "Look, I have a meeting. Let's talk again soon."

This seemed satisfactory to the stranger who swigged the remainder of his beer, glanced around with narrowed eyes, slid from his seat and, except for the turban, merged with the crowd.

Chapter 18

Hoarding: Renminbi 'disappeared'

Z HANG and The Six were growing too confident and early in the century they overstepped themselves.

Access to international shares and operating Chinese stock exchanges produced a flurry of public issues encouraging the Chinese public to invest directly in the success of their country. Even some minor state-owned enterprises were privatised.

Foreign investors started falling over each other to buy shares in China where competition was driving up efficiency. That was when some people at the top started to get too greedy.

Back when the goodies were being distributed to the supporters of the new regime, The Six did well. They had secured policy positions directing development of petroleum, nuclear energy, shipbuilding, electronics and power facilities.

Zhang arranged chairmanships of chemical, electronics, and communications companies which he considered the key to the future. Combined with his father-in-law's powerful position in public relations policy and Ah-Cy's progressive elevation, they were one of the significant families.

A PROVINCIAL electronics firm Zhang chaired had been approved to go private and The Six had subscribed to take it over personally at a fraudulently low share price they had determined themselves.

They had set the price obviously advantageously but they had not been generous enough spreading the shares around some significant local Party officials. Later they intended to go public in Hong Kong, with their personal gain made outside China proper.

Other scandals involving similar insider frauds were unfortunately exposed in the annoying free-market press in Hong Kong and Singapore. There was no trouble blocking the story of their own privatisation within China with the help of his father-in-law, but the story got out.

The Six started to panic and called a meeting in alarm. "I've got it covered," Zhang reassured them. "Your lucky break is that the share price was formally set by the senior management of the company following my verbal instructions from the board. So all we have to do is disavowed any knowledge of the process and arrest the managers for fraud."

They applauded his foresight in relief. He told his colleagues, shaking his head, "That manager was so inept not to cover himself. It pays never to sign anything."

"But remember," he advised them, "'*A crisis is merely an opportunity riding a dangerous wind*'."

Always on the offensive, Zhang portrayed himself as having exposed the electronic company scandal. They set up a commission as the national asset watch-dog, with member Zhang now one of the most powerful business officials in the country. They had created incredible licence to demand extreme personal payment for favours.

The ever-cautious Zhang had reached a pinnacle of power, portraying himself as a helpful moderate, but tactically looking for long-term personal survival.

THEIR ascent to wealthy influence could not have been timelier. The world was now looking to China for manufactured goods which contributed to more than a third of their 10 percent annual growth. The survivors of The Six were still colleagues at that point, personally debating their growing investment options heatedly like the academics they were.

Their Macau bank safely received the kick-back payments they demanded, which they directed for payment to its secure address. They never received any large funds personally, of course, nor was there any record of their personal involvement. They merely had to provide the unhappy donor with the site, plus deposit codes which changed regularly as directed by Dr Poon.

POON was dutifully building their untraceable portfolio which was diversified mainly between the United States, Japan and Europe. Recently he had found them some good opportunities in Australia and now suggested more in Canada.

He was aware before the Expo 86 international success in Vancouver they would not have given Canada a second thought, but he explained to Zhang, "A highly publicised Hong Kong real estate magnate has amazingly purchased the entire exhibition site from their government.

"Not only have the Canadians sold him control of developing Central Vancouver but their government has additionally even cleaned up the site for him. The central city is being transformed by him into a world-class residential destination. They give good deals there! I recommend Canada to be one of the easiest systems in the world for us to enter, with an especially resilient economy in which to conceal our investments."

Zhang referred the suggestion to The Six who were still personally involved in their investment plans. They dug out more data, debated furiously, analysed their findings and cheerfully authorised larger Canadian investment, reassured by the booming if overheated adjacent American economy as the new century unfolded.

Financially, things were wonderful, The Six agreed, showing

China well on the way to world domination. They were just operating within their system and it never bothered them for a second that their expanding fortune could be considered Black Renminbi by anyone.

Chapter 19

Correctness: Concerns at The Club

R ON was proud of Vancouver's socially integrated downtown business clubs but had to admit to their awful racist and sexist histories; not so long ago at that, during his father's early membership. These ancient clubs, like so many other local institutions, had enthusiastically reformed and were rigorously and visibly all-inclusive.

His father told him stories of their battles to liberate the clubs from the white all-male Anglo-Saxon Protestant cliques, with accounts of his personal heroic deeds becoming more politically correct as he aged.

It is here at The Club, which Ron considered the most senior, that the Leyland family followed their membership tradition to entertain their friends and business contacts. He had significantly given Maisie her own membership as one of her many wedding presents.

In the beautiful little crystal bar, Ron and their visiting Hong Kong lawyer Hinks attempted to outdo the martini consumption record they had established at the Hong Kong Club, which was pretty easy because they had become bosom buddies joking together about everything.

Hinks reported, "From a business point of view my clients from

China are very happy. Of course, China is now really in control of Hong Kong although they cunningly will go on allowing us to think we are still running things until it suits their purpose to take over.

"Shanghai is an incredible city with its fantastic business centre being groomed to control the world. One day Hong Kong as we know it will no longer be needed commercially, then poof. ... Poof," he emphasised waving his arms, "it will just be 'The Fragrant Harbour' again. Naturally, all the big corporations with liquid assets have long ago set up contingency plans for a full takeover by The Chinese, moving their capital away and registering ownership wherever; Grand Cayman, Bermuda and so on."

"Then," replied Ron, humouring him, "what happens to the hundreds of thousands of Hongkonger Canadians living there that have gone back?"

"Ah ha," sighed Hinks the lawyer, "that will depend upon timing and how it happens. If China is nasty, they will be stuck there recognised only as Chinese nationals and they can forget their Canadian citizenship. China's nationality law does not accept that new Canadians and their children are Canadians at all, especially if they live back in Hong Kong. Unlike Canada, China does not recognise dual citizenship. So acquiring foreign nationality does not negate Chinese nationality. Go back to Hong Kong and you are only Chinese again!"

After another long sip Hinks joked, "They all know that, especially the older folk who will need your free medical system, so they are setting themselves up to return to Canada at short notice. You will need more hospital beds and condos.

"We will continue with residential financing but that is chicken feed and not why I am here. My wealthy communist guys from the mainland have personal money coming out of their ears from the new state-owned companies. We are talking in hundreds of millions, which they need to deposit safely around the world.

"The new middle class in China has also accumulated massive profits much defensively in cash under the bed which they also want to hide but are only allowed officially to export $50,000 each per year. So, it requires a little manipulation."

"But we have your Macau bank," he whispered, nudging Ron in the ribs. "My clients will keep coming, because of your incredibly lax and trusting Canadian authorities. Unbelievable! No one asks. The guys in China can't believe their luck."

"Our trusting system, eh." Ron joked. "No one seems to be particularly interested in how money comes into the country or where it comes from as long as it keeps coming. But that will change."

Hinks smiled. "Well, for your personal comfort as a friend, clients tell me that we are now technically able to direct substantial funds to you through a local legal trust fund; no questions asked." He paused, mouthing the name, "Stumpenberg."

"So, dear boy, they will say you need have no concerns about money origins if you just go through Stump," He added ominously, "But please if you do, leave me out of it."

THEY met, at Ron's introduction, with the main Canadian chartered banks, which sensing new business, all wined and dined the popular story-telling lawyer from Hong Kong lavishly. They all knew everyone needed big banks to move or exchange significant money with trusted personal connections proving vital.

Again the martinis flowed but Ron had an empty feeling that the cheerful discussion was not entirely genuine, sensing that his banker friends were being very guarded. Hinks and Stump were obviously up to something Hinks was not too happy about.

Ron's part in the Macau operation was, so far as he could see, totally legal, at least in Canada. There were, however, some alarming gaps in his knowledge so he belatedly sought to get some free advice over a beer from his school friend and lawyer George Oikawa, who did not dispel those concerns.

"Honestly Ronnie, you need to investigate carefully before you get in too deeply with any overseas investors. Many are totally secretive and self-serving. My firm documented an acquisition by a group from Shanghai here a few weeks ago where we discovered their representatives had demanded personal side deals to agree to close for their company."

Ron said, "But you surely didn't have to continue that deal?"

George shrugged and said, "Too late; we had already committed tens of millions. From what you have told me your problem is you will be dealing with unidentified money from China. The subject is technically covered in international money-laundering law. Banks supposedly have rules but private money operations like yours slip under the radar.

"However the general law still applies to you. Prudently, you must know the identity of your clients, which means the beneficial owner not some airy fairy numbered company. You must find out if the money is derived from overseas corruption or illegal evasion, such as not registering currency conversion or paying taxes. Report anything suspicious. That's all the advice you get for one pint!"

When they had refilled he continued. "This is all covered as criminal activity in the Code and Proceeds of Crime laws. The key thing you need to remember is that it is a criminal offence to be involved in importing 'the proceeds of foreign corruption' and that is considered a basis of money-laundering. The trick is, if you don't know and the evidence is not apparent, don't worry about it. But if you do know or strongly suspect, close the account immediately."

Chapter 20

Ottawa: Enticing profiteers

WITH their senior status in Beijing and acquired wealth, the opportunity had come for Zhang and Ah-Cy Huang to travel and they could fairly be counted as world travellers.

Their academic years had also given them spare time to learn some English. However, Canada had never impressed Zhang enough to include it in their itinerary, until they started looking at personal investments there.

He recognised with a tinge of regret that it was slightly larger than China but with a tiny population in comparison.

He saw Canada as a long-term relocation objective for the Chinese population overspill but knew they must first subdue their protector the United States, a process he saw as underway.

That would take a while, he mused, as his staff briefed him, planning an upcoming official business visit to Canada.

They reported that the Canadians were attracting people from the People's Republic not just as tourists but as immigrants, playing willingly into their game plan of Chinese integration into Canada to the detriment of the USA. They did not seem to realise it was their established policy that Chinese remained Chinese wherever in the world they settled.

Zhang was now a quietly powerful businessman so the suggestion he visit the top politicians in Ottawa was received with open arms. This reaction was fully expected. Several years before, the latest Prime Minister brought a massive, fawning trade commission to China with most provincial premiers and hundreds of Canada's richest business leaders.

Recently, he had returned with an even larger entourage. They murmured about human rights but were careful not to speak too loudly or allow nasty politics to interfere with promised fortunes.

Zhang had been practising his English but his staff leader joked, "You will have difficulty trying it out on the Canadian leader because he has a French accent you will not understand. Perhaps you should take a crash course in French because some of our strongest, long-time business supporters are French speaking."

Zhang replied, with no trace of humour, "When we take over Canada, and it becomes communist, they would all have to speak Mandarin anyway. But we must do it one step at a time because, *'The sage warns that the path to Dao is long and winding'.*"

HE KNEW that large business was totally sympathetic to any autocratic government including communist, having similar objectives – profits and monopoly. His subordinates recommended meeting Canadian politicians but he asked for greedy capitalists and owners of the largest businesses who had no concern at politics.

The politicians mixed with rich business people anyway, which he commented just made them the same as in Beijing. Showing off his English he quoted, *"Crony Capitalism; crony Communism!"*

Even so, he insisted they plan very private meetings. The last thing he wanted was some Canadian politician haranguing him in public in front of their press about their ridiculous civil rights, while pressing him to make trade deals in the back room.

ARRIVING in Ottawa, he felt strangely at home. His embassy briefing was highly confidential, with his political diplomat laughingly explaining the strategy behind the hundreds of key companies they owned, controlled or seriously influenced, the politicians they had in place in the Canadian system and academics sympathetic to their political line.

In their safe room, he heard all the undercover espionage and technology theft being conducted in the country. They chuckled together that Canada was so trusting and just wanted to be loved.

The security attaché particularly said, "We need your North American companies to increase China's control of rare earth minerals. Our long-term strategy is to monopolise the world supply, aiming at controlling high-tech systems, military products in North America, the development of smart phones, electric cars and even weapon guidance or satellite systems. The government will assist buying mining and production companies outside China, especially in mineral-producing Canada, so you can make offers for companies way above market prices, subsidised financially by us naturally, causing the rapacious Canadian owners to salivate to sell."

Zhang enthused, "Once we have international control of the mineral production we can reduce prices, subsidising again by you, of course, and force all the remainder out of business. Great plan!"

The attaché was confident that China now had the capital concentrated in enormous companies to control the world. Zhang pledged his support, as always.

They parted, laughing at the Canadian Government pleading to him for trade, ignoring the warnings of their advisory secret services which did not seem to cooperate with each other and were trying to operate on impossibly low budgets.

VISITING the big cities Zhang came up against the media and some senior government politicians clearly concerned about human rights in China. He began to find the political side a bit of a nuisance.

On the one hand he had big business contacts falling all over him; on the other side, government officials speaking negatively. He understood their reluctance, since China had exactly the same policies, but he had expected to bribe his way around that.

It encouraged him, however, that Canada's real-life relationship with China was being dominated by self-dealing business people, their friends in the foreign affairs bureaux, by law firms headquartered in Toronto or Montreal, all supported by obsequious Canadian-Chinese business associations.

He entertained lavishly, speaking privately but confidentially to leaders of commerce as a fellow businessman, stroking their egos, hinting at personal benefits he could provide to them and their families in his great, exotic country.

All he secretly wanted was their minerals, expertise, company patents, technology and international contacts but he found empathy in individuals seeking power. They spoke the same commercial talk with similar personal greed as motivation. He had his interpreter along but showed his congeniality by speaking English from time to time.

"Even better," he told them, "we have no need for your money. We use state-owned corporations of various types, allowing us to supply you with cheap capital in China, providing enormous profit leverage."

At the end of a long dinner, when they were suitably friendly and liquored-up, he added, "I can give you my personal reassurance by offering our well-qualified son and daughter, the princeling Huangs, as directors. A mere $50,000 a month director's fee for them will ensure state support through me of your business."

He added with a conspiratorial wink, "We all know that leading international politicians and businessmen, particularly American and Russian, feather their family nests in this way."

He suggested slyly that they might also like to meet the venerable Huang, his father-in-law, to whom he would be pleased to make the introduction. "By the way Huang collects ancient porcelain ceramics!" he confided.

"When you bring your family to China at our expense, first-class naturally, my own household will be delighted to receive you at our mansion near Beijing."

Uncomfortable issues such as human rights were never mentioned of course. His visit to Canada was an overwhelming success, at least on the commercial side and for himself and his princelings.

Chapter 21

Sects: Dancing to the call

SOME salacious detective reporting quickly became a classic, widely circulated within the police force. It was obtained when the Mounties in Ottawa had interviewed the open and extremely forthright young woman concerned.

Late every evening Zhang left the Chinese Embassy with Lo, setting out briskly on his exercise walk around central Ottawa, aware but not bothered that their every move was always monitored by some security system.

As usual they strolled down Sparks Street where there was light and action, to enjoy a beer in the bar of a friendly bistro. As it was at the end of the visit, they were relaxed enough to have a second glass with a serious young woman of Chinese descent who overheard their Mandarin and joined in.

Knowing both his boss's taste for variety in women and his own place, Lo finished his beer and pleaded other duties. Zhang assured him he would make it back to the embassy safely but was secure enough knowing Lo would remain hovering nearby.

Alone, he turned his impressive full attention back to the woman of whose strong peasant face he approved. Her pouting, generous lips were having an immediate effect upon him.

Tight student jeans emphasised her fit legs. Her attempt at cover-up clothing failed entirely to hide her voluptuous upper body which defied modesty. She chatted away confidently, seemingly pleased at gaining his attention; moving closer now that his companion had gone.

Her Mandarin was not fluent, although better than his English, leading him to guess correctly her family had moved from China when she was a child. She added she was a college student who considered herself completely Canadian. He corrected her in a very friendly manner that she was still only Chinese to them and that she was welcome back home any time.

They talked on comfortably in Mandarin for a while until she casually asked if he would like to continue with a drink in her apartment which was a 10-minute walk away.

AS HE expected it was a simple, sparsely furnished student unit.

Once inside, in his usual privileged style, he took charge, throwing off his jacket and unbuttoning her shirt. She demurred, suggesting a glass of wine, although she did shrug at his insistence, discarding the light garment to reveal a string bra which left her barely supported but strikingly revealed.

Now she had his attention, she gestured to the single sofa, setting their drinks on the spindly table. She sat, and turning to face him nonchalantly, admitted to his consternation their meeting in the bar was not by chance.

She knew who he was having noticed his daily walk, thus simply having to follow him from the embassy. For the first time since he came to Canada meeting top officials, he felt insecure and out-manoeuvred; by a slip of a girl.

Looked at him frankly but smiling ruefully, she swayed her tantalising breasts, saying they were just a lure which would go no further, but that he might as well enjoy the show. She added she did not think he was the type of man who would try to force himself on her. Anyway, her colleagues were all close by, lodging in the building during 'the protest'.

WHEN she simply explained it was about the religious demonstration outside the embassy, he understood. She spent time manning the hutted display which The Chinese had been trying to have removed, and was protesting the diabolical treatment her religion was receiving in China.

It was all spur of the moment but this evening she had seized upon the opportunity to tell their story. Now relaxing, he nodded in sympathy, drank the atrocious cheap white wine, and played the game.

She asserted earnestly that they believed in traditional Chinese customs which through mind and body connected them to the universe.

The religious side was pacifist through truthfulness, forbearance and benevolence. Their calm, unemotional personal control would ensure that the religion inspired their eventual success.

He countered that others in their religion considered them an evil practice, while she had to admit some of their founder's claims of miraculous powers were frankly ridiculous.

She was getting flushed from the wine-fuelled argument, and her weak Mandarin was faltering so he suggested tactfully she help him work on his English.

Now more firmly directing the conversation, she replied, "All religious organisations have some beliefs not all members accept but that does not invalidate the basic principles. I meditate, perform all the exercises daily, and especially suppress sexual desires as instructed, thus purifying my body and mind. As a Canadian student I cannot understand why China, the land of my parents, is acting so viciously against such pacific, nice people?"

This brought her to a few tears so he helpfully refilled their wine glasses, this time to the brim.

Wanting to maintain the softening mood, he suggested quietly, "In your homeland we raised the standard of living of well over a billion people. In my youth there was starvation. Look at the progress we have made."

He topped up their glasses, gently slipping the clip off her bra, without her reacting.

He continued quickly, "Chinese people have many options but we chose communism which holds the needs of the many over individual rights. Some officials may have been hard on your sect and treated them badly."

When she tensed up at this reminder, he thought he had lost her, but she sat up, letting her bra slip off; her ample breasts swinging free.

Wanting now to finish talking quickly, he explained, "Religions are just one of the five problems we are very patiently working to correct, the others being Tibet, Uyghur, Taiwan and the democracies! Well, Hong Kong too. But your sect is now listening and I will help them back home."

Breaking eye contact he looked suggestively down her body. "In China we do not debate right or wrong but we act according to our feelings."

FOLLOWING his eyes, she sighed disapprovingly at her prominent, betraying nipples and knew the time had come to act. With a confidence that belied her previously innocent demeanour, she taunted him by wriggling out of her remaining clothes.

Then, in one startling motion she leapt to her feet, grabbing a tiny bell which she tinkled rigorously, progressively being joined by a similar cacophony from adjacent rooms encouraging her devotional forbearance.

She beckoned him, calling breathlessly in defiant English, "Join us. Dance it off. *All energy flows through the navel. Achieve the Fa'.* Dance it off!" commencing her naked, flowing, swirling routine in a dream-like state, accompanied by nearby chanting and drum beating from her supportive but reluctant celibates.

Picking up his jacket in resignation and leaving quietly, Zhang found the patient Lo waiting at a nearby Starbucks. He shrugged at him as they trudged off back to the embassy.

"Achieve the Fa!" he growled.

AT THE end of his official tour he stopped off in Vancouver ostensibly for a few days relaxation but actually to visit his latest nightclub, coming again under the worthy detective's own surveillance. Finally he also would be photographed inspecting the warehouse business Wong had set up to play an important role in their movement of drugs into the country.

British Columbia was famous for its BC Bud cannabis which he was informed was around a $10 billion business and one of the leading earners for the province, so they had no way to break into that established trade.

Similarly, most snorted powder cocaine now highly in demand, heroin or manufactured meth was being smuggled in from Mexico. They therefore just facilitated services for these established businesses, but progressively increasing their own share.

Rather, they were now concentrating on emerging markets particularly synthetic opioids which they had started imported from China, through Zhang's connections, as powder to press into safe-looking proprietary pills.

WHILE in Vancouver he imprudently met a representative from the consulate on the Stanley Park Sea Wall and while walking was taped by long-range equipment.

"My official report will be that Canada offers great prospects for China, where its small population will prove an advantage in the future. We must adopt aggressive policies encouraging volume emigration and I am highly enthusiastic at the success of overt political integration so far into the country. My particular advice will be to increase support of our strong Chinese beach-head now established in Vancouver."

AFTER his young missteps in Hong Kong, policeman Jack Jackman had served out some years of penance stuck in the Prairie boondocks, until his experience had been recognised and he had been moved to Mountie headquarters in Ottawa.

Now a Chief Superintendent he chuckled to himself when he saw the videos his surveillance team had submitted that a distinguished Chinese visitor had picked up a busty, pouty female demonstrator, getting back to her apartment with her in Ottawa. Par for the course, he thought; good luck to him. He laughed out loud when he read her very frank and detailed account of the proceedings.

A few days later he read the report from Vancouver that the same official, Zhang Man Lok, had several times frequented a nightclub they were watching for drug dealing, high-level prostitution and money-laundering. He initially smiled at him being a horny goat.

Then he read further that Zhang appeared to be in long, serious discussions with the manager, a Mr Wong Mai Fu, later visiting a warehouse which was also under their surveillance.

The pieces all fell together.

Chapter 22

Mounties: Getting Black Renminbians

THE call came within a week: "Corporal Pritam Singh to report personally to Chief Superintendent Jack Jackman immediately on all aspects of the Wong Mai Fu enquiry."

His envious pals in the force rallied around, so he headed for Ottawa, uniformed of course, wearing a neat dark blue turban, with a packed briefcase of evidence, plus his trusty laptop. Pleased with his new training in English enunciation he was still highly apprehensive of this opportunity.

He marched into the great man's office late in the afternoon to spend an hour being grilled about their evidence on Wong, Zhang, the nightclubs, call girls, drug dealing and warehousing.

Since the British Columbia RCMP seemed to have computer programmes which were incompatible with the rest of Canada they did not have access nor would be allowed to see each other's jealously guarded information but at least HQ had assembled it and the Chief Super was well briefed.

Dusk had fallen and to Pritam's shock his boss pulled a bottle of Glenlivet out of his desk drawer pouring them each a generous slug.

Pritam stuttered that was entirely against the rules but sipped tentatively, concerned not to offend but afraid it was a test, only to view his boss already pouring himself a refill.

"We have way enough to land the stupid Wong with his local pals but we are now after bigger fish," he explained. "Our job is to catch the bad Black Renminbian bastards!"

Staring reflectively into his Scotch Jackman mused that he had a personal reason to get Wong now he had turned up but the Zhang fellow was of diplomatic interest. He had his own orders from above to hold back for a while. Just assemble maximum evidence. Await instructions.

He handed Pritam a thick file on assembled information from outside British Columbia to read by the morning, ordered him to reconvene at eight hundred hours, slammed the Glenlivet back in the drawer and departed for the night.

"Black Renminibans?" puzzled the Corporal, worried now about keeping his stripes.

NEXT morning, this time leaving Pritam standing stiffly in front of his desk, Jackman demanded gruffly how the Corporal intended to tie up the loose ends and bring them in?

"Further close surveillance?" mumbled Pritam hesitantly, expecting to be ordered what to do, not asked.

"Get real close to the nightclub lassies. Extract some confessions?" his superior chortled to Pritam's high embarrassment, "No, seriously, your plan of action."

Pritam took a deep breath and nervously wagging his head, launched tentatively into his views.

"First, the overall criminal problem in British Columbia is beginning to be far greater than Wong or catching a few women on drugs in nightclubs. It involves the potential laundering of hundreds of millions of dollars and bringing in a deadly drug supply, much of which comes from China. Our present investigations are a minor start to unravelling and understanding entire illegal systems and networks.

"But we do not have the budget or support to continue. Obviously we are dealing with senior people from China, with international criminals, with drug syndicates but also with bent Canadian lawyers and people in authority. There has to be a vast money-laundering system which involves casinos, big banks plus some public officials.

"No one is doing anything about it, including honestly the RCMP. The new Fintrac is no help, no one seems to deal with them anyway and they only have a few people in the West. They provide rare convictions and have no budget. The financial institutions agency has told them of dozens of apparent money-laundering violations in the West but nothing happens. We can forget CSIS who are always too busy to help us or discuss anything due to it being secret. Local police forces are, well, local! So we can get no help from others."

"OK, OK," interjected his superior. "I sympathise. But what are you going to do about it?"

Finally decisive, Pritam said, "We don't get any support from politicians or officials outside the force and in fact they are often obstructive, for whatever reason, so we have to stick to our own internal principles. They claim to have their own provincial security systems but what goes on in the casinos is frankly a mystery. We must rely on proven Mountie methods!

"Considering our limited facilities, we can probe only one target at a time. Since Wong's organisation is vulnerable, concentrate our resources on that group. Dig into every line of contact, especially finding how their money moves. Give us dedicated online analysts assigned to the case. Infiltrate the bad fellows at all levels and find whistleblowers. Do not rush things and concentrate on establishing exactly how the entire network operates. Then run them in using that template to go after others."

He paused for breath just long enough for his chief to break in and reassert his command.

"Excellent. You're my man," enthused the Chief Superintendent.

ORDERED to sit and with a mug of standard coffee in his hand, Pritam could relax a bit. Now he must patiently listen to him curtly reminiscing.

"I spent many years in Hong Kong with the force, but was first cast into the boondocks when I came back to Canada. Later my Asian experience finally brought me to head office. We do talk to those other agencies at least at my level," he said rather sarcastically.

"That brings me to the reason you are here. I need a personal point man on the West Coast who can tell me what the hell is going on. No one at all is cooperating out there and I am totally in the dark about this laundering business. We have no budget, you see, so you will be very important to me personally. I will give you a direct line to call me, anytime."

Pritam's heart swelled with pride.

"We have been investigating with the Five Eyes into an international crime syndicate where we strongly suspect your fellow Zhang to be a key member with Wong his Canadian sidekick. They are just getting going in this country which is a relatively small market but a useful pathway to the States. The top syndicate leaders have been around for a long time. I have to admit to being part of the administration that inadvertently allowed those bastards in from Hong Kong back then. Wong was one of them.

"Your exposure of the expanding Vancouver money-laundering system, tying Zhang into the network has been very important. As you have revealed, they have their own shipping, warehousing and trucking companies operating on the West Coast as a perfect set up for their business."

He congratulated Pritam on his persistence, then gestured to bring him back to rigid attention. He assured him he would record the progress on the file together with approval of a generous budget to get those 'Black Renminbian bastards'.

To Pritam's amazement he stood to shake his hand and announce, "Well done, Sergeant Singh."

The new sergeant marched out proudly, with his head high. There was one objective in his mind: Black Renminbians!

Chapter 23

Wealth: Improving sources

R ON'S father Logger was rather short on the phone and he knew trouble was coming. "I had been having second thoughts about your business connections in China, so I want to discuss it with you and Maisie. Please meet me for lunch at The Club".

Getting quickly to the subject, setting the scene rather abruptly, Maisie thought, before they even enjoyed their first sparkling sip of the refreshing Blue Mountain Brut Reserve, he launched into his topic with a studied frown.

"I see immigration investor funds are in the news!" He was referring to the series of exposed multi-million-dollar frauds played by some Canadians on unsuspecting immigrants and the government.

"Can't afford to give Leyland Lumber a bad name by association, you know. Plus we are told our immigration fellas let in really bad cops fleeing Hong Kong and likely other ne'er-do-well buggers," he gruffly complained.

Trying to reassure him, Ron explained, "We are winding down the immigrant investor business because it is extremely time consuming and we agree a tad dubious. It served us well to get started and make contacts but it is too work intensive.

"We are easing out of that and increasingly sourcing real estate investors directly through Ping Kin in Macau, Hinks in Hong Kong and agents in China."

"Good to hear," Logger replied, signalling reluctant acquiescence by calling for a more satisfying large glass of full-bodied shiraz.

Then atoning for his gruffness he changed subject, which he always did tactically when he was getting his way, by graciously commending Maisie's public activity in charitable organisations, particularly, promoting human rights in the world.

Then he asked her, "I would be honoured if you would consider joining the board of Leyland Charity Trust."

This was their company 'do-good' operation, and a family duty Maisie had long coveted. He was well rewarded when she jumped up and ran around the table to hug and kiss him in appreciation.

MAISIE was developing full confidence in her relationship with Ron but it had taken a few years for her to tell him any details about her stock market adventure going on with Ping Kin.

Now as China prospered in the first years of the century, she had to tell him, because the figures had become so significant. He admitted, "I'm sorry, it already leaves me with ethical shivers, so get it off your chest!"

"Way back in 1990, when I enrolled in the Macau business school, the big topic of conversation was the reopening of the stock exchanges in China. This was a remarkable political revision so soon after the devastatingly Cultural Revolution.

"Stock exchanges were not new to China with the first exchange in Shanghai opening way over a hundred years before. They were closed first by the Japanese invasion, then again by communist revolution so reopening was a big deal.

"At the time my business school taught China was ready now to take on dirty capitalism at their own game. The new exchanges were modest, and nowhere near as active as the booming Hong Kong Exchange, but looked like a start towards a more liberal China.

"That was around the time I formed my dalliance with Ping Kin. One of the games we played together for personal gain was developing our 'fun fund' investing in shares listed on the reopened Shanghai and Shenzhen markets. We argued over which was better, laughing at our final decision to put half of our limited funds in each market.

"Then, one day we added dramatically to our small initial stake when one of The Six's hidden investment funds very simply spun off tens of millions of dollars of obscure untraceable gains which Ping Kin was not quite sure what to do with anyway. So we took it."

"I can't believe you said that!" objected Ron, absolutely scandalised.

"Honestly Ron," she insisted, "Ping-Kin is forced to work for a bunch of crooked senior politicians on the take who will have no compunction at dumping him, or worse, at the drop of a hat. He is merely looking after his future and he gets by far the larger share anyway. I am just lucky to be invited along for fun.

"Our investment strategy is very simply; follow the same instructions he receives from the market insider Six in Beijing. The Chinese stock market is essentially just one big insider trading racket, already with an amazing 80 percent in the hands of wealthy establishment investors. The average people do not really have access but prefer the booming real estate option.

"Even better for us, the insider investors controlled all the policies in the companies, knowing way ahead what decisions are being made, long before the trusting market hears the officially published good or bad news. We just are on to a good thing!"

Ron shook his head dubiously.

AFTER that, as China's economy continued to prosper, the 'fun fund' had grown dramatically. Even Ron was impressed at their investment acumen. However, after hitting unwarranted record highs the entire Chinese market crashed causing him to chortle at their discomfort.

The Chinese inside traders had naturally also seen their own investments plummet, but they busily pumped public funds back into the state activities and enterprises, quickly reviving the economy and reversing their losses.

Ron however still shook his head at the expense when Maisie happily came back from shopping with the shining new Hermes Birkin handbag she had been threatening to add to her collection for months.

Moving closer and pouting seductively she protested, "Don't be a meanie, it was only $30,000."

THE American and the world economies were also booming. Things had never been better! Requests for investments were now flowing in regularly to Leyland by way of Macau, Taipei and from China itself.

But Ron remarked to Maisie they were facing more competition because Canadian real estate agents had connections in all the major Chinese cities.

"Ping Kin says ordinary folk from China are delivering their Renminbi often in cash to the banks in Macau where no questions are asked. For an 'insurance' fee, averaging about 20 percent, the money can be changed to another currency for deposit anywhere in the world."

This was not apparently unreasonable as Ron first suggested to Ping Kin because even in Macau it was not easy to turn large amounts of Renminbi cash into Canadian dollars without question. These funds were not necessarily moved immediately to another country, however, but could be used to trade within the banks.

Ping Kin's new customers were offered several options, one of which was to buy investments remotely, such as condos in Canada, which business he passed on to Leyland.

Learning that several trades had already taken place in Macau before their involvement, Ron was pleased to see the Canadian Government was now registering tax claim on the units up front, so the taxes would unavoidably be paid in Canada by someone eventually

MAISIE broke the latest Wong bad news. "Wong and Stump have

joined forces to exploit a loop-hole. Ping Kin says they are associated with a shady Vancouver developer and have a condo racket going financed by investors in Macau, Hong Kong and China.

"Relying upon the hot Vancouver condo market and the Chinese love of gambling they have set up a 'house' in Macau flipping Vancouver apartment units. Neat, eh?

"Ever so trusting, your Canadian tax fellows are apparently not bothering to require your developers seriously to keep records or report pre-sale activity, so as the market improves they are able to flip the unregistered units off the record freely.

"They do not need to advertise or spend money on show suites because they are not selling anything to Canadians. They convinced their willing, blind-eyed Canadian bank they had pledged enough off-shore capital to meet financing requirements and then started construction."

Ron assumed, "So, once things are slowly underway their partners in Macau can have fun actively flipping condos tax free until eventually final sales have to be registered in Canada, when the building is completed and has its occupancy permit."

Absolutely," she laughed. "With those final flips, the last gamblers holding the condos, but recognised only by their confidential wagering code name of course, are registered by Stump in Canada as the 'lucky final winners'.

"The happy partners make profits, earn fees, get a rake-off on the gambling trading and charge interest on loans at exorbitant rates, mostly unobserved and in far away Macau."

"You Chinese will gamble on anything," Ron chided her.

Ping Kin assured Maisie that he had no part in this activity. "I'm just passing on the news!" All she could do was apologise again to Ron for their relationship with her criminal brother and stay far away.

RON was lunching in his Gas Town Pub when he spotted the yellow turban way down the street, heading his way. So much for undercover work, he thought.

Upon the furtive fellow's arrival, he thrust a beer into Ron's hand muttering, "My round," which lowered his apprehension.

Beyond that, the casually dressed detective went straight to the point.

Ron concentrated. "We are on to Wong, making a connection to you and Ms Leyland. He is up to strange bad things and evidence is mounting. If you have anything to report now is the time."

Beyond that Ron's careful questioning showed they did not have a clue about their formal business, nor what he meant by money-laundering, what it was, where it came from or even the volume.

Ron ended up asking most of the questions, learning they only had a handful of officers assigned to the west of Canada. The officer seemed happy to lapse into silence over another beer. Ron ended by patting him on the arm, offering any help his companies could give.

Back with Maisie he worried, "The cops have been slow but they are catching on. It is pretty clear Leyland is being watched."

Chapter 24

Leone: Off-shore shenanigans

BARBADOS had the rare distinction of having tax treaties with both Canada and China which worked well together. These could facilitate a most advantageous flow-through situation, fully recognised by the Canadian tax authorities.

Ping Kin employed Leone Lawrence on his Macau business and asked Ron to visit him in Barbados to establish offshore tax arrangements covering some real estate they were expanding in Canada. This time Maisie was with him, because, "No way you holiday on my favourite hurricane-free island without me."

She obviously knew her way around as was soon demonstrated on Dover Beach. They both preferred the south of the island with its long beaches and waves. Wearing her new Emilio Pucci designed tiny bikini, she ran ahead of him through the powdery sand. She was intercepted by a tall jet-black fellow whom she embraced fondly, jumping up and down in excitement at the reunion.

When Ronnie caught up she turned happily. "This is my husband, Ronnie. Ronnie, Charles." Charles said, "Husband??" wide-eyed in theatrical disappointment.

Then he laughed his booming laugh, producing a jug of his 'special' rum punch which, in the civilised Bajan style, they sat and chugged on the beach as she caught Charles up on the news.

"Nice fellow," Ron said as they staggered back to their unit for a nap. "How did you meet him?" "Well," she grinned, "I had always wanted to try....." but he interjected.

"OK, OK, I get it."

THAT evening they arranged to meet lawyer Leone for drinks before dinner. They were mildly surprised to find themselves invited to a small beachside bar which appeared covertly gay and filled with noisy dark-skinned locals like Leone.

"I thought you should know," Leone grinned. "Plus you should be aware your lawyer is a potential felon in Barbados subject to life imprisonment, even for acts in private."

Frowning, Ron asked, "It must be upsetting for you?"

But Leone replied; hand on heart and feigning romance, "The gorgeous Caribbean turquoise sea outside Bridgetown Harbour is my refuge from this human nonsense. I sail my little boat straight out away from shore to enjoy the solitude, dreaming alone that my salvation is nigh."

"Actually" Maisie enthused, when they had finished laughing. "As it turns out I have someone for you to meet, who is also a sailor. We will concoct some business reason to get you two together with great interest."

JUST a few weeks later, she got her opportunity at matchmaking, one of her persistent traits.

Ping Kin came to Vancouver intent upon expanding their joint business.

"How about investing in bearer shares and bonds? Is that a funny idea?" Of course Ronnie shrugged on cue. "Why?"

"Yes, I knew you would say that," said Ping Kin. "Although regulators are getting agitated there are still no security laws or regulations covering that business anywhere in Canada so you can merrily trade without disclosure, then go on trading them forever!"

"Plus," he added pointedly, laughing at his own joke, "each province has its own non-regulation, so there is non-regulation countrywide. My guys in Macau have become very keen at the potential of Canadian bearer investments. We have set up a little section just dealing with accumulating or trading bearers for sale internationally.

"It is amazing that Canada is one of the few Western countries that has absolutely no regulation on bearers which of course have no registered owner, making them safe from any form of taxation. It is difficult to design anything better for us. Both your Feds and provinces continue to allow their issue despite continuing international pressure.

"We thought you might like to piggyback on our research to start a portfolio for your new Canadian visitors. I have to assume with your own high-level Canadian insistence upon paying taxes you would not buy them yourself!"

"Not even remotely in our line anymore," pointed out Maisie winking to Ronnie behind his back, "but absolutely of interest to our banking connection in Barbados. We suggest you run this through Leone there on your way back. It could well appeal to his offshore crowd."

LEONE and Ping Kin were both rather shy, complicated individuals. While they immediately felt an emotional connection neither quite knew how to express it.

Their first meeting above bustling Broad Street in Barbados' small commercial centre was all business. They reviewed Canada's lack of controls with disbelief, both as seasoned veterans of dubious dealing to evade governments.

Ping Kin pointed out, "Canada has no limits on access to payment networks, no monitoring for compliance, no risk-mitigation standards, no penalties for non-compliance as some countries have imposed."

Leone enthused, "However, you can chose other equally easy

countries. I am aware of literally hundreds of billions flowing illegally out of Russia for example, mainly through Europe but also through some Caribbean countries.

"Payments go through complicated contortions I can often follow, involving multiple service providers who are supposed to reveal their source. But banks are also reluctant to reveal origins. Some governments are on to it including slow Canada so the present easy avoidance will soon be gone."

To which Ping Kin replied delightedly. "Then crypto-currencies and systems we have not yet dreamed of will take over. This is just like my world in China and Macau! We have a lot to talk about."

"Let's continue this over rum?" suggested Leone.

Their personal breakthrough came over Ping Kin's sometimes quaint and limited American wording choices. Leone purposely picked a straight bar where he ended the late evening educating him in rums. They raised smiles all around them with their hoots of laughter at their handheld Mandarin translation app's discovery of more explicit, raunchier words with each new rum tasting.

It would take a couple of exchanged 'business' visits before their relationship became physical but by then they were each dreaming of an escape together.

Ping Kin's needs for consultation in Barbados became more frequent. This led naturally to the joint purchase of a 50-footer sail boat which took them straight outside the constraining boundaries of Barbados, into the embracing Caribbean seas together.

Chapter 25

Canada: An easy haven

WONG'S family had settled down permanently in Vancouver but he was still commuting. He had his Asian agencies, nightclub interests and other increasing unrevealed schemes to run.

Leyland continued its immigration and money services business in Vancouver in step with its real estate activities, the volume improving year-by-year, bringing in thousands of genuine, hardworking immigrants and as planned, adding buildings financed cheaply initially by the Investor Program.

The first years were pretty straightforward, collecting names or documents, helping with the immigration process, moving money, building property, finding tenants; the usual things.

Wong still represented the unnamed tenant in their first immigration building from which he conducted his mysterious import businesses. All they knew further was that acting upon his success in Hong Kong, he had also opened his nightclubs with undisclosed partners who were financed from China through the Macau bank.

Within a few years Wong had made a cash offer for The Warehouse, buying full ownership. A worried Maisie pointed out to Ron that many of Wong's employees had been brought in by their agency relying upon his introduction and documentation.

But a few years after Hong Kong had settled down under Chinese control, the majority of their immigrant clients were being produced by Wong from China, changing the dynamics and causing their first worrying problems to appear.

Maisie, who managed their immigration side was concerned. "Ron, it has become a pattern and Wong himself is the problem. Our agreement is that once the Asian paperwork is done, the immigrants are our responsibility within Canada. Wong should have no further part but he is always hanging around, charging clients extra fees for 'special services' or undisclosed finder's fees of his own. He is a real nuisance because they all seem to be the dubious ones."

They had seen their general immigration business expanding over the years as a service, bringing valuable citizens to the benefit of Canada as well as to themselves, promoting increased staff that now occupied a full floor at the Leyland office building.

"I am getting very disappointed with some of our immigrants. As far as I can tell, something approaching a third have gone back to Hong Kong having secured their Canadian passports which is sad," Ron said. "Now I see the same trends developing in our clients from China. Those that stay are good solid citizens making me proud of our immigration service and I hope the others will return."

Ron's concerns went further. "Like all societies, however, our clients also have their too-clever wise-guy elements, that just have to beat the system but Wong seems to have gone out of his way to attract them! Far too many are making a show of settling their families here, then returning to continue earning a living in Asia or indeed whatever part of the world they were coming from."

Maisie added she was dealing with these problems in her immigration administration everyday now. "Too many clients Wong has sourced are already back at our door with problems, usually from the realisation that their application for permanent residency actually requires them to stay in Canada for years which they had no intention of doing."

"Especially also of not paying the dreaded income tax nor of disclosing their overseas wealth!" Ron reminded her. "They complain they really had not committed to stay that long on account of businesses they must get back to."

"Do you know," she asked "that spoilsport Canadian immigration officials are finally requiring proof of residence with stamps on their original passports to verify their stay? Wong is rumoured to have established a little office in The Warehouse providing 'services' for fake mailing, recording false residential addresses for entire families who have returned, with a re-documentation processes, and stamps to confuse the enemy. They apparently build up entire correspondences to prove families are in the country. One of their tricks is to misspell names so they can hide people but later claim it was all just their silly error." She paused for breath.

Maisie had learned many details from a harassed mother in their immigration process, who sought her advice because she spoke only Mandarin, having no intention of ever learning English. Wong had taken their Chinese passports and arranged new fake ones for travel.

His instruction was to use the temporary passports for travelling, while saving the clean, legal ones for later Canadian citizen confirmation. She was worried it sounded too simple but she had heard everyone so far had got away with it.

When Maisie had challenged Wong on this he had laughingly responded "The worst that happen is a five-year freeze on the application so they will just try again later."

"We do not forge passports," he had chuckled. "They are real passports bought in China on the side. Anyway they are all my clients. They have a name: satellite families!"

SHE immediately issued a written memo to Leyland staff: "*Our business depends upon open dealing with the immigration office. Therefore we will not fabricate nor deceive in any documentation nor, if asked, will imply incorrectly that our clients are complying with residency and tax requirements'.*"

"That is a very Canadian sentiment. I love you for it," commented Ron, "but we are deeply involved in all this!"

WHEN Wong heard about the Leyland staff instructions he came storming to their office in protest. "Everyone is doing this, you are crazy. Do not mess with my clients. Canada does not want to know."

Later she shrugged and told Ron on the last point Wong was somewhat correct. "So far, everyone just looks the other way. I am so disappointed and our entire immigration business involving my brother has becoming tainted. You know Ron, we can't risk being in this with him anymore and I am going to start talking to Ping Kin about pulling us totally out of immigration and personal money services."

Chapter 26

Pritam: India improves its skills

WHILE they had been working mainly with immigrants from China, people were also flooding in from India, Iran and South America; from all over the place. China produced more visitors and immigrants than India but the tens of thousands from that sub-continent were becoming impressive.

Leyland had assembled a keen young staff who were actually pushing him to expand to other immigrant countries particularly India to double their business. He had resisted, preferring to specialise on China where he considered they at least knew the lay of the land.

People from India understandably did not start moving to Canada in large volume until they felt welcome. Encouraged by the more liberal welcoming attitudes permanent immigration rapidly went up to 30,000 a year, almost as many as from China with 40,000.

Adding to the hundreds of thousands of education permits already issued, they also saw an extra 15,000 students now coming every year from India, many likely to remain, plus crowds of annual tourists. So there were plenty of Indian faces around.

"Let's double our business," the staff pleaded at a meeting.

Ron had been worried that they knew little about India, added to which the stories were that their agents were terribly untrustworthy to work with. China had its other problems but was however much more disciplined so far as documentation veracity was concerned.

While they found much of the time Chinese papers could be trusted, the best thing was to assume all those from India were suspect at least in a minor maybe a major way, due to their flexible administration!

But the sub-continent then came up from an unexpected source.

FITTING in very correctly wearing country club casuals, the intruder still stood out strikingly due to his imposing build; particularly topped by his tall and bright blue turban.

He slid onto the bench next to Ron's tennis game, crouching in vain to avoid attracting attention while signalling for a meeting by blowing his nose loudly on a large matching blue handkerchief, but studiously avoiding a giveaway eye contact.

Taking part in his charade, as he changed ends, Ron muttered, "Coffee shop; half an hour." His fellow players paused in their game to watch in amazement as the mysterious stranger kept to the shadows, to slink off the court.

"Thank you. Perfect cover," was his shouted observation of the after-school teenage coffee shop madhouse. They scored a corner table having outpaced a frantic mother with babies by clambering over piled up bulky hockey bags.

Pritam got straight into it.

"I have a big problem I am begging you to help me with. My very early police career started in Mumbai in the trendy upper Juhu beach areas where there is a lot of action," he rolled his eyes, "if you know what I mean. We young foot cops got to know the girls well, so naturally I ended up too close to one called Sheena as her protector.

"One thing led to another. She lived with me for a while although it could not amount to anything because of her low caste. Later, I moved here but when I visit Mumbai I occasionally sleep with her at friends' rate. She tells everyone proudly that I am now a very special senior police officer in Canada.

143

"Three months ago I was therefore surprised to get a notification by email from the Canadian immigration website formally advising me of Sheena's application for a certificate of nomination to immigrate into Canada.

"They copied the Visa Office and asked me to confirm my sponsorship. That was all. 'Confirm', 'Click', 'Send', no other action needed.

"Sheena was on her way, giving me happy-ending dreams of limitless fun! I was very, very joyful.

"Then, in the mail, I received an explanatory letter from her Indian immigration agent, whom I checked out to be at a good Malabar Hill address, just making his introduction to contact me by email.

"He asked me to help her out by paying a quite hefty residency fee which had taken her by surprise plus a couple of thousand dollars for his expenses. These were relatively small amounts which I knew in my dreams, she was more than capable of making up to me later.

"Then I received another email from the Canadian Government website telling me there were problems with Sheena's application. Could I kindly make assurances as to her character?

"Her agent in Mumbai supplied the words, explaining as a previous police officer I was able to assure them of her impeccable reputation, which I posted back to the immigration office; just click 'Return.'

"Almost immediately, as though waiting for my help, her agent sent me a print-out of all her many, many prostitution fines while I was a local cop. I rushed, too late: their websites and addresses in India, all fakes. Even the agent was impersonating the genuine one. I am from India, how could I not suspect?

"I then got a phone call from an Indian-voiced fellow saying that Miss Sheena needed more assistance. He suggested $100,000 would be helpful, to be transferred immediately to a wire address they would provide.

"He said the immigration people would be interested in my real family background but even more my Mountie bosses would enjoy viewing the audition tapes I made with Sheena when she was trying to become a Juhu porno star."

"Actually," he just had to add, "they were very, very impressed with my size and performance but Sheena did not get a job offer. But that's not half of it! I am also married and we have six children. My wife can be a dragon, a terrible dragon, and she cannot ever, ever, hear about Sheena."

"That's blackmail," protested Ron, "not an immigration problem. How can we help?"

But the shaken cop amazed him further by stuffing a conspicuous, bulky paper bag into his hands and saying "No. I need your confidential banking services. Send this. The financial instructions are in there."

IT WAS dusk when he left the club and Maisie at home was drinking a glass of wine when he dumped the hundred thousand in used notes on the coffee table.

"So, a cop gave you a brown bag of money and you took it? Is that some kind of reverse bribery? This is too funny."

"Not for poor Pritam," he replied. "He can be quite a goof but I rather like the fellow."

She was examining the wiring details in the envelope, noting that all was not lost because they had the contact address of the bad guys.

"Ping Kin has just got up," she reminded him. She retired with her cell phone, grabbing what was left of the bottle, to call him in Macau seeking a solution.

THE following evening they had a return call from Ping Kin who thanked them for several hours of computer fun. He had sent them a personal report which went into the detail of the Indian dark immigration side. He laughed at their rather unsophisticated but extensive fraud which he listed off enthusiastically.

"Computer scandals, misrepresentations, fraudulent applications, falsified records, visa counterfeiting, providing clean police records, unlicensed agents, impersonated agents, fake email addresses, people swaps, computer theft, and newly found families. Just wonderful stuff!"

He applauded those Indian fellows, joking that their skill at fraud was developing well. As a restricted Chinese, he acknowledged the enterprise their personal freedom allowed, but they still had a lot to learn.

With respect to Pritam's problem, Ping Kin claimed that their own expertise in Macau was way ahead having far more experience moving money. These hawala fraudsters in Mumbai anyway had proved real amateurs so he had easily tracked them down, frozen their funds, even obtained other compromising material from their records.

When confronted they rushed to comply, deleting all Pritam's evidence. He would not hear from them again. Ping Kin chuckled that they had frightened them so much Pritam was set up with freebies from Sheena for life, but probably not in Canada.

RON was worrying over breakfast about the difficulty they were still in.

"How can I, a possible laundering suspect, now safely hand back a hundred thousand bucks in notes to a police officer? Come to that explain where I got the cash? And what about the club surveillance videos?"

Laughing at his discomfort, she assured him, "We have taken care of that as well. It apparently proved child's play for Ping Kin's technical guys to wipe the club's surveillance system, and they set it up as a week's operating glitch to avoid suspicion. Pretty neat, don't you think?"

"I don't find any of this is particularly amusing, but you are just brilliant," was all the relieved Ron could say, shaking his head.

IN THE end, acting like normal trusting Canadians, they met at the pub where he assured Pritam the demand for payment had been cancelled. He would never hear from them again.

Showing remarkable common sense, Pritam downed his beer, muttered, "Thank you both," just picked up the shopping bag by the bar stool and left without comment.

Chapter 27

Clients: Troubling sophistication

A S THEY moved on into the new century, they all observed the investors from China were arriving well prepared and better organised.

Leyland was finding consortiums coming to them already formed, with detailed requirements on how business was to be conducted, many of which they just could not accept.

Their obsession of course was non-disclosure.

Ron would not deal with the more than dubious Steven Stumpenberg who was often The Chinese lawyer of choice. Ping Kin complained they had lost several great deals by being so obstinate but now a major real estate acquisition had come up through a Macau group of investors. He was begging Ron to do it with Stump.

This was big, and Ron was in two minds, resorting as usual to his lawyer pal for advice.

Vancouver is blessed with the story, slightly exaggerating the facts, it is possible to ski, play golf and go boating on the same day, which is for some weeks of the year technically correct.

This beautiful sunny day, Ron and the family lawyer George Oikawa had chosen the golfing option at their exclusive and lush mountainside club, where discussing establishment business had always been the primary purpose. Ron explained his dilemma, as they played.

"The Macau bank will provide all the capital from a consortium of their investors, allocating all assets to be held by Stump in trust to be solely administered by him, totally obscuring ownership or money movement. They already use that system which they claim to be legally available in Canada. Therefore they say it makes no sense to operate otherwise."

George agreed. "That is true, and I can set up whatever system your clients request for simple ownerships but what Stump does is not my national firm's advised practice. You are enthusiastically talking about hundreds of millions of dollars with dozens of investors. Even my large legal firm could not administer this volume of administrative work nor would try. We can cope with individual trusts but this is running a business through us which is not our function.

"If things go wrong or investors get excited they have to complain to the Law Society, which would then have to go to the court to open up the trust and to set up another capable administrator. That would be a very messy business for everyone."

He muttered that all this talk had made him miss his putt which Ron cheerful said he would have missed anyway. George concluded, "If you need to hide your identity then you are up to something and you do not operate that way."

Back in the men's locker room, with its sweeping view windows and where they tapped their own beer, he expanded on his advice. "You are facing enough unknowns from Asia, You must always know the identity of your investors to report clearly to them. Obviously you wouldn't be able to do that!"

Ron was relieved at the advice, assuring him, "Anyway, Maisie has already turned her thumbs down! So I have no real choice!"

PING Kin's amicable reaction to Ron's negative response had been surprising.

"I have assured you and particularly the beautiful Maisie, any investors we send from Macau will act totally up front with you, so it is understandable you both see this as pushing things too far."

His closing comment was not reassuring. He laughed that he already had the deal organised with Stump who had no similar scruples. Ron responded with a shrug, that was his business, but they must ensure their own activities were clearly dissociated from Stump, Wong or any of their crooked associates.

"Leyland's interests will now be almost entirely centred upon financing our own real estate business now we have decided to exit immigration and money services."

Ping Kin confirmed reluctantly that all draft documentation had been completed for them to hand off the entire immigration-related operation to Wong, whenever they wished.

Maisie responded defensively, "Immigrants come to this country specifically because that is the way of life they want to enjoy and the vast majority live that way happily, so we were pleased to be of assistance. Too many of Wong's personal clients are highly doubtful to us and some of his reported services downright illegal.

"His clients operate in larger figures and some have negative motives for moving their wealth to seeking personal safety out of China. The question keeps arising, how did they make their money? In too many cases his clients and the whole thing just does not feel right."

Ron added, "I only got into all this originally for easy Hong Kong investor immigrant dollars anyway and of course because of my love for Maisie," giving his now close friend Ping Kin the final understanding chuckle.

SHE later burst into Ron's office in anger waving an email in Chinese from Ping Kin. "Look what Wong has been offering in all the big Chinese cities with our name on it!"

He waited patiently, while she ranted on. "Wong is advertising Canadian citizenships by birth, offering pregnant women full travel, luxury hotel accommodation and hospital arrangements. Then advising that the child wins citizenship, free public education, university cost at only a fraction of overseas student fees, free healthcare for life and the bonanza, family unification rights!"

Ron objected that was silly but she went on, "Canada is among a few nations which offer citizenship upon birth in the country and thousands of new little citizens are being registered every year in Canada under that policy with tens of thousands in later family unification.

"All levels of government for years have been saying that this should stop. Politically nobody will touch it but it is not something we have to be involved in. This is the last straw. Let's go and tell Wong we want out of immigration and all its trappings. Like right now!"

WONG had shrugged at the news. "I am happy to take over the Canadian side. It will all go in The Warehouse and mix in my business."

It was a while before he realised the enormous advantage to himself that he had achieved. First, this was a legitimate business fitting perfectly into his need to hide laundered money. But second, it opened up a whole new vista to him.

He found himself sought out by clients looking for better opportunities overseas provided with cash smuggled through Macau or other locations. Soon he was happily working through his lawyers setting up loans for them in Canadian banks earning skimmed-off cash fees. His friends in China built up an elaborate underground network which Ron had resisted, with the result they were soon dealing in thousands of immigrant or visa applications.

At the staff's repeated request India had finally been added. A successful corner of the office was scented by pungent tiffin aromas and buzzed with different languages. Even more sophistication was added by hiring an expert away from a competitor who 'arranged' third world passports to act as a stepping stone to Canadian documents. If applicants had problems at home getting papers just find them an accommodating third world country where they could be bought. It was simple.

The potential boggled his mind when he needed more girls for his clubs finding it was easy to bring them in from Eastern Europe or Southern Asia if you knew the ropes.

He was aware of the very profitable human smuggling industry which several Triad friends operated in Canada, proposing partnership. Actually, they had been somewhat insistent because of his extensive shipping container business but even he had to decline involvement.

The practical difficulties in Canada were so formidable he knew that this was indeed an area he could expect serious problems. Turning a blind eye was another matter, of course allowing him to profit without becoming directly complicit.

Eventually he did push his immigration staff too far.

His manager complained, "Mr Wong, I know we are making big dollars but your latest idea to bring thousands of Chinese immigrants initially into the States on student or visitor visas and then smuggling them over the border into Canada to claim refugee status is brilliant. It does then allow them to stay in Canada indefinitely. But it is too risky with a high likelihood of exposure. Let's drop it!"

This proved to be true when non-judgemental computers unexpectedly revealed strange statistical patterns. The machines triumphed, showing concentrations of Chinese refugees from prosperous regions of China, shocking the human immigration officials into unaccustomed action.

For once, accepting good advice Wong had managed to wriggle out of that one but his life was beginning to be more complicated as he attempted to juggle all his nefarious enterprises in his own interest.

HE EVENTUALLY realised that the biggest financial advantage he had been handed by taking over the immigration business was the associated money services.

He quickly disconnected from Ping Kin's bank in Macao and linked up with his underground banking pals in Guangzhou. It certainly started out profitably, moving hidden money by the tens of thousands of dollars but he very soon found himself dealing with serious international criminals and was getting way out of his depth.

Chapter 28

China: Too big to ignore

TRADE was positive everywhere. China had become the second biggest economy with a rising middle class; a population topping one and a quarter billion people. Apart from being an exporting power they were also creating internal demand.

Leyland Lumber was exported actively to China; although Ron kept harping on that he found it rather silly to see raw lumber being shipped off to Asia to be processed into expensive building materials, for purchase back by him into Canada. He claimed that this was the non-technical role Logger's generation had subserviently accepted.

They were very busy in the Leyland real estate division, where they enjoyed an increase in the inflow of personal and investment money from their Macau bank, demonstrating that The Chinese were starting to travel widely, enjoying more relaxed, actually legal, financial controls.

The prosperity in China was also leading to the creation of thousands of illegal banks there that accepted any deposits but unfortunately were failing at an alarmingly high rate due to aggressive lending.

Their infamous grey income, earned under the table in cash was reported in the trillion US a year range. The country was awash in cash with much of it flowing to Macau, and then on as black money way beyond.

ON THE other hand the latest big thing in Canadian investment circles was the reverse: 'Getting into China'. Logger Leyland must have lost his mind, because he believed all the guff being promoted to him at the Board of Trade, of which he had naturally been president, and he decided Leyland must invest in China.

Ron lunched regularly with him at The Club and Logger was first to broach the idea.

"I want Leyland to invest in Chinese real estate!" he instructed firmly. "You know your mother and I travel extensively in China being entertained by our business contacts there. Like you we enjoyed all things Chinese. So let's invest there!"

Ron first laughed at the idea."I can guarantee right now that you have not consulted any of your Chinese Canadian friends at the board. They know better about trying to succeed in the impossibly corrupt system there."

Logger retorted, "We have not been involved in any strange stuff at all in our business with The Chinese. I have definitely not paid them any cumshaw!"

"Good for you," said Ron,"but you are just chopping up and shipping trees!"

"Well," Logger replied, trying not to get annoyed at Ron's hesitation, "as you know it's not quite that simple. Let's crack open a bottle of burgundy and chat about it." Ron knew he was serious!

"You are a condo expert and we both see that concrete towers are shooting up all over China. The two go together. Find some land, utilise your Canadian management skills and throw up some buildings. Bring home a profit. It will be a piece of cake for you, son."

Ron shrugged in modest agreement, took a deep draft of his wine, and launched into a long discussion into the pro and cons of such a venture. Finally he said, "We would need to commit maybe a hundred million because financing would be dicey. That's a lot of equity."

"What I expected," Logger informed him. "So it's agreed you will look into it?"

"Pierre," he called to the barman, closing the one-sided debate while he was ahead, "let's have a couple of large glasses of that Douro Valley Vintage you just got in, to go with our stilton!"

WHEN Ron broke the news to Maisie, whose Chinese expertise would be essential, she gave him hell. "Are you crazy? Real estate is totally controlled by the politicians through local government with their so-called courts. You can't rely on contracts; even the word 'contract' to them means a work in progress. What they call their 'court' system is part of the administration, all rigged against you anyway. It is not actually a court in our sense. Not only will you have to pay someone off for everything you do, you won't know whom to pay or how! They will take your money away like taking candy from a baby."

She paused for a long breath. "Builders will rip you off. Competitors bribe for their own projects as a way of life. They will pay friendly officials to delay and frustrate you. All in a language you don't understand, dealing with people in a system you absolutely cannot trust."

He joked, "But otherwise it's a good idea?"

But she replied very seriously, "I am not kidding. We would be investing family money and it will cost us a lot of effort with only a loss of face at the end, if we are lucky."

"There you go again about losing face," he laughed but this time she remained frosty with no happy ending.

The next morning, still angry, she remarked she had lined up a meeting with their lawyer to discuss his stupid plans for China.

SITTING serenely at the top floor law office of a high-rise office building, gazing out across the sparkling harbour at the North Shore mountains, powdered with snow, Ron should have been at ease but he found two antagonists frowning insensitively at him, obliviously sipping from their fine china tea cups.

"I absolutely agree with Maisie," said lawyer George. "This venture would be nuts. Frankly you have enough potential legal problems to worry about already. We all know China is corrupt and you cannot succeed there without bribing officials. I realise it is only in the last few years that the Western world has been taking this seriously but for the past ten years Canada has considered itself bound by the OECD bribery convention, following which we passed the Corruption of Foreign Public Officials Act. If you bribe someone overseas you can go to jail for five years!"

Ron replied this was just theory and asked if anyone had seriously been charged under the Act? George replied in the negative but muttered that it was nevertheless against the law.

"Our firm subscribes to a 'Corruption Perception' index report especially to advise clients such as you on overseas contracts and practices. I looked up China and guess what? They are halfway down the list of most corrupt countries, with South Asia making up much of that awful group. Everything, especially personal safety, is terribly risky there. If you upset some official you can be picked up, pronounced guilty on a trumped-up charge tomorrow. Then disappear."

Adding to his argument he cautioned that following international criticism of non action, the RCMP had just set up a task force to concentrate on overseas bribery. Ron laughed in reply that he had seen the announcement and there would be a few officers in Ottawa buried in politics and less in Calgary checking oil companies; big deal.

Anyway, he continued, like everyone, they would be using Chinese partners who would deal with all that so he saw no problem, which for once drew not even a trace of a smile from Maisie but a serious inquisitive stare from George.

Chapter 29

Swindled: Candy from a baby

TO START with things had gone well and Logger was confident in his decision. They had found a prospective big name Chinese condo development partner who had been heartily endorsed by their enthusiastic trade attaché in Beijing. Then they had located a prime site in a major city available for immediate construction.

On the way to meet them, Ronnie with Maisie dragging reluctantly in tow, had dropped in on Ping Kin in Macau. He immediately said Ron was "Nuts!" his latest Americanism. In his opinion it would be an unfair contest with The Chinese businessmen and their friends in politics obviously prevailing.

"They hold all the cards, control the approval processes, businesses, everything. Plus you have to cultivate the ruling families first, everyone knows that. Believe me, I see it every day."

Ping Kin pleaded, "I can find you a deal with a big friendly Hong Kong company where you can replace their bank financing in some project in China earning up to say 10 percent, then you can see how it is done."

Ron laughed, "We are going to make way more so why would we do that?"

"OK," replied Ping Kin, "but if they are building competitively next to you they will be paying bribes for every approval, while you do not even know how to do it. They will have finished with a sold-out building while you are trying to dig your hole! You have to have a big establishment name in the background supporting you, already plied with expensive gifts outside China, or satisfied in some way. You also have to set things up provincially and in the city.

"Then to get going, look after approvals, services, cops, courts; on and on. It's the way they do business. I'm not worried about ethics or breaking the Canadian law, just that you don't know how to do all that. Don't even start, Ron!"

Ron protested gleefully, "Except that our embassy has already spoken to a top- level Chinese government official on our behalf and we fit in perfectly with their new anti-corruption drive.

"Everyone likes our eminent partner who will not be asked to invest, but will provide us advice for a generous fee. They will specifically protect us against all these problems."

The Dean rolled his eyes, muttering about stupidity, while Maisie just shook her head. He excused himself as an 'exporter of money' with no knowledge of importing funds but in any event advised Ron to make sure he went officially ahead of time through his Canadian bank to get a Chinese licence to repatriate their capital later in Canadian dollars.

"That is very important," he added. "Be above board and have clean Chinese exit documentation." This turned out to be the best advice Ron received; other than not to do it at all.

LOGGER was getting impatient with the slow progress and called a family company board meeting, back in Vancouver. He was anxious to make a final decision about going into China.

Still influenced by Logger's enthusiastic, positive attitude Ron made his pitch. "I do need to warn you further about my corruption misgivings but affirm we have a fine prospective local partner, coming with high recommendations."

They also had a presentation from the Chinese Consul, a frequent speaker at the Board of Trade and friend of Logger's, who encouraged them to be part of the honesty influence growing fast in their country, to assist their constant struggle against corruption at every turn. The consul announced that the central government had just started an economic stimulus package pumping billions of dollars into urban development programmes to counter the growing international economic crisis. "Your timing could not be better," he told them, beaming.

Logger was already decided anyway. "We must not miss out on the enormous market developing in China. Now is the time to get in there," he insisted, to enthusiastic applause from his self-appointed board.

At home, he had already promised Ron's mother Jeanne another exotic luxury tour of China, still totally tax deductible of course.

THEY all made enthusiastic family trips to China at the expense of the Canadian taxpayer over the coming years so it worked out well personally but with respect to the real estate everything had gone wrong.

They launched off into a condo development by buying land which their advisory partner 'won' for them at a municipal auction, well located in a large city.

Too late, they found the so-called auction had been rigged, that the city officials and partners had shared the way above market payment. Later, it was revealed their contractor was owned by colluding officials basically blackmailing them into any price. Of course similar people owned the only property sales agent and selected the buyers.

Their partner had been put in charge of 'consultant payments' which they had agreed they should not question nor audit in any way and which got totally out of control.

They limped through the ordeal ending with large losses but back in Canada at The Club bar reporting to Logger, Ron put it down to 'the learning curve', although Logger would later claim he already had seen the writing on the wall but continued to be naive.

FOR the second project they decided to become more selective in a medium-sized city far enough away from the severe larger city competition. This was a bigger project to dominate a market still of many million people, thoughtfully planned to recoup their losses.

With an investment partner very carefully chosen through their Beijing auditors, this time Ron insisted more cleverly on a straight partnership, where Leyland held the slight majority, controlling final decisions but where the partner had half the risk, with an equal interest in success.

They also moved the most trustworthy of their known employees, a happy young accountant called Delun Fok, who spoke some English and was known to all by his given name, to be their general manager in the new project.

The partner was difficult to pin down saying they had no way of assuring that the foreigners could uphold their obligation. So it was agreed they would both fully subscribe the capital required.

The large project was well on the way up when the local bank started bouncing cheques. At the time comfortably back in their Vancouver office, project financial manager Maisie said that was not possible as she had read the accounts regularly. But on being assured their account had totally dried up, they were on the next plane to China.

Poor Delun was in the hot seat, received a blistering scolding from Maisie, which Ron could not understand but which made him cringe in sympathy for the earnest young man.

Eventually she explained, "All Delun can say in self-defence is protest that he has been battling the bank for weeks but they cannot produce the partnership money."

The bank manager later explained to them, as Ron waited anxiously for a translation, "We have been told by head office your partner had deposited the funds, but no, the money itself did not ever actually appear through into your local joint account. I regret the error but there is nothing I can do. I suggest you take it up with head office."

Delun had become beside himself in anger, raging at the bank manager and accused them of duplicity and dishonesty. He shouted, "My foreign investors are being swindled; I am personally being dishonoured."

The bank official suggested he moderate his language and be careful whom he was accusing.

He then took them to the City Hall which could offer no help except to warn they must complete the project or risk dire consequences. Even with the language gap, Ron could tell the officials did recognise the validity of Delun's arguments. They nevertheless told him the situation was closed from above, warning him not to make a nuisance of himself.

Their local lawyer advised, "I can probably get you an emergency court hearing, but the 'fee' will be extremely high. That will get you through the door, to save you face, but the chances of winning are about zero. You should save the expense."

Delun insisted, "We have clearly been defrauded and I have more trust in our system in such an obvious case."

As advised, however, being the same crowd, the court sided with City Hall that they must keep building, adding that notwithstanding Ron's 'allegation' of lack of subscription of funds, the Chinese partner still owned their percentage of the company. The judge insinuated strongly that the money had been subscribed but misappropriated by them in some way.

Delun was deeply embarrassed by the decision. Almost in tears he leapt to his feet and berated the Judge as he left the bench. A few weeks after their court travesty they were all shocked when Delun literally just did not come home one evening.

MANY months later they were back in China and had tea with his wife. "I still don't know what had happened to him but we hope he is locked away as a subject of a re-education in an RSDL lockup place somewhere and hopefully he would be released later."

"What's that?" Ron asked Maisie later.

She sighed. "That is short for residential surveillance at a designated location. It is often the first step in being 'disappeared'. They are run by the mysterious Ministry of State Security. I doubt if he is important enough to warrant that treatment and has probably just been dumped in some obscure prison somewhere for a while to scare him and bring him into line."

Maisie ensured his wife they would look after Delun's family financially, which was all they could do.

WITH annoyance but deep pockets they got the project finished but this time with an appalling loss. They had finally returned to China to close down the endeavour.

With the reluctant Maisie by his side Ron landed in Beijing. They travelled by the exclusive business class with pods of course, which was expensive but absolutely necessary for the long, tiring flight, She was now committed to carry-on travel, never checking a bag. She fought off illegal but official looking limo salesmen with a few choice Mandarin words, storming through to locate their genuine limo in its usual spot.

THE smog in downtown Beijing was so thick this trip they could barely make out the buildings. China had passed Japan as the second largest economy but at the cost of widespread, increasing industrial pollution which had spread to envelope all the overcrowded cities.

However, their usual luxury suite was up above the blanket of gloom. They at least consumed their excellent dinner, even if in silence, with the sinking sun reflecting on the few top floors projecting through.

"It's not all bad. There are 20 million people down there in the smog. We are living up here like gods," Ron risked commenting.

"They are down there, including our Delun!" she spat, and lapsed back into a long silence.

Obviously she was still giving him the silent treatment so he replied, "OK I admit defeat. Let's just finish this off tomorrow."

They were there for the final accounting. Enough was enough, so they were closing it all down after the second development. The financial results were terrible, but at least they had stopped the cash drain early and could still repatriate a large proportion of the capital.

Chapter 30

Chastened: A quiet retreat

AT their Beijing accountant's office a final shock awaited them. Fortunately Ron had taken Ping Kin's advice, arranging the original permits to repatriate their now-depleted funds but they found a lien had been placed upon it by the crooked partner in the final project.

Their ex-partner had produced bank statements recording their alleged deposits and suggested Ron's employees, probably their missing manager Delun Fok, had later stolen the money. To protect itself the bank of course agreed that was likely true.

Their logical conclusion was that Fok, who had absconded with the money, was now in Australia or Canada, living a wealthy life. If not where was he?

Their accountant lamented more respectfully that he was sorry they were not able to help the well-intentioned Mr Fok but in his favour there really was no evidence supporting the other side's case. He then dropped his voice and headed off into an intense, close conversation with Maisie, as Ron again waited anxiously for translation.

"He claims to have made our argument to the registrar who on hearing we were from Vancouver brightened up considerably. Apparently, he takes his family skiing there. He hinted he might be able to help to release the lien if he had a comfortable ski lodge for his family to attend the coming Winter Olympics there," she said.

"Even more preferable, he suggested, would be to own one, ideally by the lake at Whistler Mountain. The accountant said it was better nowadays to make 'friendly gestures' in actual assets to officials rather than use traceable money."

The whole question of bribery had plagued them in China from the beginning. Pure as they had intended to be, they found things had to be left to the locals to do it their way, or nothing got done.

Every level of approval or decision required a sweetener or it was just delayed indefinitely. All they needed to do was budget miscellaneous company funds for consultant fees, then turn a blind eye to trust they were deployed in the interest of the project. This time it had become personal.

RON tossed and turned in bed that night. This was just a bribe of a few million dollars to safeguard a great deal more of his family's money. However this time there was no escaping his direct moral dilemma.

Maisie finally switched on the light, insisting they make a decision so she could get to sleep.

"Look," she said patiently. "We agree we are not worried about the Canadian law ever catching up with us for activities in China because all Canadians investing here obviously pay bribes, directly or indirectly, or they can't succeed or even operate. And don't worry about that five year maximum sentence because no one had even been convicted, so it is pretty academic.

"I know you are concerned that this bribe will have effects in Canada where there are records and our actions can be traced. Somehow it feels different to bribe a person in China where it is expected, compared to Canada where the thought makes us cringe."

"Once again," Maisie sighed, "you want me to be your conscience. I have to set up the deal with Macau. But absolutely not on your father's company. We must not involve Logger. We will pay this through Macau; personally."

All it took in the morning was a call to Ping Kin to arrange a transfer of funds by them to Stump, which would be followed by him making a purchase in Whistler, delivering the deed to another bent lawyer colleague.

And then yet another numbered company would own a lodge in the best ski resort in the world. "The records will be totally untraceable back to anyone, with us totally in the clear," she assured him.

When the purchase arrangements had all been set up, they met again with their accountant. Ron nodded wearily that he had arranged the ski lodge, ironically concluding their China debacle with a bribe.

THEY returned to Vancouver and walked together into The Club for lunch with Logger, dreading the China project windup. Ron had insisted she come with him for moral support but Logger could see they were amazed by his cheerful greeting in the Bar.

He already had a bottle of Grand Cru breathing and was in a good mood. "What's going on?" they asked, incredulously.

Savouring his burgundy slowly, to let them suffer, he explained, "Your adventure in China had already started, as you are well aware, when it turned out the rest of the US-influenced world was headed for the big recession."

He patted Maisie's arm affectionately and reassured her, "I knew, of course, that wise Maisie was against it from the beginning and has helped get us out of it."

Turning back to Ron, he continued, "When I agreed to invest in your overseas venture, I had several alternative business options being proposed to me by your sister in our lumber business, which I was actively considering but which would have proved devastating!

"We lost way less by putting the money into your real estate ventures in China than we would have expanding our lumber business here, which actually all collapsed due to the recession. So, Ron, you not only saved us money but conserved your sister's management reputation."

He toasted them with a broad grin. "Good show, Ron and Maisie."

"WELL, that was sure a relief," Maisie said, as they walked down The Club steps; hand in hand again after some weeks. "However, I see it has become your venture into China and they are now your sister's lumber proposals."

He just gratefully squeezed her hand and they walked back to the office deep in their own thoughts, simply relieved to have that experience behind them.

Chapter 31

Maisie: Confirming convictions

THE Leyland family ski log-mansion was buzzing with activity and guests during the Winter Olympics at Whistler Mountain in 2010. It was admittedly very grand but they excused it and justified it tax-wise as a 'business essential'.

It was an enormous event for the entire family and they entertained all their friends and business contacts constantly. It was a coming of age for Ron and Maisie's adult teenage children, Cathie and Johnnie, who had of course been brought up skiing in the mountains.

The publicity thrust British Columbia further into the international limelight and finally established it throughout the world as one of the finest places on earth to live.

Now pretty much freed from domestic duties and from looking after children's interests, Maisie found herself becoming totally immersed in the affairs of the company and in her charitable interests. Their business grew in step with British Columbia's international status, with their connections expanded not only in Asia but throughout the world, giving them the opportunity to travel extensively.

MAISIE'S life in Canada was becoming a dream.

Vancouver itself is one of the world's most beautiful cities with a style of living envied everywhere. On top of that she had a spacious new home now actually on a beach in the smartest part of town, nurturing two very active teenagers.

Then there was her patient, so Canadian Ron, who obviously adored her, happily still introducing her to his beloved Canada. Ron knew enough about her background to be proud of her successes but with his privileged upbringing she thought he could not really understand the depth of her appreciation of the Canadian way of life.

She really had not known anything about China initially because she left as a refugee child but her time studying in Macau had forcefully ingrained in her the amoral depth of the Communist brutal lack of human rights in China.

When her studies had ended she could not wait to return to the safety of the British colony where those rights were guaranteed, even if far away by their democracy in the United Kingdom.

Now, here in Canada she felt she had completed her journey and was safe. She was an independent woman who could meet with anyone or express herself freely without fear. Ron took it all for granted but she actively valued it.

MAISIE'S constant worries about her personal 'fun fund' investments in the Chinese stock market still caused amusement and concern to Ron. He had to admit, however, the value was growing appreciably, augmented by the occasional large sums of capital Ping Kin just found lying around somewhere.

With help from the top politicians, the stock market in China had hit a record high, only then to encounter the recent world economic crisis. Once again it halved in value, but now it had bounced back due to the required political stimulus and financial manipulation.

Through their insider information, they had been lucky enough to get in early on two of the world's largest initial public offerings in China, producing overall results of which they were finally beginning to be quite proud. On the record at least, Maisie had become a very wealthy woman!

SHE discovered Canadian federal politics with Ron at an impressive political dinner, where the ladies were all resplendent in long dresses and the gentlemen in their black jackets. There she met the charming current Prime Minister.

Possibly her statuesque beauty, enhanced by the daringly low, slit sided and tightly fitted, red Versace gown caught his eye. She had made her entrance with an admiring Ron walking proudly a pace behind her. He had enjoyed selecting and deciding upon buying the dress creation for the event with her at a recent Harrods fashion show they attended in London.

The Prime Minister and his wife went on a tour of the reception, where he clearly focused his total attention on Maisie's opinions, which prompted her to offer her business card in further support.

Ron laughed, "This is a fundraiser. He is only interested in your dollars!"

However, she did hear from the local party organiser, finding herself on an 'ethics in politics' committee, a burning issue concerning strange dealings, of course by the other parties. She had been nonplused at that first formal event seeing Steven Stumpenberg hovering at the edges but apparently knowing everyone. He turned out to be a shadowy backroom wheeler-dealer and fundraiser for the Party, himself a very generous political donor.

She worried about the myriad dubious financial things in her life but at least she had agreed with Ron that they gradually extricate themselves from the money services business with its source and movement of funds way beyond their knowledge.

Eventually she wanted to sever any direct financial dependence upon China which she felt Canada could well do without.

Ron's reaction was, "You worry too much." but she was serious.

"I have lived under the other system. You try being afraid of having an opinion on anything, in case it goes against Party interests. I mean deadly afraid. You just didn't understand. I know I got you into all this, but now I see the dangers not only for us personally but for the country. We have to defend Canadian values more seriously."

They did nothing about it, of course, because every time they paused to consider reorganisation, a new bigger, better deal came along.

She consoled herself with the knowledge she spent at least half of her working hours on the business of the substantial Leyland Charity Trust, which had been founded originally by Ron's grandfather.

Maisie had become very close friends with Ron's sister and between them they ran the trust. Logger was lucky if he managed to get in another word after, "Ladies, may I bring the meeting to order?"

They supported a wide variety of 'good works' across the country. In recent years Logger's daughter had convinced him willingly to help gay and lesbian rights organisations and other 'genders', which he freely admitted to puzzle him but which he whole-heartedly accepted.

However, he especially backed Maisie's desire to champion democracy and general human rights causes in Canada and around the world.

Several charities and social interest groups had invited Maisie to join their boards since she started working on the trust, keeping her very busy and frequently travelling. Of course, they are were also looking for generous financial support. Naturally she focused upon the scene she well understood and became a public advocate for human rights in China.

CANADA'S attitude to China had also hardened with that Prime Minister, Maisie admired so much. He had become so publicly critical of Chinese human rights violations, a concern of several of Maisie's public service groups, that Beijing had cancelled face-to-face meetings with him.

There was a battle over Chinese state energy companies investing in

Alberta and he continued to have a poor relationship with China over labour standards and environmental protection. Nevertheless trade kept ballooning with the imbalance in China's favour progressively widening.

Maisie joined an international trade committee in her new political group but contrary to their leader's public stance on human rights found them to be only intent upon promoting more trade with China; giving concessions in order to get it.

She argued at the committee, "My experience is that China blocks trade with any industries it can run itself while encouraging partnership with others it is trying to learn or take over. Once they have the technology from us they will obviously dump us and do it themselves."

However her committee retorted it would become the strongest economy in the world. Canada had to deal with it. Most of Canada's goods exported to China were by extraction or commodities and whatever North America did it could not compete with China's lower labour costs.

To her disappointment it was just becoming a matter of the all-powerful Renminbi.

RON strolled way too nonchalantly into her office.

"I have been invited to Toronto to talk at the annual dinner of one of the Canada China business promotion organisations in view of our connections with China and Hong Kong. What do you want me to do?"

"Why are you asking?" she glared. "You know very clearly what I think, unless you are going there to tell them the truth: widespread corruption, despotic government and systemic violation of human rights. Is that what you will talk about? You are so Canadian! All politically centrist and only wanting to give politics a passing thought when elections roll around."

He mumbled an excuse about business promotion and slunk from her office. He was still recovering from the business venture into China and knew retreat was the best tactic.

She called after him, "Ask them if they will accept me as the speaker instead?"

At least that made him pause in the doorway and turn to give her an amused grin, in acknowledgement of her now well-publicised stand on human rights.

Then he came slowly back into the room. "We all agree with you, in principle, Maisie. I love the way you face up to humanity problems and deal with them yourself. I trust your judgement totally.

"I was brought up with Kissinger's theories and have the excuses of realpolitik to let me overlook what happens in China or other countries and just to go on with business as usual. But times have changed since the 1970s and now I agree they are starting to become aggressive and are trying to control us.

"There is a lot of negative self-interest at play and we all have not yet developed your depth of conviction. We are working on it!"

Softening slightly, she responded sardonically, "One day you will find that taking a firm stand is critical to your own interest too. It's a simple question of principles or profits, Ron. You will find the risks outweigh the profitability."

She emphasised, "I have experienced the personal fear of the other oppressive system. It's probably easier for me to comprehend. So I have decided."

Chapter 32

Ah-Cy: Securing status

ON THE other side of the Pacific, another woman, Ah-Cy Huang had also found herself becoming engaged in politics but at a very senior level.

Her parents had desperately wanted a boy but by the time she was in her early teens they realised they had something of a prodigy on their hands when she qualified for the top-level gymnastic teams. But she was still female!

It was not until she took the chair of the University Student committee her father recognised some personal political talent in her. He saw Zhang as a useful support, jockeying him into the commercial world, retaining Ah-Cy for more important political manoeuvring.

During the Cultural Revolution it was tricky but he had Ah-Cy accepted into State Security, at first with a very junior undercover start in the national publicity headquarters where she was used as a casual mole reporting on loyalty among her privileged set.

She was quietly impressive and moved quickly up to deserve senior trust, specialising in using all the new technologies to stifle dissent and control thought.

Her special security role was to be divulged to no one, including Zhang. She had continued her fierce loyalty to the Huang family, with her quiet insider knowledge and easygoing personality helping them through several difficult situations.

POWER had changed Zhang, ending any physical relationship between them many years previously. She had just shrugged off his first few affairs but not when she learned that he was regularly using his position to force sex upon vulnerable women who were brought under his control.

She found their family charade useful while he still had Huang's and Party support, so they maintained a publicly cordial relationship but living mostly separate lives.

She was informed officially about her now-influential husband's continuous liaisons with other women, even with the occasional man she noted with a smile. She had her children growing up and enjoyed her own affairs, one lasting for years providing satisfaction on demand.

She had taken a fancy to Zhang's long-standing bodyguard Lo. One safe afternoon she simply ordered the impressively muscular officer onto her bed, surprising him by her assertive direction of her own desire for prolonged activity, which left him in anticipation of her frequently recurring demand.

He immediately had to adapt to her curious instruction, in direction of his rhythm, when she sang marching anthems to herself during the early action. This led him to dread the constantly repeated long verses but trained him dutifully to speed up when she approached the final inspiring chorus.

Then, breaking into strident song, she directed an ever-increasing tempo which she rode to a triumphant patriotic conclusion.

AH-CY'S personal progress had been publically unobserved but she found herself playing a senior part in hosting the 2008 Beijing Summer Olympics in which she helped organise her beloved gymnastics and particularly manage public relations.

She arranged the closure of strategic industries on rotation to reduce the smog which usually obliterated the cities. The now-pervasive industrial gloom would have ruined their carefully publicised fiction as a green and clean country.

Her success at the Games, coupled with the family name, later found her invited to head publicity, representing the country at an international trade conference in Canada.

She now quietly had a very senior Party status, not known to Zhang but way outranking him. The delegation was flown to Ottawa in an impressive state aircraft. They were given the full Chinese Embassy VIP treatment.

From their Parliamentary diplomatic gallery she watched with absolute amazement as opposition parties harassed the Prime Minister ceaselessly, even calling themselves the loyal opposition as though that made it all right.

Even worse, they continued those disputes on all the media, opening up the government to criticism which they were stupidly prepared to tolerate. There was no help from the police or the courts which seemed to operate independently.

Her leaders' policy at home was always right. With an incredibly large and potentially volatile population, dissent must obviously be stifled immediately with any prospect of destabilisation eliminated. How ineffectual these Canadian politicians looked by comparison!

Individuals may not be allowed to ruin things for the vast majority. She saw immediately why the Western world was so weak, so obviously running into major problems; conversely why her country was so strong.

THESE wonderful weaknesses were all discussed at their briefing back in the Embassy prior to the conference with a clear explanation how the mother country was taking advantage of the situation.

She heard that thousands of students from China were soaking up Canada's technical education. It was amusing that they bribed the trusting universities with fees, donations and loans, while the few

Canadians studying in China pursued mainly Chinese ancient culture, dancing and artefacts.

They already had established well-financed intelligence units with special service officers embedded in all advanced education facilities throughout Canada, ensuring their returning students were not in any way influenced by the decadent democratic system but also spreading the inspiring communist word to Chinese Canadian students generally.

They now had almost total direction of Chinese language radio stations, media and newspapers in Canada, progressively switching them over to Mandarin with censored news in accordance with their dictates.

Ah-Cy clapped her hands in delighted support. "This is just the beginning. At home we are making extensive use of the internet and modern technology to control any misguided anti-authority sentiment. In Security we now have tens of thousands of people around the country working on this program.

"We are now progressively infiltrating the North American social media systems and you will find also in Canada we soon will be asserting powerful social control. This will be extended to all Chinese people overseas, of course."

A staff member wondered, "But will Canada be sufficiently gullible to accept this?" Ah-Cy laughed. "They already know and call it the Great China Firewall. It will all be introduced innocuously through chat and news apps apparently owned by North Americans but providing direct connections and reporting fun things in China."

Their envoy agreed enthusiastically. "Our technology and face recognition science is now beginning to allow us to track every individual Chinese person outside the country and link them back to domestic families giving us enormous personal leverage."

AT THE delegation's private pre-conference lunch, she aroused the executive group by jumping confidently to her feet and pronouncing in her entertaining style that in the previous years they had emerged as world champions.

She asserted that dramatic economic growth, crowned by the nation-building success of their magnificent Olympic Games, (she dramatically held an imaginary torch up high), and the massive failure demonstrated by the American-led recession, (she make a rude sound, grimaced and gesticulated downwards), had highlighted them as leaders of the world.

Raising her arms in triumph, she pronounced, "China is on the podium and everyone is begging for our winning attention!"

As one man, which they were, they leaped to their feet in wild applause.

THE conference proved her right! The international meeting of governments indeed showed Canada begging for more trade with China particularly as they were just emerging from that financial crisis.

Even this Prime Minister, she noted with glee, had been making a nuisance of himself about their so-called human rights nonsense but was now bowing to big business, pushing for trade.

She observed, "It is clear, greed and personal profit is their real motivation while ours is solely the wellbeing of the motherland. Remember, every citizen, public official and company legally owes allegiance first to our state, subverting personally to instructions from Security."

She had a strange thrill that they had heard rumours, of which she had been advised, that she was in more than public relations and had a role in Security. Even though she was speaking in her usual cheerful, encouraging manner she saw apprehension in their eyes and that they were deadly afraid of her.

SHE pleased their envoy, advising that on return to Beijing, "I will report to State Security that I see advantages in increasing political and public relations activity in Canada. I will ask that they provide even greater budgets so you can continue to make inroads into Canadian society, especially getting sympathetic politicians elected. We must essentially promote Chinese ideals to the already welcoming population to pave the way for vastly increased emigration and acquisitions in the move to control Canada. I am now sure the profit obsessed Canadian establishment will not stand in our way,"

Chapter 33

Lawyers: In vino veritas

THE Leyland family had known George Oikawa since he and Ron were at grade school together. He was a very correct lawyer in the Japanese Canadian tradition, but also a very practical person. So it was remarkable that he arranged the dinner they would all remember. Ron could recall it vividly, notwithstanding the quantity of alcohol they all consumed.

George had heard many stories about the flamboyant Hinks from Hong Kong. He was also guardedly aware from the local Law Society bar chit chat that Stump had apparently gone somewhat rogue.

His legal responsibilities to Ron, Maisie and to the Leyland company overlapped in many ways with the other two lawyers from whom he normally tried to keep a considerable distance. But when Hinks came into town it was just too great an opportunity to miss.

"Ron, you want to join me for dinner with Stump and Hinks, when he is here? It obviously can't be at The Club, with Stump there, but I'll find somewhere hidden away."

He booked a table tucked at the back of a quaint harbourfront restaurant which he knew to have a fine cellar. They all had enormous egos with a knowledge that only came from day-to-day practice in the fray, but as one accord they kept only to generalities of the law, not anything client specific.

It was a stimulating evening, that got off to a very noisy competitive start, which brought the restaurant owner running in concern, but when it proved to be a show-off argument to select the very best wines, he mellowed immediately.

They settled down initially to civil, mostly legal discussion but their intensity increased by the end of the second bottle when they were all shouting at the same time: Black Renminbi had raised its head.

Hinks prevailed, breaking in loudly, "Canada is only the sixth or seventh favourite place for The Chinese to put money anyway but they come here because they love the passport. Money is money; no one knows what is laundered. Make investment difficult for them and they will invest somewhere else. But they will still want your passport and the long-term visa! When you have easy immigration into a country at the top of the ethics chart from others at the bottom, you are obviously going to have some fun. My Hong Kong is caught hovering in the middle."

He hopped around making frantic wing movements with his arms accompanied by loud "Caw, caw" noises

AS THE evening progressed the focus of their loud discussion centred round Canada's total lack of preparation for dealing with that real, nasty world out there. They ranged over immigration, money movement, laundering, crime generally and the law, plus all the day's political problems, particularly from the increasingly assertive China.

Getting into the cheese and liqueurs, it all turned a little technically legal and Ron lapsed into silence, listening, just warming his brandy. By this time the lawyers were all talking loudly, competing for attention.

They laughed uproariously that obviously guilty criminals walked away in Canada because the courts were too slow. Judges could not get around to the trial in time. Then they chortled about the poor cops, after months of diligent preparation, so often losing out because of obscure evidence technicalities.

"How about when the dog wouldn't sit?" asked Ron. Hinks said he had read that story. "Surely it is an urban myth?"

He was assured by a smirking Stump, "A judge actually let a criminal go, even though he was caught red-handed with tens of thousands of secreted Fentanyl tablets, because the sniffer dog did not actually get her bum on the ground when pointing, as was technically required."

Hinks' antics and loudly barking "Woof, woof, woof" had the nearby table scrambling for relocation. When he had calmed down he claimed that Canada had too much administration anyway.

"Recognising Canada is a big place does it really need 14 competing major national administrations? They are not capable of exchanging information between themselves or with commerce, with no way of sharing vital data to expose criminal activity.

"The key thing is to know who owns what and your Canadian multi-systems seem designed to prevent this. They have a total inability to track beneficial ownership or put together national open registries, for instance of real estate ownership."

THEN they all got more technical, actually agreeing the Canadian courts were in confusion trying to control administrative law across the country.

"Don't get me wrong," Hinks insisted, "Although I practise in Chinese Hong Kong, I believe firmly in the rule of law but I have been told it is not being well served by the Canadian courts so far as administrative law is concerned. I've looked at the cases and see that the judges are all over the place. In fact they bitterly contradict each other right up to, and amazingly including, your senior courts."

The others agreed there were regularly conflicting decisions producing total disagreement. "How can we expect all our levels of administration to work to catch the money launderers for example if there is confusion about the simple definition of the crime?" asked George, indignantly.

Stump shouted that immigration administration was so relaxed he could get a Chinese panda admitted, which raised a big laugh.

George replied with a smile, "You probably could at that, because the Canadian common law is based upon the pursuit of individual justice. Some idiot would argue that a panda had rights too. Then it would go up through all the courts wasting time as always."

He agreed seriously though, that the administration of Canadian law was in a terrible pickle making beating the system too easy. "Delay, delay, delay!" they all chanted slowly in triumph.

Stump jumped up, prancing around the table supposedly like a robot shouting "Robocop, Robocop!"

When the laughter died down Stump insisted that visa and immigration decisions were now moving over to computers rather than officials.

"With half a million people a year now coming into Canada as immigrants or on some visa or other, we can't decide on immigration quickly enough when humans are making the decisions, so now we are asking robots to do it. Next we will need computerised judges to second guess the robots!"

Hinks pontificated dramatically, "*Quio custodiet ipso custodes?*" leaving George muttering in Ron's ear, "*Screw you whatever; I'm the boss!*"

Hoots of derision brought the maitre d' running again.

As they quietened down, Hinks changed the subject and launched onto his pessimistic view of his home, Hong Kong.

"My observation is that China is not waiting for the end of the 'One country two systems' term, to start taking over. Major trouble is coming but your Western world is slowly seeing China as a malevolent shadow over the horizon. Canada however is looking more and more attractive."

LAYMAN Ron finally broke in on the lawyers to general noisy jeers.

"So in your view, so far as bad foreign investors are concerned, Canada is a wonderful place to operate. We have ended up with a barely functioning administration and court system; with no idea with whom we are dealing due to poor registration; with ineffectual policing or security authorities; facing online transactions so advanced we cannot trace or understand them anyway.

"And they all have no budgets, plus we are being taken over by robots!" he concluded as they all hooted, but objecting that it was not as bad as that!

"The only ones with the big pay cheques are you lawyers." shouted defiant Ron, over mounting friendly derisive boos. "There are far too many of you! You all have your fingers in the pie, one way or another."

"I move," responded Stump, standing dramatically, rising his finger, "that in penance for those ill-advised remarks, Ron pays for dinner!" which motion was passed by noisy acclamation, all secure in the generosity of tax deductibility.

However, as lawyers they all lived with these background concerns every day in their working lives. They would continue to administer the law as they saw fit. These serious thoughts did not deter them from knocking back a final round of drinks or from cheerful back-slapping goodbyes.

Then they staggered off individually into the night, each alone with his conscience.

WAITING bleary eyed to hail a taxi, Stump could have sworn he saw a ghostly pink turban hovering in the shadows down a nearby street side alley, but when he looked again it had gone.

Chapter 34

Wil: The Canadian way

R ON KNEW that Logger was a tad disappointed when he selected urban land economics as his major at university because he wanted him to go into the lumber business.

Leyland had a real estate division for him to take over, however, and his engineer sister was already showing interest in the forests, so Logger had accepted and encouraged his decision. Ron had done very well and that side of the company had eclipsed lumber and wood products in profitability.

At the end of university years Ron acquired his real estate licence which pretty much went with his business school real estate option. He kept it up and it had always come in useful.

Right from the beginning when Ping Kin had proposed extending their real estate activities he had been as good as his word, and money for capital investment across Canada had started appearing. Now it increased dramatically.

They decided upon a diversified portfolio for some of the larger investors but many were just interested in a couple of prime properties. This was fine and they also set up a management division to look after them, over several years building up quite a portfolio.

The business also picked up Canadian clients of all ethnic origins of course but particularly Chinese by word-of-mouth. They became known as something of a 'Chinese' real estate company despite being called Leyland.

The surge of investment from mainland China was not without its problems Leyland's managing salesman, Wil Choo, requested a meeting with Ron to discuss company policy. This was highly unusual because the ageing hockey enthusiast Wil was not one for protocol or unnecessary bullshit.

His grandfather's Chinese forebears had been abandoned in the middle of the prairies during the railway construction but had prospered there as farmers and traders. His grandfather had volunteered without coercion to fight for Canada in the First World War, celebrating returning from the trenches with only a severe attack of gas poisoning.

He was received joyfully by their neighbouring Métis homesteader's daughter who was immediately pregnant with Wil's resultant father. His father in his turn married a girl from a nearby German farming family, explaining Wil's mixed appearance together with the perverse Wilhelm Choo name.

Today Wil was unusually serious. "I absolutely compliment you on the increasing property business the company is enjoying but I worry about the way the deals are shaping up. Just because I look sort of Chinese and sometimes try to converse in generations-old Cantonese, which gives them a laugh, they assume I think the way they do. Actually my German is better from my mother and there are more people of German origin here than Chinese!"

"No way!" responded Ron incorrectly, relying on visually evidence as would most people.

"But these new wealthy business ginks from Asia are all looking for kickbacks," Wil continued. "They come here representing companies or groups of investors but expect substantial personal giveaways. This is not just now and then; this is always! What they are doing is just plain stealing from their investors who pay for it in their deal. It just does not sit well with me. They also spend all their time hiding their identity, particularly to evade any taxes. When I tell them this deprives Canadians like us who have to pay more taxes to make up the difference, they just laugh."

Ron brought him an obligatory mug of Tim Horton's to calm him down with the suggestion, "We have come across this sort of thing previously in dealing with Canadians as well. Remember that government official's wife who came and asked for a free condo when her husband was buying a dozen units for government use? And then when we turned her down he bought in a competing building? Or that briefcase of cash demanded by the CEO for that big company rental?"

"Yes," the salesman agreed, "but those incidents were years ago and the fact we remember them shows how unusual they were. Anyway we didn't do them. Everyone has stories like that. They are the exceptions that prove the rule. There are always deal sweeteners but they apply to the main negotiation and not to personal profit, other than dinners out, or hockey tickets of course.

"What I am worried about is that we are being exposed to a total cultural change in the way we conduct our business lives. Honestly it scares me. It is not the funny money itself that is coming in, nor the corrupted people themselves, it is the kickback, dog-eat-dog culture they are introducing around the world like a virus."

It was now very plain to see where Wil was coming from considering his family background, embracing his love of Canadian traditions. He was obviously totally serious to impress upon Ron this was a matter requiring company policy, which could impact upon their success.

"I will have a chat with the boss" Ron quipped, attempting to lighten the mood, "but I do agree this is big stuff. We will be right back to you."

"WHAT do I keep telling you?" asked Maisie, "You Canadians are so naive. Now the rapacious real world has arrived. Like his grandpa, Wil is on the front line with the insidious gas creeping around him. We have already stated a clear company policy that we respect the Canadian way of doing business which insists upon following established rules. But of course everyone says that.

"What we have to do is put in writing that we are extremely serious about this; that any employees not upholding the most exemplary Canadian standards of behaviour will be dismissed."

" OK," agreed Ron, "and while we are about it we will set up a top-level vetting committee which will check all deals to ensure these standards are maintained. We will likely lose sales in the short run but we can only hope that Wil and his team stay with us."

Ron met again with Wil, reporting their decision. His response came after a very brief reflection.

"Fuck 'em. We will do it the Canadian way!"

IT HAD taken many years of steady business after Ping Kin had introduced them to his source of equity, before the scale of business had grown from China, but finally a very big deal came up.

The usually calm Ping Kin sounded somewhat excited. "Meet me in Shanghai to talk about a major real estate investment proposed for Canada." They were on the next plane.

They limo-ed through the dense smog at the port of Shanghai to a surprisingly pretty waterfront office for a conference at the head office of the shipping company, Maisie very smart in a new Michael Kors suit, designed to impress professionally.

Chinese shipping activities were expanding around the world, particularly along the Belt and Road program but this company had decided to be contrarians away on the West coast of North America, with Vancouver as their head office location.

To make an initial impact they had resolved to look for a major waterfront property to establish their presence. They wanted Leyland to seek out that property.

Maisie and Ron returned to their hotel suite for an evening of frantic emails, returning the next morning with a proposal. This suggested the initial budget would have to be in the region of $2 billion to develop the type of establishment the shipping company had described.

They required excellent office buildings, warehouses, a container port and transportation connections. They advised that was just the beginning; container and dock expansions could be added as needed. However, Ron stated pessimistically they would never get this through the Harbour Authority.

The bouncy, friendly little chairman Luk Man Tok told them to get to work, just leaving the politics to them. They had the obligatory male only banquet that evening leaving Ron so wasted on whiskey that they had to delay their flight back by a day.

NATURALLY, everything was top secret. Ron dealt with the initial negotiations personally, seeking to option the vital pieces of land confidentially and of course through surrogate companies.

Anything on the waterfront in Canada had myriad conservation problems which he warned the Shanghai clients would take a long time. They told him not to delay but to exercise all the options before they expired.

Then came a surprise. Ping Kin emailed, "The entire budget has been funded in Macau and that I will be arranging shortly to have the money sent to a Vancouver bank."

Ron's bank manager later called with great excitement.

"Ron, a considerable sum has been deposited from a not clearly identified source into a restricted account to fund an enterprise of which you are reportedly aware."

Ron thanked him, assuring he was indeed working on that confidential enterprise.

His banker friend nevertheless continued, "Are you prepared to sign a comfort memorandum just confirming that to your knowledge the funds are from a reliable source, intended for a legal purpose?"

Ron replied virtuously that he would be very happy to vouch for them.

The mysterious bank account was administered by a well-known national Vancouver law firm which duly authorised the funds to exercise the options on the properties but on Ron's instructions did not make any public announcement, at the request of the shipping company.

Progressively over the coming months they acquired extra properties at increasing prices as the rumours started. Eighteen months from their start they had the entire required property assembled. Architects and engineers had been hired, although hidden away in a corner of their office where the master plan was being assembled.

THE banker administering the fund was the first to raise an alarm.

"Many hundred millions of dollars have been transferred from the mysterious account," he reported guardedly, while lunching with Ron.

"This should be confidential between me and my client of course, but you are sort of the client. I am alarmed we were instructed to send the money to a bank in Cyprus which we regard is a bit dicey. Do you know anything about this?"

Ron just numbly shook his head.

When he reported the conversation to Ping Kin the explosive response was "Oh, shit," in very clear American. This was followed by a long silence.

Then, "I will have to think about this but I can't keep it to myself. Don't do anything or tell anyone. Just carry on with the project."

Chapter 35

Corruption: Tigers and Flies

THIS TIME it was not a dingy back street strip dive but a dining room in his staffed private suite atop a luxury hotel in Guangzhou. Now clearly respected by his colleagues, Zhang nevertheless greeted the invited Dr Poon effusively.

What transpired was still obviously on Ping Kin's conscience when he had related it to Ron and Maisie much later, during a warm holiday together in Barbados, but he claimed the situation left him no choice.

Zhang had asked, "Do you realise it is almost a quarter of a century since we first met! I do enjoy our occasional meals together, but affairs of state keep me busy. Let's chat while we enjoy dinner. I have a big favour to ask, which will also be to your advantage."

Then they enjoyed a gourmet meal, looking out over the city lights, chatting as though old friends about current affairs, especially regarding the rise of the new political establishment in Beijing.

Zhang got down to business over a couple of snifters of cognac, which he courteously poured himself. "The new state controllers are consolidating their power. I have extremely confidential forewarning that in the coming months they will introduce the most sweeping anti-corruption assault ever announced."

He chuckled. "They claim to be going after criminal *Tigers and Flies,* all the way through society. I suspect The Six are Tigers, so we have to be especially vigilant. This gives us six months warning to protect themselves, ensure all our lose ends are tied, and especially that our international activities will remain undetected."

Ping Kin assured him that was always the case but that he would work full-time in the coming months to double check everything.

Sipping his cognac thoughtfully Zhang continued. "We Six are getting on in years. Please review our overseas assets for easy family division or access in the future."

Then his boss poured them a touch more cognac with the warning he had one more rather personal matter to mention.

"I offer my apologies in advance, but as a standard precaution I recently checked all my associates for loyalty, including you, and it revealed some interesting activities in your private life."

Patting him in a friendly manner on his arm, which made Ping Kin secretly cringe, he admitted, "I have suspected all along but now know that you are gay. Also I know that you have a close, perhaps inadvisable relationship with our black lawyer in Barbados. No problem to me personally, I assure you.

"However, I am also most intrigued by your gay cover arrangement in Macau with the talented and reportedly beautiful lady now our associate in Vancouver. What is her name? Ah yes, Mai Xi."

Ping Kin explained that it had been Mai Xi's clever idea with which he had subsequently just played along. Zhang congratulated them both on their deception which was practical and simple.

He contemplated his swirling brandy and then pronounced, "*The teacher can open the door but the student has to go through herself.*" Chuckling to himself at his subtle gender adjustment to the old proverb, he added, "I hope to meet her one day."

WHEN he had finished speaking, after pausing tactfully, Ping Kin thanked him for his sensitivity but admitted also to having an apology to make but coincidentally one which could also benefit the situation.

In an abrupt change of subject which took Zhang completely by surprise he talked about the shipping development in Vancouver knowing he was a director of that corporation.

"You have to be aware of the shipping proposal in Vancouver, Mr Zhang. Unfortunately I must advise you many hundred thousand of dollars have gone missing. My apology is that it happened many months ago but I did not known how to deal with it because Mr Luk Man Tok is one of The Six and he took the money personally.

"It just occurred to me you might consider exposing that situation as a placating gesture to the new controlling powers in Beijing, providing them with an example to use but simultaneously dealing with this unfortunately revealed risky in-house deceit."

He finished, lowering his eyes to signal his suggestion was made with the greatest of respect. Zhang's expression did not even flicker but he revealingly tapped a finger in annoyance on his snifter as he asked to be provided with the evidence.

He sighed, finishing his drink abruptly; their conference over.

ALTHOUGH the Harbour Authority was making Ronnie's life hell with their endless meetings, the approvals were moving along. The shipping company was heading towards an impressive announcement and they had opened a small Vancouver office.

Then came a total shock.

It fell to their local manager to respectfully invite Ron to dim sum where he impassively announced, "Mr Luk Man Tok has retired. There is a new company chairman whose policies simply do not include a facility in Vancouver harbour. So a freeze has now been imposed on all capital expenditure. Leyland will received instructions from Shanghai to sell the assembled property and to wind down any related business.

I have been instructed to settle all the outstanding accounts including of course the brokerage and management fees Leyland has already earned."

It took another year to dispose of the land with Wil and his team happily earning more fees now on the sale. When everything was settled Ron asked Maisie to enquire what had happened back in China. She knew the ebullient Mr Luk had been removed from management on short notice but they both hoped he had not 'been disappeared' as they so acceptingly put it back there.

Their worst fears were possibly confirmed later when they met Ping Kin. He reported *sotto voce*, that a voice he would recognise anywhere called to announce on his cell phone, with a sinister chuckle, that The Six was now reduced to Four.

THE years had been hard on Zhang although he portrayed himself as a tough character. This was necessary for survival, but he had misgivings over many of his actions, over-thinking harsh decisions. What he actually did about all this was never reported to Ping Kin but he gradually pieced it together.

When he had told Zhang about Luk Man Tok's stupid misbehaviour he had left him thinking quietly. As always Zhang had felt totally alone but this time overwhelmingly sad.

Man Tok was a close friend from undergraduate days; an especially loyal member for the clandestine Six when they worked so dangerously on their secret economic plan. He had thought him a friend.

It was not so much that Man Tok had not contributed his skimmed capital into The Six funds according to their agreement, but rather that his unsophisticated method was so easily detected.

Their assets were now in the billions. To risk things for this petty gain showed a terrible lack of judgement or worse that he no longer trusted The Six, deciding it was necessary to build up his own private funds.

The whole point of keeping the group together was mutual protection, justifying the very expensive technical organisation in Macau which went to great lengths to hide their assets and the owners.

He thought about the rare situations where he or his colleagues, in their constantly recurring management problems, had to resort to someone who was being impossible just disappearing.

Emotionally, Man Tok was absolutely not in this category but he was privy to all their secrets. No doubt he had a failsafe plan exposing them all if he should be under threat. Zhang certainly had hidden defensive records himself to reveal for that purpose.

Thus Man Tok could not simply disappear but neither could they risk having him arrested to be interrogated formally. Could he follow up on Dr Poon's suggestion to expose him as beneficial to the 'corruption' reforms? It had happened months previously so Man Tok undoubtedly thought he was in the clear; he could be surprised.

Zhang finally decided that was in fact the best solution but he must bring his father-in-law Huang in on his proposal. The old fellow was obviously pleased because it apparently fitted perfectly with *'Operation Fox Hunt'*, a new secret process they were launching to expose unhelpful corrupt officials.

Together they discussed the action required with a friendly senior Party member and a shocked Luk Man Tok was picked up without notice but by Zhang's own private security. Now, Luk could either cooperate or it would be the worse for him.

The official called to thank Zhang profusely for his helpful exposure in loyal support of the new Party anticorruption policies, leaving him smiled quietly to himself, that they caught a *'Fox'* but missed the *'Tiger'*.

Chapter 36

Cash: An endless flow

WONG HAD shocked Ron into silence, explaining his problem of excessive cash in his nightclub business.

"A million dollars fit easy in a hockey bag but that is a problem for the casinos. It ties up the cashier and counting machine for three quarters of an hour. You need a sealed sack for chips or they have to count them again when you get a cash-out cheque ....after winning! Ha."

Ron had never felt any interest in the casinos Logger had visited, mainly on family vacations, tagging along in the choking, smoky atmosphere. The smoke was gone but even though they retained the seductive female drink pushers, now a few male ones, Ron never went inside their doors.

Thus it was rather a surprise when Wong had laughed at the lax money control. "People have bags of cash. It must be bad money. How do you get all those notes? They have cops and government guys but they are not often there. Nobody cares."

He went on to boast he had actually converted millions of dollars of cash into gambling chips in several of the casinos but Ron had shaken his head in disbelief.

"It is true. Everybody knows" had been the answer.

"WELL, I believe it." replied the increasingly cynical Maisie later. With two children around she spent time at the club gym and in the supermarket with her lady friends. "The insurance corporation says they have over 2000 super luxury cars covered here. My friend's husband has a car showroom. They sell dozens of cars way above our income level, often for hundreds of thousands of dollars in cash."

"So what do they do with the cash?" asked the still sceptical Ron.

She replied, "My friend says they just take it to their regular bank, to be paid it in as 'car sales'. They even hire Brinks trucks when the bales of money are alarming. But that is the last they hear of it. How is the bank to know or really care how the car buyer got the cash?"

"Well," he replied, "everybody knows the banks have to report any cash deposit over ten thousand, so they get caught!"

"No," she chuckled, "that's a myth. What they have to do is take notice of any cash deposit like that and report if it is considered suspicious. That's very different."

This made sense to Ron because he was well aware contractors on small projects regularly took cash for some jobs, just dropping it off at the bank as acceptable construction payments.

Maisie had the last word as usual. "From now on we are going to know our clients. That is the key. We will not deal with anyone using serious cash unless we know why and how they made it."

RON mentioned her determination about cash to his local Canadian banker over poached salmon and an excellent New Zealand sauvignon blanc at The Club.

"Money is just money, Ron; it has no ethical measurement. Cash is just one thing though. It is a miniscule part of the enormous amount of money being laundered around the world. Way less than 10 percent of 'money' is cash and most of that is in general circulation for daily use. So small contractors, cars and gambling chips are just chicken feed. I applaud Maisie but that is not the problem although useful to small thinking politicians because they and their electorate all understand the size of it.

"Don't turn down big money just because someone you don't know from China or any developing country offers it to you. They most likely have made the capital legitimately, or what they consider legitimate there.

"We bankers are aware that China has recently changed its policy and is beginning to offer Renminbi, mainly so far through Hong Kong, as a currency for general use throughout the world. This is a big policy change and obviously aimed at direct competition with the dollar, euro, yen and pound sterling.

"They appear to be concentrating less on selling manufactures abroad and are more concerned at opening channels for directly access to their domestic market. Hong Kong is very important in this financial process so far and you have your foot in that door. But watch out for Shanghai!"

Ron broke in, "My big concern is how you banks seek out and trace the origins of all this money you move around?"

"Well," replied the money expert, "regarding the origins of any capital, right now the Canadian authorities have to prove, and don't forget beyond reasonable doubt, that you actually knew it came from an illegal activity. If, similarly to other spoil-sport countries, they only had to prove you knew there could be a strong risk of the money being obtained illegally you could more easily get into trouble.

"They call it the 'measure of recklessness' but while we will surely have that here soon, if you suspect, don't get involved. Actually, that brings me to the purpose of this lunch apart from our long friend-ship. Joking aside, Canadian banks are straight, Canada being one of the least corrupt countries in the world. Our bank has to choose our clients carefully and obviously know how they are making their money."

Even with this assurance, Ron was still suspicious about all the big banks' obvious role, somehow, in laundering money. Having approached the subject several times obliquely over lunch, he finally said in exasperation, "You keep evading the subject but I need to know how these major illegal sums are transferred through the banks? They have to be. Explain it to me."

His friend chuckled. He assured him he would never get a senior banker anywhere to discuss that subject, so that was all he had to say. Ron pointed out that just refusing to talk made him sound guilty but he responded laughing, "See what I mean?" which closed the subject.

Moving on smoothly, he turned serious. "Just a warning, Ron. We are becoming very concerned about your Macau association mainly because we can find no records of their financial dealings; anywhere. It's actually strange. The cash keeps flowing, big cash. There is nothing bad of course because there is no paper trail.

"Nothing wrong with your own activity in BC, in fact you have done well, except for the China development jaunt of course. But a warning: we may have to pull out, honestly from puzzlement about your Macau partner. But that's not likely!

"We find it more difficult in the States because they have 'safe harbour' provisions in their privacy laws which require banks to reveal or exchange information about customers suspected of money-laundering. Here that is not specified and we are protected and cannot hand over information without the risk of being sued."

"Don't worry, Ron," he added with a helpful smile, "if Fintrac comes knocking on the door we will tell them to bugger off as usual."

As they walked out of The Club he got to what may have been the real message. "I have to say, personally Ronnie, that we have been doing some checking. Your brother-in-law, M.F. Wong, is a real loser. A confidential warning came in from security in Ottawa which caused us to consider closing his accounts with us. You have to distance yourself from him."

Ron nodded glumly.

THEY confronted Wong in his home office where he could, then actually did, rant to his heart's content. Eventually he realised he had no audience.

"You say the Canadian bank will close my account? I must have the bank for face. No can do," he insisted.

He shouted that he was just getting settled in Canada. He needed upfront companies with regular bank accounts for some business. He must have formal banking with China for the flow of capital to keep going. "Where do I put the cash if no bank?" he asked.

Ron just abruptly informed him, to Maisie's nodding approval in the background, "We have told all our banks Leyland Co. are severing business connections with you or your businesses. From now on you have to arrange your own financing."

They left with a tirade in foul Cantonese ringing in their ears which set guard dog Wanchow howling excitedly.

Wong worried about the pending problem with his own bank for several days but then the inspiring answer came to him in a flash of memory. Of course, he thought. It was the same bank! But whatever was that young banker's name? Some simple research produced the answer.

NOW the general manager of the large Canadian bank, James Quincy Inglewood, Jimmy Q, awaited the arrival of client Mr Wong Mai Fu, with great interest.

Having just been fully briefed on the account, he was now sipping his Earl Grey tea in contemplation while gazing thoughtfully out over his wide Lake Ontario vista.

He knew he had every reason to be cautious. Traditionally the Canadian banks had praised themselves for carefully monitoring their clients to reveal any dubious money acquisition practises. They could reasonably claim to know their clients well but in real life he knew this often applied only to those that chose to be open with them.

Everyone who had something to hide often did so behind corporations, trusts or just simply through their lawyer's trust accounts. It then became a question of how far did he as a banker want to dig in order to find a reason to refuse business. Kind of a silly question to a banker, he knew.

He was also aware the business would just move across the street to another Canadian bank if he refused it, so there was the question of offering lucrative fees to competing banks, which was totally stupid.

He had however become aware of 'the signs' by which all shrewd bankers could immediately recognise a dubious client: the willingness to please the banker; the lack of concern at suggested iniquitous interest rates or terms; the over-assertion of fair dealing; a certain vagueness about business activities.

This client exhibited all of these warning signs but it had become a personal matter.

WONG had aged considerably since that dark evening of the crushed vendor incident many years ago in Hong Kong but he was still recognisable as the smarmy fixer in his memory.

Jimmy Q rose to greet him cordially, ushered him to the corner coffee table and settled in for their discussion. He congratulated Wong on his increased command of English since they had last met but asked whether he would like an interpreter, knowing full well Wong would prefer a personal discussion.

To lighten the mood he asked in a joking way, "What became of that tall, skinny lad I remember in Wanchai? You have filled out a lot." He certainly had the comfortable corpulence of a successful executive.

"Now prosperous!" countered Wong, patting his tummy ruefully.

It quickly became apparent that Wong had adopted a more subtle approach since coming to Canada. He merely chatted, in his strange fractured English, about the coincidence of noticing Mr Inglewood's name as a senior person with his Canadian bank, remarking he had dropped in to congratulate him on doing so well.

Jimmy Q listened politely, trying to understand him. "I have a successful business in Canada, with good Chinese partners. You give us good service; thank you. Much more business is coming. Thank you. Thank you!"

That was it. Having helped him back into his winter coat Jimmy was served with several obsequious head bows as Wong took his leave. Back in his office Jimmy reviewed the video recording of the visit with his chief of security, from which they both agreed it was an obvious shakedown.

The bank's record of the long ago car incident in Hong Kong clearly showed the local police investigation had determined it was an accident as also confirmed by the RCMP officer in the colony. So Wong's implicit threat was merely an embarrassment but even so was to be avoided.

Jimmy Q also made a note to check up personally on Leyland and make sure his friend young Ronnie, an heir of their very old clients, was not getting himself into too much trouble associating with this scoundrel.

They decided to look very carefully into Wong's business activities but also to report the matter to the RCMP, plus Fintrac just to be on the safe side.

THUS, another report implicating Wong arrived on the desk of Chief Superintendent Jack Jackman at RCMP headquarters. This one reminded him of the 'accident' involving the drunken young banker in photographs of the totally stationary, demolished food stall which had been the site of the crash.

Respecting the rules of the Canadian establishment old boy's club, Jackman naturally added nothing to the bare-bones report which made its way into the record but which was copied to Sergeant Singh in Vancouver.

The Chief Superintendent consoled him, "I know you have been steadily building up a convincing case and are chafing at the bit to move on Wong but we need the whole gang and to bring down the international cartel. A bit more patience please and we will get them all!"

Chapter 37

Respectability: Increasing status

WHEN WONG first arrived in Vancouver he had headed for the casinos which had become established in the city over the previous 30 years.

Wong's acquaintances in the Hong Kong nightclub business had given him introductions but he quickly learned from Stump it would be impossible to break into casinos from a business viewpoint.

"The government, indigenous people, establishment figures, the unions and other mysterious investors have long had an unbreakable grip on casinos. Pity, because they are such a loosely supervised industry."

"Good nightclubs on the other hand," Stump said, "I am told, are sadly lacking."

"What does that mean, told?" asked a puzzled Wong.

"Simply that I wouldn't ever been seen dead in one. But I am told they are tame compared with your uncontrolled behaviour in Asia. You could look into it."

OF COURSE, unrestricted nightly activity indeed abounded back in Asia. Wong still ran the club in Hong Kong for Zhang, and had quickly confirmed for himself that the Vancouver business was wide open.

He passed on the opinion to Zhang who agreed to back a venture in Vancouver.

It had opened offering raunchy girly entertainment way beyond anything in the city but so long as he kept to the 'no touching rule' (at least when any strangers were around) all had gone undisturbed.

Wong was a very practical man with years of experience dealing with the Triad drug dealers in Hong Kong. While he was not stupid enough to compete in any way, he offered his whole cooperation in his clubs, being rewarded for compliance and with a partnership rake-off deal.

With their first modest nightclub budget they had settled for rented premises but with success he decided their second would be set-up in its own property. His particular problem was the alarming build up of cash which the first club was generating so he consulted a contractor his pals told him was 'accommodating'.

He was advised, "What we have to do is build as much as possible of the new property through cash payments. It is actually quite simple so long as we all keep quiet. We sign a formal construction contract for the record, at roughly half the cost and we will find a way to spread the balance in cash payments over an 18-month period. It is my problem to share it around the dozen banks I deposit in, and to employ cash-happy consultants and subs."

It worked like a charm.

The second club was also highly successful, especially due to Wong's now- renowned, expanded Titty Bar. Then he built the third club in another part of town but on the same basis with the flood of untaxed cash from the two clubs no one appeared to care or ask about.

When they had become involved in their own developments they had sensibly been advised to design for other tenants also, so that they could mingle rental income with their own nightclub cash in confusion. Each complex presented well as a mixed-use commercial centre establishing Wong as a responsible local developer.

By the time the third club property was opened, the cash build-up was again becoming embarrassing so he did not renew the lease on the first club but built an even larger one nearby, soaking up cash as usual.

The accommodating contractor had also become wealthy, now accepted as a close friend revelling in his debauched visits to the clubs; complimentary of course.

By now, Wong had become a member of the Chambers of Commerce, recognised as a successful businessman who owned three sizeable properties. Local councils respected that municipal taxes were always paid on time. His established property managers with their impressive auditing accountants ensured that income taxes on third party rental earnings were fully satisfied.

But nothing could satisfy the incessant cashflow, so he decided to build his mansion. Once again, the $10 million edifice was contracted formally at six, but built over a longer than necessary period to allow the balance of payment to be was spread out in cash to the various players.

"Construction payment," was all that needed to be explained late Friday afternoon for cash deposits at the local bank and for the transaction to be completed. The title for the mansion was again held by a nominee company of which his lawyer was the sole director so no one could ask any questions.

In this way, Wong had created his little palace with the magnificent sunset swimming pool overlooked by the grand dining room where he was destined to preside over his final Black Renminbi banquet.

WONG had received only a rudimentary education. In fact he had been lucky to escape with his young life to Hong Kong but his tough experience had left him street wise.

His lawyer Stump had set up his nightclub and warehouse companies so obscurely, however, that Wong needed a personal accountant in his private office to keep track but particularly to explain things to him. Maria was loyal and highly competent but Wong, of course, expected more.

He sidled into her office with that look on his face, she now well recognised. Before he could make his move, she jumped up and thrust a bundle of papers into his hand.

"Stump!" she exclaimed. Greed prevailed and he paused; "Stump?"

She asserted professionally, "He makes a lot of our proceeds disappear into his own pocket but this audit indicates it has risen to at least 30 percent." Backing away carefully she asked, "Is that the deal?"

His ardour visibly diminished, Wong grabbed her audit to storm out of the room, leaving her sighing in relief.

She had assumed from experience that providing sexual favours went with the nature of any highly paid criminal accounting job but he was such a nuisance, always wanting it during the busy working day.

Even worse, it was always under the distractingly soulful eyes of his ever present attack dog Wanchow, although reassuringly accompanied by the animal's approving, wagging tail.

In his office, Wong barely understood the mass of figures but her conclusion was clear that Stump was ripping him off 30 percent which he determined must be confronted. Might as well pay tax he thought grimly as he drove over in a fury.

AS CHEERFUL and friendly as always Stump cleared a space for him to sit. "Sorry, but for total security I do all my own clerical work. It piles up a bit. What's new, Mai Fu?" Wong spat out in rage, "Thirty percent?"

Stump explained patiently that his fees came also with expenses or pay-offs he could not always reveal. He had his instructions too which added to the cost of doing business. His inclination was always to help out but this time he had nothing to offer.

Wong made a bad mistake. "You cut the fee or I will tell the lawyer chiefs what you do."

"Are you blackmailing me?" asked the lawyer very quietly.

"Cut the fee or find out," raged Wong, as he slammed out of the office.

THE success of Leyland's real estate division and of young Ronnie had not gone unnoticed in the boardrooms of the great banks in Toronto.

Maisie had bubbled with excitement during her early years in Canada when they were first invited to their bank chairman's table and reception at the highly prestigious Daffodil Ball in Toronto.

"This calls for a trip to Christian Dior Couture." she enthused. "Paris here I come!"

They quickly found elite society doors opening across the country and within a few years the bank had them firmly within their cultural circle continuing their long association with the Leyland family.

Now, Jimmy Q set about safeguarding his business interest. Ron was invited east for a gourmet rare-cut chateaubriand lunch in Jimmy's private dining room, sharing a bottle of his specially imported medoc. After the main course the great man got straight down to business.

"Ronnie, our grandfathers did business together, then our fathers and here we are! So let's not beat around the bush, although things look good, you have some problems with Mr Wong and with your Macau connection, possibly involving money-laundering and sources of capital that need sorting out. The bank is here to help you through just another historical period unscathed.

"What I am proposing is that we painstakingly move all your Macau accounts and China business into legitimate contracts within this bank. By the time all our experts have combed through things and the records have been documented, the money transfers will all be confirmed as legitimate and you will have no further worries."

Ron hesitated before replying and then said, "Thank you for your concern Jimmy, but we are not at present actually aware of any money transfer illegalities. If so we would report them."

"Of course," replied the banker equitably, "but it's what you don't know that is going to bite you in the ass, and that means one day

Wong and Macau! Let me tell you a tale....." and he launched off into his own version of Wong's history in Hong Kong when he was a youngster there.

"It is interesting that I met him back then, eh? Although it was a pretty small business world. You know the bank has been checking up on him and he frankly is a criminal from whom you must distance yourself. Unfortunately, everything you have been doing all these years through the Asian connection is suspect and you have to expunge it very carefully. We can do that for you!"

"You do know he's Maisie's brother don't you?" asked Ron and the banker nodded that just made taking action even more important.

"Our chairmen fathers, the old fellows," he joked, "have said we need some action on this but I'm not pulling rank! They haven't a clue what is going on technically these days, no idea about money-laundering or political threats from other countries, so it's all up to us. And you have it easy. I have questionable money flowing into Canada from countries all over the world.

"We know all the top decision makers in the country. For heaven's sake, they probably have their own low interest loans right here in the bank! At least we need to work together on this."

They had a couple of glasses of the bank's famous vintage Portman's with their Louis Cyr prize Quebec gouda and the lunch ended very amicably with the agreement they would bring finance manager Maisie into the discussion and start thinking about Leyland's extrication from direct Asian banking links.

Chapter 38

Strategy: The Scheming Dragon

MAN LOK and Ah-Cy, to their Canadian establishment friends, were now at the stage where social integration between the Canadian and Chinese decision makers had reached a highly cordial level.

The Zhangs played their part by becoming renowned for their hospitable personal attention provided in their country. Families had become integrated to enjoy vacations together around the world financed by their amazingly generous state companies.

The princelings had come through famously providing the Canadian investors and financiers with all the top level Party contacts they required to establish their businesses there.

The scions of prominent commercial or political Canadian families, in return, found themselves invited to serve on Chinese company boards naturally at the apparent going fee rate of 50,000 a month.

Since many of the wealthy Canadians lived their lives in the same residential areas, schools, clubs and rarefied atmosphere to which the senior politicians had become accustomed, it was more difficult for the political types to speak out in public against the widespread human rights violations taking place in China.

ON ONE of their now-regular visits to eastern Canada the Zhangs were invited to dinner at the embassy, to be preceded by a chat in the Safe Room.

Zhang was a little miffed that his wife was accorded sufficient status to attend but was reassuringly patted on the back by their envoy that this was also his personal opportunity to talk about public relations and policy with a member of the Huang family.

Privately, the envoy was delighted that the ever-cheerful Ms Huang would be there to lighten the evening and he was personally aware she operated from State Security. He courteously waited for her to open their discussion.

"Our leaders in Beijing are expressing serious concern that countries around the world are not respecting Chinese domestic and international political policies." she began. "It has been decided that business leverage will be used, with countries forbidden access to the Chinese market if they do not promote Chinese political communist values in their home countries." The envoy nodded in agreement.

She reminded him enthusiastically of her role in Olympic sport. "Canadian professional sports teams are beginning to appear in Chinese tournaments. They must understand if they make public statements anywhere in the world contrary to Chinese policy they will be prohibited from visiting China together with their sport. Another subject bothering us is that the internet internationally is presently controlled far too much by the American value system and this has to be broken for our eventual domination."

The envoy responded enthusiastically, "That is a subject I wanted to discuss with you too, Mr Zhang. You are doing your duty to take Canadian expertise back to our homeland but I would like to see you playing a more hands-on part in moving to control North American technology here.

"We need your tech companies to get serious about buying assets here by overbidding if necessary. Also by winning more government contracts and partnerships by underbidding or by promising delivery prices that no one can match. The embassy will subsidise costs, of course. It is now absolutely essential to our strategy we penetrate local technologies to enable our potential control of all networks. This is easy here due to Canada's insatiable desire to go faster and faster.

"That is their vulnerability. They will allow all their systems to be manipulated remotely just as we wish. I assume you have been thoroughly briefed in the essential back-door technologies we are inserting?"

He was rewarded with Zhang's vigorous, enthusiastic assurance. Seeing Ah-Cy also nodding they exchanged quizzical glances but refrained from comment.

She suggested amusingly that they should just get their export-import banks to offer more of their generous un-repayable loans that were being gobbled up around the world by unsuspecting countries.

"Debt-trap diplomacy!" she announced triumphantly in English.

"With money you are a dragon; with no money, a worm!"

The amused envoy closed on a lighter vein, suggesting that Chinese companies should also be seen investing in popular projects such as shopping centres and urban complexes or amusement parks to secure the support of the general public.

Could some of Zhang's financial groups invest in this way? Zhang responded enthusiastically, "That is a very interesting idea."

The envoy smiled that this had all sounded rather serious. "Let's now enjoy a quiet relaxing dinner together."

Ah-Cy jumped to her feet and broke into a rousing patriotic song conducting her arms in time, to Zhang's high embarrassment but to the hand-clapping envoy's complete delight.

THEY graciously allowed their various Canadian business friends to provide them with a week of entertainment in Ontario and Quebec, before heading off back across the country to give Zhang's own business managers the good news of their expected expansion bonanza to come.

Chapter 39

Umbrellas: Raised in Hong Kong

UNBELIEVABLY to them, Ronnie and Maisie had been together in Canada for 20 years. Then on a memorable day in 2014 she had burst into his office, with the disturbing news of huge demonstrations in Hong Kong expressing political concerns.

"The provoked political unrest certainly took me by surprise because I could not fathom why China had not just left things as they were," she said. "They are calling them the 'Occupy Central protests'. Apparently China has become impatient, and is pushing a decision to deny universal suffrage, interfering in the electoral process and effectively starting to take political control. Why ever would they do that?"

Hundreds of thousands of previous immigrants were known to have returned to Hong Kong as Canadians, many being youngsters with university degrees initially unmarried and mobile. The city was obviously booming economically, offering everyone opportunities and progression in prospering companies.

Things looked stable under the 'One country, two systems' arrangement and their Canadian passports also gave peace of mind with long-term options. Those who had returned seemed happily resettled, with Hong Kong itself set for decades of prosperity. Now things had suddenly changed.

Ron saw a spike-up in business from Hong Kong after those first demonstrations which increased with the succeeding mass 'Umbrella parades', the interest in Canada measurably starting again. People were reluctantly recognising it was only a matter of time.

They found some were returning to Canada for personal reasons such as raising young families or nearing retirement age. Some were just retiring to enjoy a quieter lifestyle. Some had ageing parents living in Canada. Some just decided it was time to go.

NONE of this directly affected Leyland's continuing expansion of its real estate business with the company now doing its own developments and also offering a full spectrum of property services to well-vetted clients.

They could now afford to be much more selective. Just chatting on their regular call with Ping Kin, he mentioned, "The Six had founded several dicey big P2Ps around China and internationally, riskily using my bank as a front." Then he paused, awaiting Ron's query.

"Actually," laughed Ron, "I know what that is! We turned down a direct approach ourselves financed from China to start a peer-to-peer lending company. The investors get their extortionate interest rate, the weak borrowers get their capital but with high risk of failure. Dubious money from China is going into those types of loans here but they can degenerate too easily into loan sharking. We are not in the leg-breaking business!"

"I have the same sentiment," Ping Kin agreed, "but The Six had attracted enormous funds from thousands of small-time investors around China and listed similar companies in Hong Kong and in the United States. There are alarming Ponzi characteristics and even the Chinese regulators are starting to step in. It is very concerning."

"But," he continued, "I mainly want to talk to Maisie about our stock market 'fun fund'."

Over the past decade the Chinese stock exchanges had grown enormously, vying for second or third place in world standing, with

Shanghai passing the $5 trillion mark and Shenzhen at about half that much.

Maisie's private 'fun fund' with him was significantly now no longer the brunt of Ron's amusement and Ping Kin continued that he had some big news he wanted to pass on. His English was by now way better that Maisie's Mandarin so they often communicated in English to Ron's relief.

"The Chinese exchanges are now officially linked to the Hong Kong exchange through the Connect programme, with mainland investors being able to invest in Hong Kong while similarly opening up the Chinese market to direct foreign share purchase.

"So for a variety of reasons I find it a good time to split our 'fun fund'. I will arrange a personal account for you in Hong Kong, but just to keep you speculating, I am sending my half to Barbados!"

They were both aware their main concealed capital, which he jokingly called their 'rainy day fund' remained hidden deep within his computer programme, accessible only to him.

"You can have investment fun on your own, kiddo," he informed her, applying his latest American movie lingo.

Then he reverted to Mandarin to remind her that her stock exchanges in North America had over a $30 trillion share value to offer with lots of variety. Frankly, without their insider market tip-offs, she would need the far more honest information provided to make decisions.

Then, taunting her in English again he continued, "You may well want to sell some of the shares and move the money, but for the moment it is all parked in Hong Kong at your disposal. You can declare it all and pay all your stupid voluntary taxes as you seem determined to do!"

Ron just shook his head in horror at the prospect of another problem of riches to explain. These quite considerable capital assets just suddenly appeared in Hong Kong formally documented through Hinks as a gift to Ms Maisie Leyland from a bone fide benefactor in Macau.

Their tax advisers in Vancouver said it looked good to them so she simply declared the value of the investments in her next tax return in Canada.

Delighted to have someone actually disclose an overseas asset, particularly from Hong Kong, the Revenue Agency positively assessed her tax return with gratitude.

MAISIE'S direct connections with Macau and Hong Kong were gradually fading and her interests in Canada were expanding. If anyone asked she just replied she was Canadian.

When yet another early connection with Hong Kong disappeared, Ron mentioned, "You will be interested that the Canadian Government has decided it had enough of Investor Immigration and is closing it down. Except for it agreeing to a continuing sweetheart deal just for Quebec as usual. Anyway, immigration is no longer our concern and we can thankfully just expand our real estate and protecting our current interests. But it's another of your links with Hong Kong gone."

With a grin, he asked her, "Were you sad to lose the immigration business? After all it was a connection with Hong Kong and brought us together? Or were you just waving your beautiful naked boobs around in public in Macau to get me excited in order to buy a ticket to Canada?"

"You mean, *'Softly softly, catchee monkey?'* Absolutely not so." she laughed. "It was the myth of your Gweilo sexual prowess that attracted me. Before I knew better, I was pregnant. Imagine a little girl, half-starved, being smuggled into Hong Kong? Taken in by an unknown older brother, everyone strangers, Mom and Dad far away, lost forever but making their sacrifice too.

"That is why I helped you with immigration; why I value being Canadian so much. The colonialists never welcomed the idea of Hong Kong Chinese people being free to reside in the United Kingdom, actually supporting the mainland's racist approach.

"We were called Overseas British Nationals but being Hong Kong Chinese were unable to live permanently in England or pass on the privilege. When The Chinese took over, they also created a new status for resident Hongkongers. They can apply for a special administrative region passport but they must be Chinese citizens. If born there the general rule is they have to be of 'Chinese descent.' If not, they have to be 'naturalised' first and China is very selective.

"The kicker is that there are still about three million people holding a class of nationality called Overseas British Nationals. The Chinese say if you are of Chinese descent you belong only to them and every-body can only hold one nationality."

Ron agreed. "In China it is not a question of personal decision but rather doing what you are told. Will the Western powers support the Hong Kong folks? It again becomes a simple question: what is more important, money or personal rights? Both countries traded the 'Chinese' people with the property."

"You got it." she admitted sadly. "Maybe Britain will put that right one day and offer them full nationality when they see China in its true light. The Chinese always regarded Hong Kong as a part of their country which it obviously is, so it's only a matter of time before they impose their terrible system of government on the people there. I didn't see any future for them.

"That is why I value so much being welcomed into Canada and will stay, come what may."

Chapter 40

Trauma: A coercive proposition

WHILE their earlier money services connections still sourced funds through Ping Kin in Macau, they had no immigration distraction, being now exclusively involved in real estate deals.

Clients from China and many other countries were also just walking in the door with pots of money they already had in Canada, many looking for long-term investments but others trying to park the money in loans or mortgages.

It proved a simple business putting these investors together to acquire properties but usually there was no knowledge of the actual beneficial owners, nor was their source of capital ever questioned.

Ron and Maisie had also becoming concerned that many of their clients tended to trade properties amongst each other which was a classic money-laundering manoeuvre, although good for their fee business.

Thus it should have been a pleasant change when the charming Zhang couple came into their lives, representing a solid Chinese company.

Zhang Man Lok and his wife were evidently well into their sixties despite her trim, fit figure or his well-maintained jet-black hair. He spoke courteously and slowly in English

"We are visiting Canada informally from Beijing for a major state corporation. I am a minor director but with some influence. We intend to diversify our real estate holdings throughout Canada. My wife is in a government service and here on vacation."

Mr Zhang apologised with a smile they only spoke a little English. Friends had recommended *Mai Xi* as a knowledgeable Mandarin-speaking person and because of her background in the real estate market. He addressed her by her Chinese name which he emphasised.

Maisie's expression remained impassive but her memory reverted immediately in shock to that day long ago in Wong's bar when Zhang made such a negative impression on her, although he did not appear to recognise her; how could he?

She still knew this could be no coincidence and she immediately recognised the identity of her brother's mysterious financier.

HIS wife Ah-Cy Huang smiled in apparent understanding when Maisie explained her preference for using her Canadian name. They went off for three friendly days sightseeing, shopping, or doing girly things which allowed Ah-Cy to relax but merely increased Maisie's apprehension.

Zhang had also been busy. His corporation did have an off-the-record group already established in Vancouver, working closely with the Chinese Consulate, casing out Canada.

His colleagues were highly respectful, as they needed to be of a member of the ruling class but he was merely addressed as Mr Zhang. During a general discussion he directed them he had selected Leyland Co. for their acquisitions, where he found the Mandarin-speaking Ms Leyland very charming.

He also slipped away for a personal clandestine meeting with Steven Stumpenberg. At Stump's office they were joined by Wong, who came in quietly by the back door, the subject of the conversation being their deadly fentanyl business.

Zhang conversed in studied English with attempted assistance from

Wong's limited Mandarin, which just made translation efforts more complicated.

"It was easier for me to supply you before China decided to make fentanyl sale illegal and to cooperate with the States. I have the chemical production in China but now have to be very careful. We are not soft like Canada and are have immediate death sentences and executions," Zhang said.

"The Mounties are getting involved because they now know Canada is being used as a port of entry for redistribution to Mexico, the US and even down into Australia."

"So, you say it is too dangerous. We should shut down?" worried Wong.

"No, absolutely not. It is becoming a North American epidemic; profits will rise with bigger risk. We must take over more of the market."

Stump worried, "One day politicians will decide they have enough votes to decriminalise drug use and treat it within the medical system where it should be. Until then our market will keep growing, but more people will overdose giving us more police and potential exposure problems. Heads will inevitably roll."

Zhang shrugged. "It is our job to separate ourselves from risk and not be traced."

Stump nodded, affirming that was what he did, but Wong did not appear to fathom his own increasing vulnerability.

Wong was then courteously dismissed from the meeting on the explanation Zhang had other business to discuss with Stump. This involved generously financing higher level connections in the Canadian establishment that Stump was making on Zhang's behalf, for further expansion of their interests in the province and throughout the country.

THE anticipated day inevitably came for Maisie, when Ron presented a preliminary real estate report to Mr Zhang over a light salad and white wine lunch in their private office dining room, with her impressively having to do most of the talking, in Mandarin, of course. Mr Zhang just sat quietly listening.

AH-CY had been working hard on her English but professing ignorance in her public life, spoke in Mandarin. Maisie quickly found her out while they had fun playing with the languages, particularly to decide upon a North American name for her.

"I suggest Arcie because '*ie*' is at the end of all my family and best friends' names."

They quickly found too, that of Maisie's adopted languages, her English was now fluent, by far stronger than her Mandarin, and they enjoyed the conversational interplays.

Maisie had become close to her with the realisation she was her own woman, not dominated at all by her assertive husband. They settled down to a happy routine of afternoon margaritas which left them half cut before dinner. Sitting at a bar on the seawall they licked salt from their empty glasses, giggling to the toned waiter for a refill.

Ah-Cy observed that it was amusing they were sitting there in Canada, two Chinese women, chatting away in Mandarin. It was a good sign for the future that China was clearly beginning to subvert North America.

Equally equitably Maisie replied in English, "We are only able to speak frankly and openly here in such a public place because we *are* in North America. It is only a matter of time before your communist system in China goes the same way as the Soviet Union with your rising middle class insisting upon more personal freedom."

Ah-Cy laughed, replying in Mandarin that was a hopeful American dream because the system in China was very different. She said it was becoming clear that Beijing was succeeding where Moscow failed. They were developing a successful economy in China that was becoming an alternative for North America's liberal democracy which was failing, perhaps due to lack of direction.

She agreed that there had been some human cruelty along the way although that had also happened in the European colonisation and industrial revolution but China was changing quickly with increasing nationalism which had everyone pulling together.

Maisie countered, pointedly back in English, "You still have a long way to go and you have many weaknesses. Look at your deadly ageing population demographics for example, together with evidence your export surge is levelling off. Many of your brightest like me, ha!, have departed and you have already enjoyed your best years of development. Now you have emerging nations breathing down your necks!

"Then there is the increasing pollution, new coal-fired power stations opening every week for example with reports carbon use will keep accelerating for at least the next 20 years. How about your miles and miles of depressing concrete middle-class towers that will all become slums at the same time? All enormous difficulties in the future you still have to face."

She bit her tongue restraining herself from getting on to her pet peeve, human rights, deciding this was not the time.

Still, not their problems to solve that afternoon they agreed knocking back their margaritas cheerfully. "Cheers!" said Maisie. "*Ganbei!*" replied Ah-Cy setting the tone for their future partying.

Ah-Cy explained, "Anyway I had no personal political choice. Do you recognise my family name, Huang? When I married I retained my original name, Huang as is our custom, but I insisted our children also keep the name. Outside of China I reluctantly answer to Mrs Zhang, which I hate!

"My grandfather and particularly my father who was a revolutionary hero are extremely famous in the Party. Growing up in Hong Kong I expect you were probably not aware of Chinese politics. My husband Man Lok started out as a nothing and owes everything to my old dad, 'The Patriarch' Huang, who has brought him to power. Without our family he would be finished and would lose everything."

The new drinks arrived with Maisie snorting in English, "So he better not piss off you or your father, right!" which when translated into Mandarin started another fit of giggles.

AT THE end of the visit the two teams assembled together at Leyland's office to review all the investment options they had been discussing, with hopes of arrival at some firm proposals.

They had got to know each other well and chatted at lunch, eating their sandwiches, drinking their coffee and even having a few beers or glasses of wine to celebrate a productive week. After all it was Friday.

Ahead of the group, Maisie went with Zhang to their map room to explain the layouts of their proposed investments. They sat together examining plans, with the objective of him selecting an important option.

Admittedly she was wearing a signature, very short Kate Spade summer dress that emphasised her shapely long legs, but she was completely unprepared when he slipped his hand up between them, demonstrating his skill at concurrently reaching quite another objective. He was totally confident in his approach, expecting no resistance and obviously being accustomed to abject female compliance.

Before she could even react, his assault was interrupted by Ron with the rest of the group entering the room talking cheerfully. The expressionless and unemotional Zhang just unhurriedly moved his hand away, continuing to talk calmly.

The presentation went on with a subdued Maisie interpreting but wondering how to deal with this turn of events. The sexual aspect of his approach did not bother her in the slightest because she had lived daily fighting off much more physical assaults in her young life. She knew that Ron would just have walked out of the negotiations if he had seen what happened but she knew how much these deals meant to him.

The problem was that Zhang's move was clearly proprietarily, signalling to her that she went with the deal. As the group continued to discuss real estate, her mind was in turmoil but she convinced herself it was no big problem, that she could deal with it and she decided to keep it to herself.

What bothered her even more was that she was on a slippery ethical slope. Either she was Maisie Leyland or Mai Xi Wong. Was she governed by principles or riches? Like all good Canadians she would avoid a confrontation, hoping for both, just waiting to see what transpired.

THEY entertained the Zhangs and his colleagues to a very long and cultured Chinese dinner that evening before they left, with Maisie strangely subdued but striking in a black Prada outfit which she had designed for the occasion, to emphasise her professionalism.

When Zhang announced, in a slightly inebriated rambling speech at the end of the dinner, translated dutifully by Maisie, that they would look seriously at the acquisition of the two big shopping centre-anchored complexes they had considered in the range of a few billion dollars, they assumed it was the free-flowing wine talking.

Then the Zhangs disappeared off back to China, with sceptical realtor Ron fully expecting that was the last they would hear of them, but leaving Maisie still apprehensive and wrestling with her conscience.

SHE was steely eyed when she rushed to report to Ping Kin, protesting about Zhang's unexpected appearance. She described in anger his remarkably accurate hand manoeuvre.

"This is not all a coincidence because I remember him from my childhood at the Wanchai hotel. He must be financing Wong's crime. What were you thinking, springing that evil man on me? He insists on calling me *Mai Xi* very personally in Mandarin, which is spooky."

There was a hushed, long pause before he admitted, "This is very concerning because Zhang is the unidentified powerful head of The Six. I never told you because I am sworn to secrecy. It is the essence of our set-up that none of the principals is ever identified.

I had no idea Zhang was visiting Vancouver but I am aware he had ongoing personal business with Wong in which I am not involved, probably to do with drug dealing, so you must be very careful. I also never told you for your protection. Why did he come directly to you and why bypass me?"

Maisie knew she had to tell Ron about the identity of Zhang but she limited the account to having seen him earlier with Wong in her Hong Kong younger life, making him his likely financial connection. He agreed it was odd but always positive, suggested they wait to see if there was any follow-up business before worrying too much.

ALERTED by Chief Superintendent Jackman to Zhang's public reappearance in Canada, Sgt Pritam unbelievably had a call from CSIS. They had found themselves tripping over each other, literally, disguised as back street vagrants conducting surveillance on the meeting lawyer Stumpenberg had with Zhang and Wong.

Finally, they agreed to pool their resources but by the time they had conferred, reached agreement on the protocol, run it through their lawyer and received approval from Ottawa, the Zhangs had already long ago packed their bags and gone home.

Chapter 41

Olga: Gratifying cash use

WONG had not heard back from Stump, so when nothing was said at the secret meeting with Zhang he assumed gleefully he had backed him down on the fees grab. He decided the brief talks with Zhang when he was in town had gone well, confirming his support.

Then his mind switched to Canada's 10-year multiple re-entry visa that had just been introduced and he knew he had yet another business bonanza coming.

Once again Canada was going for the money. They were not only offering the visas but pushing them through special visa offices in many large overseas cities, particularly in China, where they were being snapped up.

If the applicants had known the Canadian visa offices were being run by Chinese government agents they might not have been so eager, but they had quickly moved into issuing millions, roughly half in China, causing a very profitable surge in tourism and capital investment.

Ron too was profiting from the increased interest in property speculation, particularly in his condos, where tourists had been casing out the market in Canada with their easy visas, enrolling in his marketing schemes conducted back in Chinese cities.

They soon found they could sell out most of the units in prime Canadian locations through agents in China without even having to offer them for sale in Canada. Then, since they were investment buildings they either managed empty apartments which made life easy, or looked after units the poorer investors needed to rent out.

Their brokerage business also noticed the increase in investors from China looking for manageable hotels, shopping complexes or apartment buildings preferably in areas with lots of Chinese faces and name signs.

Still, the happiest had been Wong, who had seen his immigration business prosper and who spent most of his time travelling.

His wife Olga, son Ivan and daughter Sasha had become committed Canadians with the kids' high school educations completed. Their talented girl was excelling at a music degree with the likely objective of a scholarship to the Julliard Conservatory. Sasha appeared to have absolutely nothing in common with her father and rarely spoke to him.

Olga had completely taken to the West Canadian lifestyle, with no debt of course, enhanced by an adequate but steady cash income from Wong, the source of which was never questioned. She feared him, particularly his temper, so she submitted to his rough sexual demands when he was in Vancouver, but spent as little time socially with him as possible.

She had met Wong as manager of entertainment in his Hong Kong nightclub. Olga had always been a highly distinctive beauty, who quickly became known as Wong's bought woman, although she was paradoxically quite cultured. Typically of a White Russian she spoke English, Russian, Mandarin and also native Cantonese fluently.

Early in the previous century her Slavic forebears had been forced eastward out of Russia to form the extensive White Russian colony in Shanghai, only again to be moved on to Hong Kong by the Chinese communist revolution. Their attractive, accommodating women had developed quite a reputation for their ability to entertain: Olga excelled.

Flaunting her surgically exaggerated, although tastefully exposed body at the nightclub, she was obviously no innocent but he had always claimed her exclusively as his own, jealously monitoring her friendships.

While she was attracted by the high standard of living she enjoyed with him, he had always controlled her expenditures carefully. This had continued after they moved to Canada.

She was a fit, vigorous woman however with her own demands. While he was often away she devised a private business to supply herself with a useful hidden source of income. She had worked for him from time to time, between pregnancies, in his immigration business with access to literally hundreds of contacts. These were now useful for her 'jeweller cash business' as she liked to call it.

Her client list was augmented by her friends in the travel industry who introduced tourists, often short of Canadian cash which she offered to provide quickly with no questions asked. The business proved so simple when her Mandarin network supplied her quickly with the names of jewellers eager to cooperate.

Jewellers suited her case best because they were traditionally used by cash launders such as drug dealers in the simple process of 'buying' jewellery or watches from one source at an inflated value for cash, then by arrangement selling it back at below market to another, receiving a cheque in payment. The discount was horrendous but the money was now legitimised.

The jewellers could trade the same pieces back and forth indefinitely with no risk. However, the originating jeweller still had the recurring inconvenience of a stack of hot notes in the safe. It was here that Olga saw her opportunity.

She identified tourists who were short of Canadian cash for unrecorded purchases and put them together with the cash rich jewellers. The scam simply provided the cash by Renminbi debit card payment in place of sparklers, for which they provided a fake jewellery receipt, just in case.

Jewellery was extremely difficult to trace. Such transactions were never questioned. Naturally, the jeweller got a good deal for his money, while Olga left with her well-earned commissions, trying to cram all the banknotes into her oversized Longchamp Roseau tote.

Her smile of anticipation indicated she had a good use for her additional cash.

A WOMEN friend had recommended a strong young masseur who she advised was prepared to offer extra services in the privacy of their country club athletic centre. "He's fantastic." She rolled her eyes. "All it takes is a standard club massage booking, subject to their monthly couple of hundred dollar fee."

But the signal was to be a much more substantial upfront cash tip, which Olga laid coyly on his table. Smiling encouragingly he murmured quietly, "The rules are to maintain complete silence, always total relaxation and allow my unrestricted manual access to your entire body."

His professional massage was then augmented skilfully to produce breathtaking surges of on-the-edge sensation. The eagerly anticipated last session of each month was his opportunity to earn that really big cash bonus. Then he performed his usual process but continued, to induce prolonged waves of pure pleasure, which engulfed her totally relaxed body finally leaving her absolutely spent and satisfied for weeks.

She was acutely aware that he was introducing a subtle monthly escalation into the process involving his personal participation. She increased the gratuity in silent encouragement, happy that the jeweller cash was being put to such a good use.

WONG travelled constantly, running his Asian businesses and immigration agencies, mainly leaving the family alone. So they thankfully had little to do with him, with the exception of his son Ivan who hated him with a passion but was involved in his business.

For one thing, although he understood Cantonese and had taken Mandarin in high school, he had insisted on speaking English from a young age. He grew to ridicule his father's still broken English although carefully not to his face. Wong had not paid much attention to his children, being totally absorbed in his schemes until Ivan had graduated from high school with a comfortable university-entry level.

"No," insisted his father. "leave school. I had a business at you age. It is time for you to go to work." With that he was sent into a nightclub where he was employed starting at the bottom.

Now he was in his twenties, managing one of the clubs with his life totally involved in cash. As a young, educated Canadian he was acutely aware that he was a criminal, deeply absorbed in the laundered money business.

He laughed defiantly to friends that he drove the expected Lamborghini Spider of a nightclub manager. He had paid his 200,000 bucks in cash, just like in the legend, without a peep from anyone.

As expected, he was also seen openly living with a slinky girlfriend in a luxurious Yale Town penthouse condo he had bought for cash, with payments spread over a period, broken into easily bankable deposits.

He had become so skilled at smurfing, the science of breaking funds into manageable small parts, that he was in charge of all their general laundering programmes, handing out packages of cash regularly to staff members and other 'straw men' as they were called.

For a fee, they took their allotted cash to one of the casinos, where they were personally acquainted with the right people. They returned with a laundered 'winnings' cheque or at the least all the cash converted to easier bundles of $100 bills.

He knew well a casino 'work around' as they called the laundering process could not happen, in theory. It required the cooperation of the cashiers, croupiers and security people but also for the management to be looking the other way, to avoid anything revealing going into the record. They all had their systems, teams and varying times perfected.

His father had his own mysterious laundering system, for years having them load bales of big notes into his car, for his regular visits to the casinos where he was renowned as a high-roller.

To be on the safe side the nightclubs never deposited any casino cheques or drafts, but signed them over to Stump who used his trust account to eventually credit them into their bank, less his fee as agreed.

Ivan also ran a quickly growing loan-sharking business out of the nightclub back office to facilitate gamblers with lines of credit in cash, which were not provided by the BC casinos themselves. One way or another he was moving the cash!

HE WAS a bright lad and Ivan formed a working relationship with Stump, who became something of an advisor.

As a personal side business, they initially set up a series of hidden corporations which they used to purchase barely profitable fast food franchises which were cash businesses and perfect for depositing carefully laundered, illegally earned cash.

They had a vast network of criminal contacts between them needing their services. They had recently added a couple of successful large downtown restaurants to their network and a chain of massage parlours, all offering additional employment to "your young ladies", as Stump called them, never having met one and staying personally far away from any of their establishments. Ivan, on the contrary, had become a busy, visible young man about town.

He had a sick feeling the authorities would one day get their act together, with him ending up in jail. He blamed his father, but he still feared him way too much to desert. Plus he was becoming accustomed to the lavish life style!

AS A club manager, Ivan had met the majority owner Mr Zhang several times briefly on his visits from China but knew his bodyguard Lo quite well because they often ended up drinking together when the bosses were meeting. They had a bit of a language problem but managed to communicate, resorting to his schoolboy Mandarin.

Ivan knew the friendly but taciturn subordinate had to be suspected as an intelligence gatherer which was the case, but he knew Lo could also be used to return messages. He had a lot to tell.

As they drank, Lo divulged rather more than Ivan felt he needed to know about his mother's wild young life in the Hong Kong nightclub business. Lo laughingly revealed, "Did you know that she was one of Zhang's especial favourites in the club but your possessive father always denied her to him when he visited, even when offered large cash incentives."

Lo managed to convey the message that Mr Zhang was now very impressed by the educated, bright young man looking for him possibly to replace his father in the organisation in due course; perhaps heading up Canada.

They discussed Wong's growing intemperance which had caused fights with others in the group. Lo regretted he had heard that Wong was becoming something of a liability creating the possibility he would be retired soon. "Mr Zhang told me it is far too long since he personally spent time with the beautiful Olga, and asked me to pass on the request that you bring your mother for a very private dinner out with him one evening soon, for the three of you to discuss your future career in his organisation."

Chapter 42

Principle: Influencing Canadians

'WE HAVE created a friendly monster," Ron suggested to Maisie and Logger at a regular Leyland meeting. "Wil is in the paper again today, with a picture, stirring up trouble over potential real estate fraud and money-laundering as usual."

Since Leyland had introduced their tough rules of conduct, Wil had become a fanatic in the industry, claiming privately it was not only about ethics but self-defence, because everybody had to work by the same rules.

"He is taking this real estate business very seriously, blaming all the easy money that has been flooding into the country. He doesn't think he can do much about the deep rooted institutional establishment fraud. Nor about street crime which is all bad stuff that everybody hates.

"But he says he has over 25,000 loyal fellow real estate salespeople in British Columbia backing him. He thinks they can make a difference. Twenty five thousand!"

They had encouraged Wil and his supporters who were on every committee possible, making a nuisance of themselves pushing for honesty. Once they had got started the press jumped on the bandwagon with Wil becoming something of a minor celebrity.

Ron continued defensively, "You know I have always done my bit in the real estate industry, serving on all the right councils, boards, committees, panels, conventions or whatever is going."

"Didn't achieve much," Maisie replied, "but I don't really blame you. More than a thousand people are moving into the city every week, many with money, making the pressure on real estate continuous.

"While the income gap is widening alarmingly, the overall standard of living and employment is high, with our socially progressive state supporting everyone in safety. No wonder people from around the world are scrambling to gain admission. We are just all caught up in exploiting the growth."

"Still," Ron retorted, "at a professional level, on my various committees there have been mounting rumblings of concern about business ethics. Too many people are turning a blind eye to un-Canadian practices that are happening. We worry if we let things just continue, they could become a way of life.

"We talk about all the minor avoidances of taxes including resultant money-laundering going on around the industry. Everyone sometimes makes cash payments for services but we preferred just to ignore the tax significance to get on with everyday life."

"You are too busy being important and successful," Maisie kidded. "So nothing is done."

WIL had exploded onto the scene demanding that the real estate industry become proactive rather than hiding away from these mounting problems, which he could see being severely exacerbated by the influx of foreign capital, with different business practices providing too comfortable profits.

He did not believe the dozen or so regulatory bodies should any longer get away with their claim they were only qualified to protect the public in their specific profession because their expertise did not extend to detecting fraud or money-laundering.

He enthusiastically addressed his fellow thousands of registered real estate professionals, insisting they could deal with such bad business practices themselves but that it would have to come from each of them personally.

"Most important," he demanded, "you must insist upon knowing with whom you are dealing, to ensure the real ownership is honestly registered. I have been negotiating all my life and I know all you have to do then is look your client in the eye and ask how he made his money. But the real question is, do you really want to know?"

He asked every single licensed professional working in the industry to accept a personal responsibility to expose money-laundering not only through their companies or associations. That had also to include appraisers, home inspectors, mortgage brokers, insurance personnel, builders, reluctant notaries, and lawyers; in fact anyone in the know.

Wil was waking up to the fact that money-laundering had become significantly dangerous to the society. Cash alone got a lot of press, but on his fast-growing website, writing proudly as a prairies lad, he called it small potatoes in the overall market.

The main source of black money being laundered was tax crimes, fraud, embezzlement, drug dealing, theft, bribery and corruption, often with the proceeds sitting in bank accounts earning interest, or parked in temporary investments waiting to be legitimised by laundering through a stream of transactions. Real estate was ideal.

Around this time, his highly polished obligatory senior salesman's Bentley mysteriously started developing flat tires and deep scratch marks down its sides.

He went further, starting to enjoy the publicity, by criticising widespread cash being increasingly used in dubious ways by the entire society. It was bad enough mouthing off about the profession that fed him, but then he got really into trouble attacking the lower end construction industry.

He reported stories of acceptance of significant cash payment by clients in smaller construction projects, passed on through the system to willing sub-trades, then on into the general world as cash wages, subsequently on to down to the McDonald's or Starbucks level where it again discovered the tax system.

"All the money parting hands in that chain is potentially laundered but is shrugged off by everyone involved. And where did the cash come from in the first place?"

That was when he got his first big load of messy construction excavation dirt dumped in his drive.

On his social media site, he turned this into good press to the delight of his thousands of followers, by tweeting, "My grandfather fought in the mud of the Flanders trenches. I can bloody well put up with a little crap on my drive in a matter of Canadian principle!"

AROUND that time, Ah-Cy Huang dropped into Ottawa on official business on her way back from Europe.

She was now operating at a Party political level at State Security but with an unidentified public status, in which she had observed a conference in Brussels. Then she had attended serious briefing talks at the Chinese Embassy in London regarding the new Brexit referendum upset.

She had been speaking English for a week and when she lunched with her friend the security envoy in a safe room at the Chinese Embassy, she surprised him by cheerfully showing off by greeting him in English.

"Hey! Good to visit you again!"

"Ms Huang. Great English! I welcome you back to frigid Ottawa. It is always an especial pleasure and uplifting to chat with you," displayed his immaculate accent and nuanced command of their language.

She explained, "I can tell you confidentially and not for publication, that I recently took an executive position at State Security."

"I am very impressed. Congratulations."

Ah-Cy nodded acknowledgment. "Among other things, I am now involved in vetting and editing the production of the *Global Times*. I spend a lot of my time working in English and last week everyone in our London office spoke it."

They reminisced together about the remarkable success of the propaganda newspaper published internationally in dozens of languages by the Chinese Communist Party's daily official tabloid, out of Beijing.

"You know here we are concentrating on the Mandarin edition?" he asked, to be answered by her enthusiastic nodding.

She continued impressively in English, "That is not what I want to chat about. I am travelling to give an early warning of a new program we are about to introduce internationally and I would like you personally to work through me when we get going on the Canadian push."

"So you are checking out my language ability. Plus assessing how far you can trust me; if at all?" the seasoned diplomat chuckled. "Well. I am prepared to admit, life in Canada is extremely pleasant, although their system of government is totally impractical and indecisive, at least the way they play it."

"Ah," was her grinning reply, accompanied by a disconcerting flash of her brilliant white teeth, "don't they call that *'backsliding'*?"

"Not at all. It's called *'Know thy enemy'* which is my job," was his totally unconcerned smiling rejoinder.

"Have you been working on anything interesting?" she asked, to make conversation. He replied enthusiastically, "We are pushing to buy into any mineral companies around the Arctic to assist us position ourselves strategically for future control of those Northern waterways."

"Yes," she replied enthusiastically. "In Beijing we are taking this global warming opportunity seriously. Our people in Europe were laughing about the big advantages the new Paris Accord gives us."

She got back to business. "We are intending to introduce a volunteer policy to be enacted by all embassies, consulates or representative offices around the world but which I consider particular important to infiltrating Canada.

"We will be recruiting local ethnic Canadian Chinese people into a corps of volunteers playing a role to be our 'eyes, ears, mouth and hands', ostensibly to protect the lives and interests of citizens of China in Canada."

"And nose?" he interjected to her delight at his unusual relaxed humour.

"I propose you conduct training seminars for volunteers which will call for careful long range planning. The voluntary work is to be an honour to all people of Chinese background, to improve our relations with Canada but also to earn rewards for their families back in China."

The envoy was doubtful. "We can expect virulent press attacks here that this action is building a communist network in Canada." But her answer was, "Give them the explanation this is just a helping hand from regular folk. They will gulp anything."

"Swallow!" he corrected gleefully."Swallow! I have been waiting for a mistake to pounce on." Her genuine laughter encouraged him to think he may have found a reliable contact in Beijing.

Surrendering she switched back to comfortable Mandarin. "The basic idea is to build up a vast hidden network of reliable Chinese people sympathetic to the motherland across the country, which we can use for many purposes," she chuckled, comically wiggling her eyebrows suggestively.

But he ended their conversation very seriously. "Canada is finally becoming defensive and it is getting more difficult to deceive them. They have realised that your State Security '*Operation Fox Hunt*' for example is not confined to alleged criminals but has extended into Canada to stamp out political dissent. Canada is getting increasingly edgy about their silly human rights. There is trouble coming."

AH-CY had thought of stopping off in Vancouver to see *Mai Xi* for a few Margaritas on her way back. Zhang had said nothing further about pursuing investments in Canada and although the envoy knew about the proposals the subject had not been raised. Also she had a nagging conscience about misleading her so-trusting pro-democracy friend about her clandestine activities in her mistakenly adopted country. She suddenly admitted to herself that she missed Maisie; a feeling she had never had for a friend or indeed for anyone.

"What's the matter with me? Getting soft!" she admonished herself. Then she broke into a ruefully smile realising that she had returned to think about her in the English she spoke.

Chapter 43

Warehouse: Murder, she said

THE Warehouse property with which they had started their Immigrant Investor programme so very long ago, was still of concern to Ron. He felt there was something fishy about Wong's activities there although it was obviously busy.

There were always uniformed guards, providing tight perimeter security and the entire property was brightly lit and operated around the clock.

Since they had sold it to Wong it was no longer any of their business but they remained curious. There was an impressive, constant flow of trucks and goods at the property. Moreover the yards around the structure had never been extensively built upon because Wong apparently needed the land for container storage.

He had assembled an all immigrant and Cantonese-speaking senior staff, running the activities in the property that were totally loyal, possibly due to the nightclub privileges they were awarded. Everything was shrouded in secrecy.

That was the extent of their knowledge about the activities there, other than the immigration business, but it was a Mexican not one of these Cantonese employees, who spilled the beans.

MAISIE appeared to be the sympathetic ear in the organisation. A dark-skinned, plumpish young lady slipped up to her nervously at the supermarket to enquire if she could talk to her privately.

She wheeled her buggy over to the coffee bar, with a broad smile asking "OK, what's on your mind?" only to have the smile replaced with a look of deep concern as the story unfolded. The woman claimed, "A really bad immigrant Cantonese guy is running it all for his gang from Guangzhou but Wong is in with them. Do you know what goes on in The Warehouse?"

Her name was Maria Carmen and she worked as an accountant in Wong's private office. She admitted she was up to her neck in "illegal stuff".

Maisie was aware Guangdong province on the Pearl River estuary, her original home, had quickly become a major manufacturing hub for China attracting more than 50 million permanent residents with additionally as many again unofficial itinerants, producing a significant percentage of its exports. Thousands of merchant ships with millions of containers were involved making detailed document checking a massive problem.

Maria explained haltingly, "I trained in a straight shipping company but my team now basically falsifies bills of lading for volumes of goods being imported into Canada mainly from Guangdong. There is an extensive system of bribery with professional involvement of course, but we have it all down pat, because we starting slowly way back when The Warehouse was built.

"We also repackage goods in The Warehouse with the employment of large teams of cheap, mainly migrant workers, where my Mexican comes in very handy. We also have our own legitimate trucking company which pays significant taxes to keep the Feds satisfied. In fact, we operate one completely correct import company providing just enough legitimate tax cover.

"Our vast cash income is made from evasion of duties or import taxes but additionally by facing no income taxes on sale. It now amounts to hundreds of millions of dollars which are sent to the Chinese bank in Vancouver with no questions asked. I assume it goes to the Guangzhou gang.

"I thought I had a good relationship with him allowing him unlimited kinky sex on demand and giving him warnings about other criminals ripping him off."

She rambled on about the Stump percentage dispute and other issues.

"Things got more alarming. Wong now smuggles in large barrels of Chinese white chemical powder which goes into a highly secure lab area, but comes out pressed as pills for American and Canadian use. They recently started re-exporting down to Asia and Australia."

The distraught woman sobbed that things were going smoothly but there was a big fight about under-paying the migrant Mexican workers, who realised they were taking terrible risks. "Wong stupidly allowed it to get out of control. I was brought in speaking Mexican to sort things out but became implicated by taking their side."

She moved close and grabbing Maisie's hand, whispered, "Everything got worse and I think someone was killed,"

"Killed!" exclaimed Maisie in horror. Maria was now openly in tears so Maisie just abandoned her full shopping cart to rush the crying girl out of the store.

MAISIE did not know what to do next, so she bundled Maria into the Range Rover Sport V8 and conscious of her LAPD television education, called urgently for Ron to meet them in a hidden corner of the supermarket parking lot. He sat in the back seat, at first totally puzzled but quickly appalled as the story was related.

"Killed? How did it happen?" he gasped.

"That was the scary part." Maria answered choking on her sobs, "Their leader Jose was with the other Mexicans for their usual after-work tequila, all protesting about the pay, but he didn't turn up for dinner. No one has seen him since.

"Wong fired some of the others but hinted to me I am in trouble as well. I am very highly paid, and admit I know all about the activities. He has always considered he has sexual rights on me whenever it suits him, which I can put up with, but not this.

"The Mexicans have told me they will get even with him which I want no part of and I know everything so I am really scared."

BACK in the privacy of their office, Ron lamented, "We know that criminals from Guangzhou probably Triad are involved with your bent brother. Even Ping Kin has had dealings with them, although indirectly on the financial side, but all of them have documented Leyland connections.

"Now we were personally aware of drug-dealing, major fraud, smuggling, money-laundering, rape and possible murder. This is terrible!"

Maisie took the calmer lead. "We can't even discuss this with George. We have to sort it out ourselves, but our first priority is to protect Maria and her family. They can undoubtedly track her down but if she disappears, no longer posing a threat, they will likely leave her alone. I will cash her out and send the family back to Mexico."

They also agreed that confronting Wong would not work due to his unpredictability. Going to the authorities was out of the question. "That leaves Ping Kin," they both agreed.

As always cool, Ping Kin first pointed out their original joint ownership of The Warehouse was long obscured in Stump's tactical registrations but especially severed by Wong's purchase which followed.

Reverting to quick, worried Mandarin Ping Kin agreed absolutely the girl must leave the country with her children, everything carefully arranged so that it could not be traced back to them. They should definitely not mention this to Stump who could not be trusted. Finally he assured her he would check through all the existing records to ensure any of their involvement in the property or anything remotely connected was erased.

He continued in English, "Don't inform on them because it is way too complicated, with the likelihood of coming back on you. Anyway, they are too blatant and will eventually be discovered. Stay far away. When The Six hear, as they will, you will not be involved. Wong, I am afraid, is running into deadly trouble."

Chapter 44

Laundering: Running unchecked

R ON WAS glumly parking his most recent Porsche Carrera at the office in the morning when Pritam crouched, squeezing unexpectedly into the passenger seat.

Knowing not to speak too excitedly he enunciated, "Ron, something serious is going on. I shouldn't be here but we have just set up a team to bring down Wong's drug dealing. Your Black Renminbians in Macau are implicated. I advise you to come in and tell all. I will get you a deal."

"First Corporal, is this drugs or money-laundering?" replied the puzzled Ron formally, giving himself time to think. "Second, what the hell is a Black Renminbian?"

"Sergeant Singh," he announced proudly. "We are after Wong with his drug importing bastards. Actually there are no officers in any service looking seriously into money-laundering in British Columbia, so far as I know.

"We are not racist in the force, so my friend the Chief Superintendent has educated me never to use racial words but to refer to the bad money guys as Black Renminbians so there is no confusion. But we always get our person, whatever we call him! ....them?" he corrected himself, looking puzzled.

"You have to take this personal warning very seriously. We have enough evidence for a search warrant but my Super has instructed me to hold off for the moment. For head office policy reasons!"

With that he tried to slip quietly out of the car again but muttering to himself in frustration as he got his tall turban caught up in the low door opening.

IN HIS office a concerned Ron reviewed their situation. Although no longer directly associated with Wong, he knew they were involved in a dicey situation. If there were a deep probe into their capital activities over the years what would come out? He rather suspected a lot!

But, he was also aware, decades after the problem was internationally recognised, Canada had done little about laundering regulation. The amount of laundered money was enormous but could not be established due to ignorance of the subject, exacerbated by an inability to keep up with much better financed criminals.

In Canada a wild estimate was $50 billion a year, perhaps 10 in frontline BC, but honestly no one really had a clue. Obviously stuff was going on around him but they were in the clear; weren't they?

He reported the new encounter and his worries to Maisie when she arrived at the office.

"Pritam is getting serious? Come on. He is lots of talk but no action. He's a weird fellow. Black Renminbians? That's kind of neat but a bit of a mouthful. You know I always prefer to promote lower case for clarification as in French. I still reserve 'Chinese' for Mainlanders, but all the rest in the world I call 'chinese'. That makes me distinctly a chinese Canadian which clarifies everything perfectly, although I have to admit my idea hasn't caught on much yet.

"Whatever he calls the baddies, I can see him out to get Wong for girls and drugs but why would they bother us? Just for possible money-laundering? That's almost statistically impossible. Fintrac have tens of thousands of reporting agencies to study but only look into a few hundred every year.

"They have grand-sounding laws to quote with no budget or personnel to follow up. They have hardly had anyone charged let alone convicted. Forget it. Pritam is bluffing. Why ever would they bother with small fry like us?"

"Precisely because we *are* small fry," he insisted, "easy to catch due to weaker legal defence funds but providing needed political publicity. The unassailable establishment guys always go free!

Still, we have never been consciously involved in crime but quite possibly in dubious money, so potential laundering claims are possible if they do investigate Wong's buddies."

IT TURNED out later that Maisie really had taken it seriously. She had been doing some research.

"You know, I really didn't know what laundering actually is."

"Bit late in the day." Ron laughed, "Obviously, turning bad money into good."

"But precisely!" she insisted. "People bandy it about but look blank when you ask them. We do most of our money acquisition out of Canada so are we in the clear anyway?"

Ron muttered, "Well, we have been involved with hundreds of millions of dollars so something is going on. I suspect we are in the shit however you define things. Some of it has been Black Renminbi.... look Pritam has got me going now!"

"Nevertheless," she read from her notes, "everyone commits an offence who transfers property or proceeds knowing they were criminally obtained. Including by tax evasion.

"Now listen to this Ron. It says specifically that a crime that takes place in another country is a valid predicate offence provided if it had taken place in Canada it would have been a designated offence. I agree that one can really get us into the shit, as you so delicately put it."

"But," countered her ever-patient Ron, "you can't surely charge someone in Canada for evading taxes in China so how can that be an offence in Canada? Perhaps it could be an indictable 'type' of offence? Perhaps 'the proceeds of corruption' would catch it but it seems awfully vague to base a complicated case on."

She just shook her head. "One thing I am doing right now is to take George's advice. We will have him draft up an anti-money-laundering compliance programme to keep us on the straight and narrow!"

"And demonstrate that we always have been!" she added, as she stalked out of the room.

"HONESTLY, stop worrying," George advised calmly, as he could from behind his imposing oak desk. "In retrospect we are all wondering but the truth is we were not paying sufficient attention."

He went on philosophically. "We might as well face it. There is so much big money and influence involved that the politicians will not act aggressively until there is overwhelming public opinion backing them and they have covered their own asses.

"Look at the States recently where a major bank agreed to be penalised way over a billion dollars for alleged money-laundering but no charges at all were laid, presumably because that would upset their financial system. At present whatever the facts, I think you are probably safe.

"The law too, on the subject, is very complicated. With the resources you have I could find ways to defend you and appeal endlessly until we are all old and grey! You are anyway totally back to real estate investment again, dropping out of the money transfer business.

"Yes, get an anti-money-laundering compliance programme in place. As a lawyer I would of course never counsel the destruction of evidence but I suggest you might look seriously at all your past files. Conveniently lose everything that is not essential particularly computer records. No need to clutter up people's minds unnecessarily!

"But sever all direct connections with Macau! That is where the danger lies."

They assured him that their Canadian bank had progressively

assumed the documentation of all Leyland's Asian business accounts and Ping Kin was only involved now bringing individual deals and in personal business with Maisie.

"Unfortunately there are 20 years of online documents somewhere out there and past financial dealing can still come back to haunt you. The records regarding your long-term association with Wong can clearly still involve his criminal activity and any financial connections with Macau may prove dubious."

"What I don't understand," asked Maisie "is why the authorities have not moved on Wong already? He lives openly as a conspicuously wealthy man, but has no declared source of income. They must have on record he pays little income taxes. He is renowned for owning three of the raunchiest nightclubs in Vancouver, with women and drugs obviously available, boasting his awful titty bars.

"My young nephew Ivan roars around town in a Lamborghini, for heaven's sake. Why don't they investigate him and Wong directly?"

George shrugged. "That is what would happen in England. There he would be slapped with an unexplained wealth order but like everything on this subject Canada hasn't worked that out yet."

RONNIE slumped in his office chair worrying about the trying day. He reflected that at least the climate change was improving the Vancouver weather and an early summer had arrived, yet again.

Maisie slipped quietly back into his office. She whispered into his ear, "Let's go home early, open a bottle and forget about your silly worries."

Regular hard exercise had maintained her firm body and she still never wore a bra. He had just happened to notice that morning, when they were dressing, that she had also returned to her warm weather practice of not wearing panties either.

This provoked his grinning comment, "You have to be extra careful in those Chanel summer frocks you just selected. They look awfully short to me! My observant sister has made a few risqué comments."

She had just smiled enigmatically in reply; very aware that the shared knowledge she was not wearing panties always turned both of them on.

"Yeh, global warming!" he shouted happily.

Unimportant things like money-laundering vanished from his mind, he gave her a long kiss, grabbed her hand and they left hurriedly.

Chapter 45

Reality: Their game discovered

WONG, unlike Ron, had no ethical business misgivings to concern him. He could not believe how cheap his business was to run in Canada compared with Hong Kong or China.

He was able to operate in Asia without being harassed so long as he paid off all the necessary officials to keep everyone happy. That was very expensive. Yet in Canada, he did not even have that problem because strangely people in authority were not on the take. They indeed had lots of laws forbidding things but no apparent interested in enforcing them. It was quite puzzling to him.

He was also bemused that anyone could apparently bring any amount of money in various currencies into Canada so long as it was declared. Hong Kong airport was difficult but Macau and a number of locations in China were a good jumping-off point, where airport officials could be bribed, because the only problem was getting the money onto the plane, not getting it off.

The Canadian officials seem to believe the cash movement problem was taken care of at the other end but where there was always someone to bribe or many mules happy to bring in a bag of money. They seemed to dream that the rest of the world lived up to their agreed international conventions. What a laugh.

And that was just bringing money into the country. In Canada itself he carried wads of cash around every day without anyone being seemingly concerned. His car trunk was always stuffed. He had a storage room in his house piled to the ceiling with bundles of Canadian bank notes.

His nightclubs were very rarely visited by any sort of official or cop and he knew the casinos also did not have full-time law enforcement in house so the money-laundering simply happened when they were not there watching.

If only his personal situation were as positive. He was belatedly realising that in Canada he was the fall guy. He had upset too many forces in the organisation which were beginning to align against him.

There were even snide rumours that the affair he had feared for many years between Olga and Zhang was finally happening, with nothing he could do about it.

Unknown to his partners, of course, he had stashed away a considerable fortune off-shore in Asia arranged around several national identities.

Ever since he had been in Canada he had provided services for Asian 'friends' accepting payment back in their currencies. He also did not need an intermediary bank to 'transfer' money internationally. He simply appropriated stacks of Canadian cash locked away in his basement to hand out to those Asian colleagues who needed dollars, in simple exchange for currency back in their homeland.

Getting passports was no problem. It could be time to think seriously about moving permanently back to mother Asia where he felt at home. He decided to make some contingency arrangements.

He looked across at his shapely, detached wife, taunting him pointedly in a flimsy, revealing lounging gown while quietly drinking her coffee. He sighed as his only friend in the world, Wanchow, rested his large head on his knee and licked his hand.

RON, in contrast, read the changing general situation very differently.

He fussed to Maisie that the authorities were indeed starting to get serious about checking the source of Renminbi conversions.

"The fellows were even talking about it at The Club bar."

Things nevertheless were going well for China, with the Macau bank overwhelmed with cash as usual. Ping Kin, who now travelled the world constantly on business, started making frequent visits.

His English had improved immeasurably, so he and Maisie rarely now conversed in Mandarin. "Money is freely available from successful business people in China anxious to safeguard their earnings overseas. Official figures are that more than $200 billion a year is flowing out of China annually but I think that is way too low. Canada has almost no regulations and I can shovel money your way!

"The majority of my cash is legitimately earned, I just have to devise ways of reassuring now-suspicious international authorities it is all genuine. Nothing wrong with that? Canada for one, particularly British Columbia, seems delighted with the surge in prosperity it is all bringing.

"Look at your real estate market, Ron. No vacancy, everything selling high, low interest rates. Lowest mortgage default rates ever. A high percentage of residences are without any debt. Your prime buildings throughout the country owned by secure Canadian institutions.

"It shows the amount of free cash just sloshing around in your system."

"Sloshing," he repeated, rolling his latest English word around his mouth. "Everyone wins."

"Depends where you are on the pay scale," objected Maisie who still followed Canadian politics, now being influenced by the strengthening left-of-centre Provincial Party.

"We do not have enough local wealth generation to justify these prices. Our values are based on income levels and capital acquisition elsewhere.

"Our median household after-tax income is around 60,000, way down the North America scale, but we have one of the highest real estate costs, pushed up alarmingly by laundered money. It is a beautiful place to live and more people will keep moving here but we are building to the luxury market and advertising by issuing literally millions of visas.

We are selling super condos and penthouses for obscene amounts of money. Admittedly Leyland now insists upon regular upfront payment through formal sources but many are not even financed and often stand empty. Who are these people and how did they make their money? No one asks."

The wise academic Dean responded that the money would nevertheless keep flowing to safe, friendly Canada in the years ahead.

"You are particularly noticing China at the moment but other countries will become prosperous. People with money will want increasingly to move to safe Canada, from India, South-East Asia and Indonesia for a start; then from all of the Middle East, Africa and South America.

"You just need to suck it up and work out a way to look after everyone so you all share in the prosperity!"

"Suck it up!" he repeated, pleased with his latest English obscurity.

WITH Ping Kin in town, they decided finally to confront Wong directly.

When they demanded a meeting, he surprisingly suggested dinner at an idyllic West Vancouver waterfront restaurant down from his mansion. Canada geese strolled around on the fronting lawns pooping excessively, while seagulls squawked overhead. They hoped, incorrectly, that his selected setting would keep Wong less voluble.

Most of the conversation was conducted in English because it was their only common language but with bursts of Mandarin or Cantonese to explain missed understandings, followed by muttered explanations. So it was not a comfortable encounter to begin with, but quickly became heated even before the first bottle of wine had been totally consumed.

Maisie listed the few areas in which their business still overlapped with Wong, mainly connected with previous immigrant investments. She handed him a contract and told him quietly in Cantonese, "We can no longer afford to risk association with your criminal ways. These separation papers are very much in your favour, and Leyland Co. has signed." He just glared at her and stuffed the documents into his pocket.

He sat brooding and by the time dinner had arrived, he had switched to brandy, then to questioning his sister bitterly on why she told everyone he was involved in criminal activity?

Now upset, she was shouting in harsh Cantonese, asking where all his cash came from, protesting that it was obviously laundered and demanding how deeply he was involved with drugs.

Still in their childhood tongue, she protested, half crying, "You have got us involved with some nasty people we frankly know are crooks, so we want nothing more to do with you. It is so embarrassing to have you as a brother!"

He responded loudly with a stream of choice Cantonese invective directed at her specifically as a promiscuous, hustling, lying whore but then headed off bitterly into a tirade containing so many harsh profanities even Ron recognised the forbidden words.

Wong leapt angrily to his feet. "Bitch. You are no Chinese. Diu lei goh hai," he shouted over his shoulder as he lurched out of the restaurant.

A nearby table of wide-eyed Cantonese family diners, continued to stare in riveted, shocked silence as the three of them nodded their apologies, returning sombrely to assessing their overall situation.

Maisie berated Ron, "You have to go and see Wong and convince him we are absolutely cutting off all connection with him or any of his gang. Make him sign that contract. Tell him never to come to our home or office again. I am officially no longer his sister! Get him out of our life."

Chapter 46

Riches: Come with submission

ADDING to all this drama The Chinese connection was bringing into their lives, Zhang had in fact come through with his promise to have one of his state corporations invest in Canada in a very big way.

He had also required that Ron, particularly with *Mai Xi* as he insisted upon calling her in Mandarin, be personally involved in the action working directly with him. They had reportedly budgeted 'about' five billion dollars for investment in Canada which he would oversee personally.

For three months a highly efficient team of experts from Beijing visited. They analysed the prospective deals with Leyland's realtors to make final recommendations to their revered leader Mr Zhang.

Soon, the private announcement came directly from the company's executive suite in Beijing that they had decided upon the two large-scale mixed use investments, one in Toronto and one in Vancouver. Then, the conformation that Leyland may start negotiating confidentially but within legal instructions from the corporation's distinguished Vancouver lawyer, Mr Steven Stumpenberg, QC, JD.

Stump followed up by regretting his small office was too much of a mess for a meeting but that a quiet lunch in theirs, with a couple of their excellent bottles of merlot, would be most acceptable.

He arrived paperless as was usual and first proceeded to demolish a bottle of their best vintage, chatting urbanely about nothing. Then he laid out Zhang's ground rules.

"First, I have been informed your friend Ping Kin will be involved which I assume accounts for your luck in getting this deal," he said.

"I will do all the documentation but you should not be surprised if you do not recognise any of the corporations or organisations I create. You will just have to accept this is the way they work with my job being to obfuscate. No one chases down the beneficial owner in Canada.

"Leyland's first part in this is solely to secure the investments and earn a fee from the seller. If there is a broker in place you will have to make arrangements to share their fee. With the massive value of the investments that should be no problem although making a fee deal of that size with an owner will be interesting.

"Now comes the part you might find problematic. There will also be an advisory agent earning a very substantial fee for assisting the company in tying down the deal on behalf of the buyer. That will be one of the names you will not recognise nor meet.

"The fees involved are substantial but I have not found a way to exclude them from the documentation such that you would not be aware of them. So I have to tell you."

There was a period of silence, before Maisie exclaimed, "But by telling us, we are compromised and complicit."

Stump replied good humouredly that this was not in his opinion legally a problem, because the company appointed the advisory agent.

"It is up to them to decide to whom they pay fees. I am merely advising you in advance so that you do not start getting excited when you see large chunks of money at closing appearing in columns you were not expecting or paid to a company you've never heard of. That's all."

THEY were both indeed compromised but in more ways than Stump appreciated. They were not surprised, of course. They had experienced this as the way many foreign investors sought to do business but they were upset to see it happening in Canada on such a large scale.

Indeed it was up to Zhang how his corporation spent its money, They actually had no idea where the agency fee was going, just a suspicion. But if Ping Kin, and it followed The Six, were involved, then through their Macau connection they could be indirectly associated with the deal.

Plus, in truth, they were being handsomely paid to keep all this information to themselves.

They of course reported this to Ping Kin who responded, "I am indeed now fully up to date on this project and I will be in Vancouver soon for meetings with Stump on the subject. Our Macau bank will in fact be receiving that advisory agency fee on behalf of a client but I should not elaborate."

The months of negotiation went by quickly with the two magnificent properties purchased. Leyland earned a full fee from the seller on one, sharing on the other but in both cases enjoying enormous profitability.

The terms were easy to negotiate, with full prices, because the buyer was so keen to spend the capital. The closings went without a hitch, all the obscured ownerships were duly registered, fees were paid and the deals completed.

Leyland now moved into the lucrative longer-term contract of managing the properties.

Maisie, controlling Leyland documentation, was very aware the questionable agency fee had been paid. She also learned the funds themselves had not left Canada, which was not unexpected.

Instead, Stump had been instructed by his undisclosed client to spread it around a few dozen Vancouver luxury condos. Apparently he was to hold the assets vacant and in trust until further notice, although Leyland were not consulted in these dealings.

Ping Kin called. "I have been advised by Stump of a list of obscure condo owners and titles together with values, which I have recorded here as the consultant's derived assets in Vancouver. That's all I have been told."

She saw all the closing papers and she realised Zhang knew she was aware of the bogus consulting company rip-off fees. What he did not know was that she had prudently preserved paper copies of all documents relating to the fees for storage securely in their safe.

He was obviously aware she suspected he was personally financing Wong's illegal activities, but was relying upon fear of his power and their mutual interest, for security to prevent her from exposing or defying him.

Now, he was just playing with her personally. She was highly stressed.

Wil was having his Bentley vandalised right outside their office, standing up for their ethics. Her brother was involved in unspeakable crimes of which they were aware, possibly financed by Zhang personally, although Ron rather pointedly had not broached that possibility.

With Ping Kin, she had more than a hundred million hidden away in the Macau system. Leyland itself had probably dealt with laundered money over the years. Now they had documented evidence of a suspected major fraud. Heaven only knew how much the persistent Pritam and his fellows knew. It was all her doing and it was her responsibility to deal with Zhang.

THEN to add to her problems, she received a cheerful message from her now regular correspondent, Ah-Cy enthusing that they were returning to Vancouver for the grand opening of the company property after its renovation. She added how much she was looked forward to a week of fun and margaritas together.

It indeed turned out to be a trying week for Maisie who read mounting sexual intent in every glance from Zhang. She realised that the riches the deal was bringing them could involved submission to Zhang now and in the future. Like Canada she was in danger of selling her soul. She must find a solution.

The days of company festivities went well, which was easy since expenditure was no object. With ribbon cuttings completed the men spent days on the lush mountainside golf course while the ladies shopped, regularly renewing their margaritas.

EARLY in the week they had arranged a formal, luxurious dinner dance to entertain all Zhang's new Canadian business contacts, at The Club as expected.

Zhang's harassment reached a new level when he grabbed an opportunity to edge her into a side room, where he ran his probing fingers slowly up the front her stunning Mikhael Kale silk gowned body. When she held him off, trying to keep her protests muted, he smirked, "I know all about your life in the Hong Kong whorehouse and your gay boyfriend in Macau. Don't stay too close to him, his days are numbered!"

She was saved by nearby activity and trembling badly slid past him to rejoin the party, but now with the bitter knowledge that Zhang was taking control of her life.

It was therefore no surprise when he later gripped her arm to steer her to the dance floor. There, obscured by the swirling crowd, he slid his tongue into her convenient ear and clasped her silky buttocks to him, his intention affirmed.

Easing away from his probing intrusions, she admonished him and whispered in quiet Mandarin, "This is not the place but I will contact you."

WHEN an opportunity arose, later in the week she phoned Zhang, just leaving the message, "Vancouver Hotel, tomorrow, Suite 801. Three o'clock."

Unannounced, but precisely on time, he came wordlessly into the room.

She had a tea trolley prepared which he ignored. He threw off his jacket, striding straight to pull her roughly against himself, demonstrating his pent-up anticipation and exclaiming, "I finally have my little *Mai Xi.*"

He was tearing off his clothes in frantic haste, so she moved quickly away from him across the room, checking the door and turning to pose in a provocative stance.

She dropped her long Oscar de la Renta-designed jacket slowly to the floor, stepping out in a revealing little matching sheath dress which clung tightly to her body, still trying to appear calm but betrayed by her anxiously heaving breasts.

He moved to claim her but paused; a picture of classic, evil warrior domination fully aroused and focused upon her mesmerising posture.

She closed her eyes, holding her breath in mounting alarm at her fast dwindling confidence in her strategy.

THE door to the suite banged open to dramatise the entry of a tall, bearded hotel plumber, wearing oversized waterproof overalls, and struggling under a huge bag of tools.

His appearance was made even more outlandish by his tall orange turban which had unfortunately been knocked awry during the hurried entrance.

Her startled eyes immediately took in the scene. When she glanced back at Zhang, she saw that the sudden interruption had left him looking down in disbelief at his prematurely deflated ego. A flash of revealed white curly hair brought her nervous giggles that she had way over-estimated his black-haired, coiffured virility.

She grabbed her La Renta jacket and retrieving her prized Chanel 2.55 Classic handbag, scurrying out of the suite, leaving the bearded, turbaned fellow mumbling an incoherent excuse to the still motionless Zhang, about wrong rooms, while scrambling to retrieve some pipes which had escaped his bag to roll across the floor.

LATER that day she received a secretive call on her cell phone from the voice she knew to be Pritam.

He affirmed very professionally, "I am sending you a clear video of the relevant events in the suite as requested, as my personal service for your very, very good help before."

He apologised profusely."I got carried away watching the fascinating proceedings on the monitor in my service closet. It was a bit of a rush to make the planned entrance on time. I hope my late arrival did not cause you any concern."

Chapter 47

Enigma: Searching for answers

EARLY the next morning, Ah-Cy was unexpectedly called by a security officer at her Vancouver Consulate asking subserviently if he could come for a confidential meeting. She had slept separately for many years with her own suite but she replied it was better if she came to the consulate.

Moving way into retirement, her father faced far less dangerous times, now beginning to be regarded merely as an ancient figurehead. Conversely, her status within the ruling class had become established and she was quietly accepted as an accredited colleague in the covert National Security ministry.

This was a semi-private visit so she was curious why she would be contacted, especially by a junior person. She was indeed received at the consulate by a highly unsure young security officer who did not know how to proceed.

"I have been instructed by the embassy in Ottawa to look out for you personally but they cautioned me against contacting you unnecessarily. Since this is a private matter I thought I really must discuss it with you personally."

He then obviously lost his nerve, caste his eyes down and lapsed into embarrassed silence. "All right, just tell me," she advised gently.

He reported formally, "At three o'clock yesterday I observed Mr Zhang going into a hotel room to meet Ms Leyland alone. I am not suggesting they did anything together. In fact Ms Leyland exited the room only 15 minutes later in a highly agitated manner.

Before Ms Leyland left the room they were briefly joined by a bearded hotel plumber, who hurried departed from the room a few minutes later, only to return after Mr Zhang had gone." He paused to make his point, adding triumphantly, "I identified him as a member of the Canadian secret service!"

Using her motherly charm Ah-Cy laughed, patted his arm reassuringly and said, "I know about that meeting. Ms Leyland is a friend of mine and was engaged purely in business matters.

"The Canadians have been outwitted in our business deal. Ms Leyland set up a hotel room meeting hoping to make a last-minute very personal plea to my husband. It sounds as though she even brought in a Canadian undercover officer to pressure him.

"But as you observed the Canadians got short attention from my loving husband! Being the experienced executive he is, he just laughed at her immature attempt so she stormed out in embarrassment. He is followed around by the Canadian undercover people like faithful dogs. It was logical they would have checked out the room, as no doubt you yourself did."

Continuing her maternal pose she suggested he never accuse a well-connected person, especially a senior one, without solid evidence; even then with extreme caution.

She added, rising decisively, "This is commendable work, but it must go no further because it could put unwarranted suspicion on Mr Zhang. I will record your fine attention to duty during this week when I returned to Beijing."

Walking back to her hotel she wondered what had taken place in that hotel room. She smiled ruefully to herself, remembering how often she had been left frustrated by Zhang's fleeting tumescence; but that fast, with a beautiful woman like Maisie? But perhaps she satisfied him even faster than she could, she chuckled to herself.

Come to that, she did not believe for a moment Maisie was that sort of person. It just did not ring true. Her background connections with The Six in Hong Kong and Macau were now well known to her and she still thought of her as the *Mai Xi* who would remain forever ethnically loyal.

She understood that there was more going on than the real estate deal in hand. Puzzles were risky and she was disturbed.

THE remainder of the week at the Leyland office had gone smoothly and towards the end of their visit Ron and Maisie held a farewell cocktail party at The Club for them.

Maisie caught Zhang standing alone and palmed a copy of the video tape into his hand. She smiled briefly, stood close to him to whisper, "Man Lok, here is a little reminder of our brief unfulfilled time together, for your future viewing."

She held her breasts provocatively close to him, looked him seriously in the eye to demonstrate her defiance and then strolled away, trying desperately to appear casual.

PROLONGING her ordeal, that same evening after the cocktail party, as a return gesture, Ah-Cy had a limo waiting outside The Club to transport just the four of them to a private room at a favourite Chinese restaurant she had found.

She triumphantly announced, "Peking Duck with all the trimmings!"

She was worried when the bottles of Dom Perignon she had ordered did not produce more animated conversation, particularly with Zhang in a philosophical mood, often a cause for alarm.

He had switched over to tumblers of whiskey so she knew trouble was coming but his general discussion appeared just quizzical. As the last dishes were being served he did move to a frontal attack. Ron's measured responses however kept things in check.

Zhang said directly to Ron in English, "I am upset that our investments did not have positive acceptance in the press. There were negative demonstrations but worse, anti-Chinese sentiment all over Canada. Even senior politicians expressed regret we had bought prime property.

"So why does not Canada make up its mind if you want us or not?"

Ron's calmly responded, "Our press releases were positive and the business community fully supported the purchases."

But Zhang was not satisfied. "That is not what I heard from my embassy. You have personally been critical of the Chinese system of government, promoting human rights and the rule of law. I know you invested in China but then rejected it. You Canadians are even questioning the source of money from China so why are you so prepared to except my Renminbi?"

Equitably, Ron explained, "This is complicated. Money is money. I understand we are dealing with a state-owned company. If I had really worried about human rights issues enough and how your state money is made, perhaps I might have had second thoughts myself."

Maisie and Ah-Cy were both looked down at the table at Ron's quite firm reply now expecting an outburst, but Zhang switched calmly to a personal question.

"It is an accepted practice when a man in China lands a big deal like this, becoming rich, that he is entitled to enjoy one, or several lady friends, whom he sets up around the city.

"There are millions of lucky women in China and Hong Kong being looked after in this way as they had been for centuries.

"So I am wondering, just out of curiosity, now you are wealthy, whether you have a few young beauties hidden away?"

Ah-Cy made play of hitting him and shaking her head in mock anger while telling him to behave himself. In their defence, she half laughed that he only spoke like that with friends!

The pause had however given Ron time to collect his thoughts. He answered in a measured way, "I have loved Maisie from the moment

I met her and I would never be unfaithful to her. Consorting with other women is not my way of life nor will it ever become an accepted practice in Canada."

Ah-Cy sat with a stony expression on her face as Maisie gripped her hand; almost concealing her concern at the direction Zhang's dialogue was taking.

She looked into her friend Maisie's stricken face and saw something had been going on justifying her husband's sneering laugher at Ron's genuine response. She now knew whatever intimate activity had happened in that hotel room it had somehow been forced upon her.

Fortunately, Zhang, full of himself and whiskey, was still talking loudly, intent upon keeping their attention by launching pompously into a proverb stating that, *'The virtue of a woman does not go deep but her passion knows no limits'*.

Speaking quietly, to lighten the tension, Ah-Cy countered in pointed English, a warning that, *"The first decision of a woman is the most intelligent but the last the most dangerous"*, receiving a dismissive wave of Zhang's hand.

She then laughed, "Man Lok always resorts to obscure proverbs when he runs out of points to make," allowing them to end the meal in a guardedly cordial fashion.

LATER, alone in her luxurious suite, Ah-Cy could not sleep.

She was very disturbed by the events at the dinner, recognising the depth of fear Zhang produced in Maisie. Something had happened between them, apparently to Maisie's detriment, which led him to gloat at his control over her.

She shook her head in realisation of the evil man he had become. She recognised he had always been just a practical convenience in her loveless life, but now not only was his usefulness over but he had become a problem. She determined she would look more closely into his activities, realising it was becoming urgent for the family that she dealt with him.

Chapter 48

Fidelity: A rare commodity

ONE afternoon, trying to appear nonchalant but on shaking legs, Wong just made it back into his own office at The Warehouse to collapse into his easy chair.

He had just staggered from his mature but athletic, blonde accountant who had replaced the unfaithful Maria but who entered into her additional duties with enthusiasm. Like Maria she was self-assured but this time Wong had lucked into something of a nympho who followed him around hopefully with beseeching eyes just like his always faithful dog, Wanchow.

She unfortunately took great joy in knee-tremblers which he did not want to admit his ageing legs could no longer support. It was terrible. She had become the everyday aggressor, killing him with her uncontrolled, athletic stamina.

He so missed the motherly, comfortable Maria who had abruptly disappeared when he had discovered she had been personally skimming substantial amounts of cash out of the payments to the itinerant Mexican workers, causing untold problems. This created the need for substantial additional compensation, plus stern action to get them back under control.

How she and her family, together with her boyfriend Jose, had managed to just disappear from the country with an obviously fully professional cover-up, he just could not understand.

Now, he barely had time to calm his heartbeat, when his out-of-town provincial lawyer called with the appalling news he had just been visited by a big-time Vancouver lawyer called Stumpenberg, asking probing questions about the confidential condo sales. Somehow his personal laundering deal had been exposed.

Things were just not working out around here anymore. He was exhausted and slumped in despair. He was in big trouble.

THE blame for the deal actually originated with that new assertive accountant who had confirmed Maria's figures with a clear explanation that Stump's percentage grab of profits was in fact increasing. She had observed in her innocent style that everything was in cash which the partners did not know existed until Wong told them.

"So why hand over so much?" she asked, widely opening her large, innocent blue eyes quizzically.

The second part fell into place when the new provincial government imposed their taxes to discourage Renminbi foreign speculation, driving down luxury condo values overnight.

He overheard his Cantonese management at The Warehouse laughing about the plight of some of their colleagues from Guangdong who had just finished a condo building that was losing a fortune, when the idea came to him.

Still with ballooning cash surpluses he had moved onto buying suburban properties like small strip malls or warehouses from people who would take generous cash, so he understood how that worked. The skill in laundering investing was to move the originally cash deal through several transactions and to represent the eventual asset as legitimate.

Why not, he reasoned, buy more small cash investments, then offer to do straight swaps for groups of their losing condos, all in the spirit of good money-laundering practice?

He took a very private trip to the pretty provincial lake resort to view the almost empty new waterfront tower with the local law firm representing the Guangdong group.

The earnest young lawyer proudly confirmed, "My clients built the tower without debt, with equity all subscribed from China. They intended to gain maximum profits from the ever-rising market so they decided, unfortunately as it turned out, not to pre-sell. It is common knowledge the new taxes have swept away their profit margin forcing them now to face the prospects of selling at a loss."

Wong told him he had a potential solution but insisted for confidentiality he would send his representative to conduct the negotiations in their office, rather than in Vancouver. He knew he could not personally risk the exposure having so many Guangdong contacts so he brought in the one person he could trust, his son Ivan.

Putting the actual deal together was much simpler than it would appear as Ivan quickly optioned the half a dozen investment properties he needed at very full prices, with sellers prepared to accept the excessive payment in cash over a period.

They then swapped the commercial properties for equal value packages of condos with the Guangdong investors at their cost. The investors had their original equity outlay back intact, admittedly with no profit, but with diversified investments occupied by good 10-year tenants. Even better, they now had legitimate laundered investments in Canada which was to be their next step anyway.

Wong of course had paid for his total investment in cash. Then he set about renting out the residential units, having conveniently laundered his cash into a declared, upfront apartment building. Later, he could openly sell the condos when the market improved.

PERHAPS really beginning to age, Wong had however made some mistakes.

The first was to instruct Ivan to appropriate cash from the night-club consortium to hide in this undisclosed venture. This was all really out of ego rather than necessity. Engaging other investors from Guangdong just proved thoughtless.

He should further not have employed Ivan in the deal at all, although initially the damage had been caused by his visibility.

Having a clandestine negotiation conducted by a handsome Harry Rosen-dressed young man, arriving dramatically outside the small town legal office in a red, open Lamborghini with a bratty exhaust, accompanied by a showy tall model wearing an almost transparent designer top, did not encourage secrecy.

Even so, Ivan did not betray his father initially. One morning his mother Olga left a message simply to say that Man Lok, as she always called Zhang, had phoned her about a serious problem she had to discuss with Ivan urgently.

He met her for lunch at her gym, as it happened just after she had enjoyed her monthly happy-ending massage. He found her in a corner of the bar with a pleased, silly smile on her face, so relaxed she could hardly lift her large glass of pure Canadian Iceberg vodka off the table.

She sighed in frustration at their stupidity. "How could you possibly do a deal with known crooked people from Guangdong stealing Man Lok's money, without him finding out about it? Just because it was taking place in a remote British Columbia resort town?

"But you got a very lucky break because although he is still pursuing me hard, I haven't put out to him yet. So I guess it's Mai Fu out and Man Lok in!" she slurred unconcernedly, taking another deep swallow of the icy vodka.

"Man Lok is prepared to overlook your misguided loyalty to your father in order to finally get his jollies but you now have to make a decision. Tell Stump in detail what happened. Then stay quietly in the background because things look really ominous for Wong."

He nodded. He had no choice.

IT WAS edging towards evening. Wong's dark office was empty and silent.

The dramatic events of the day had exhausted him to the point he was actually dozing off in his comfortable chair.

A movement startled him into full consciousness. His office door was slowly and ominously being eased open. His eyes widened in fearful anticipation and he muttered a frightened "Aiya!" in final resignation.

The revived athletic blonde crept determinedly towards him, her eager apprehensive panting and guard dog Wanchow's welcoming tail thumping, the only sounds. Her aroused, naked body glistened in the gloom.

He groaned. Everything was overwhelming him. He looked around frantically for escape but there was none.

ACROSS town, Ron was engaged in a regular chat over a quiet beer with his friend Pritam Singh. They each had the motive of extracting information from the other, but a curious friendship had emerged.

Ron was aware a few beers loosened Pritam's tongue and discretion but was totally taken aback by his unexpected and unguarded revelation, apparently intended to get his sympathy.

"Seriously Ron," he confessed, "I would hate your wonderful wife Maisie to be dragged into the sordid Wong affair. Particularly considering the courageous way she dealt with that evil Zhang person."

Seeing the shocked questioning expression on Ron's face, he put his hand to his mouth apologetically.

"Oh dear. Oh dear. You don't know? Well, nothing bad happened!" he hurriedly assured him. The whole story came tumbling out to defend Maisie, including her account to him of all the earlier harassment and then he gabbled on, indiscreetly revealing their entire Zhang police background dossier.

When the dejected detective officer finally left, Ron's first reaction, staring morosely into his beer was incredulity, followed by annoyance. As he thought about it, however, he realised it was an unselfish act because she had nothing to gain herself and a lot to lose. It took a lot of courage for her to try to fix the Zhang problem all on her own.

He decided to let her tell him about it in her own time. "Scheming little devil," he muttered to himself, sinking the remainder of the pint with a rueful grin.

Chapter 49

Extraction: Fleeing the Dragon

'SHANGHAI is taking over. Time to move on," exclaimed Ping Kin, dramatically opening their regular Leyland conference call, speaking carefully in his improved English.

"Now the International Monetary Fund has equated the yuan with the dollar, euro, yen and pound sterling, China will not need Hong Kong or Macau much longer and will build up Shanghai as the money centre of the world.

We are on a slippery slope and our bank's days around here are limited. I had to scramble to extricate the bank from the 'Panama Papers' source exposure which led back overwhelmingly to Hong Kong and Macau. Our offshore dealing is getting tougher."

Maisie thanked him for his recent personal advice and confirmed she had pulled all her investments out of Hong Kong, as he had also done himself, worrying generally about increasing instability.

He explained that the recent gold situation there had finally decided him.

"We put no bullion business your way because it is very specialised and we work directly through Hong Kong and international gold brokers anyway. It is illegal to export gold from China and physically difficult to sneak out anyway.

We watch the level of gold retained in Hong Kong as a measure of international confidence in the future of the city and now see it progressively being taken to safety. That was another warning sign!"

Maisie concurred. "America's transgressive new President is aware China will not liberalise your autocratic system of government. He knows you are actively raiding the Western world economies while integrating yourselves politically around the globe."

"Well, there are a lot of reasons," he responded. "A major trade war is starting with the powers of the world taking sides, and I don't intend to be caught in the middle!

"US trade retaliation has already begun to hurt our prosperous growth but more to my concern in Macau at the moment is China's depleting US cash reserves causing them to slap on foreign currency controls but admittedly with little effect.

"To my dismay, Zhang informed me The Six are upping their personal cash extraction programme from China by hundreds of millions for which I need to find new investments. I sense I am running into a very risky personal situation.

"I have financial matters to settle internationally but dealing with our personal 'rainy day' investment fund Maisie, has become critical to my plans and I will visit you in Vancouver with something specific in mind."

HE RESERVED dinner very privately for them all in Vancouver giving signals a serious discussion was coming. For one thing it was at the prestigious Il Giardino. Then he started by ordering her favourite Veuve Clicquot, La Grande Dame no less, which was served personally by the charming Tuscan celebrity restaurateur.

Ping Kin did not rush their drinks or hors-d'oeuvres, being his usual courteous self, and they just chatted amicably for a while. It was obvious however that he had a lot on his mind. "They are getting too greedy. They will go down. I will be the first to fall with them," he finally exclaimed.

"The Six and I are reaching a parting of the ways. My young hands-on fellows manipulate new processes like crypto-currencies far more efficiently than I can. They are beginning to work with new virtual money exchanges in unexpected countries all over the world.

"Inventive hidden capital manipulation is going on. We have been bypassing banks anyway for a couple of years now as they became obsolete for many of our purposes. Since Maisie and I became involved together the world has changed dramatically as have we.

"I have become part of the international business set which has developed over the past couple of decades. I attend MIT alumni dinners, for example in Boston and last year I even went to Davos. I have friends all over the world and I enjoy the comradeship. It is increasingly a global world with us wealthy professionals from all countries flying frantically around trying to keep up.

"Times have changed. Leone and I, an openly gay and very wealthy couple, can travel the world together; take ski trips to Biarritz or scuba dive in the Maldives. Originally Maisie and I were isolated in Macau playing alone with my computer but now I am a citizen of the world and quietly a member of the one percent.

"The problem is the world and technology has gone global, now beyond my abilities, with the international dynamics changing constantly as the rising middle classes of the world emerge. But China, and my existence there, are intolerable and I have to be free.

"As well as becoming expendable, I fear I know too much but have to stay in China until this is resolved because there is no way of running away from these thugs anywhere in the world. We must regrettably dissolve our relationship while I find a way to get out before I am 'disappeared'. I have it all set up and with your agreement we can deal with it all tomorrow."

Then he shrugged philosophically and called politely for another bottle of the very special Veuve Clicquot.

NEXT morning, when they were on their own, he told Maisie that he had the strangest unscheduled call from Zhang a couple of days previously.

"He chatted briefly and then quoted one of his proverbs, that Yuen Zing Chon in the Old Book of Tang advised them, *'A player may be lost but the watcher will remain lucid'*.

"I took it I was the player but did it mean he could manage without me? It was either a veiled threat or a warning to leave, with the safest being to leave!" Then he laughed ruefully. "*Extricate* is my American word of the month. I am working on my own personal *extraction* urgently."

She knew it was now vital she told him about Zhang's sexual harassment and the hotel room encounter but she felt strangely shy to relate to Ping Kin what had happened.

Ron could never, never know. He would not understand because it was 'a cultural' thing. Ping Kin would however appreciate her tactic and know how to use the marginal leverage she had obtained to influence Zhang.

Maisie said, "I can explain," and launched emotionally into her story.

"THE moment Zhang walked into our office in Vancouver I realised it was not a coincidence. When our eyes met he knew exactly who I was and I realised that I had been the prey since I was a teenager. Remember how I gave you hell when he nonchalantly slipped his hand up between my legs in Vancouver?

"I had become good friends with his wife so I thought I was safe and anyway they went back to China. Then they returned with their billions of dollars. He made serous moves on me but I still thought I could just humour him. I knew how significant the big deal was to Ron although definitely not that important.

"The climax was reached when Zhang quietly backed me into a corner one evening, passing his hands over my body, saying with a sneer he knew all about Macau and that I could forget about you, my gay friend, because your days were numbered.

"My first thoughts were for your safety but then about Leyland's potentially dubious financings with Macau over the years, complicated by the need to extricate ourselves carefully. I knew Zhang had to be Wong's long-time criminal financier right from the beginning. Then I despaired at the impossible situation if he personally controlled our financial arrangements with Macau instead of you.

"Ah-Cy had told me that he totally relied on her famous father for political support so the plan to compromise him with the family had occurred to me.

"I assumed that Ah-Cy and the family could not be close to him considering his attitude to other women, but that filmed evidence of an affair could surely cause him serious loss of face with the national icon Huangs? At the very least he would know I had evidence and was a woman to be reckoned with.

"When he arrogantly grabbed my ass on the dance floor I took it as too good a chance to miss, immediately deciding to set him up. So I arranged to meet him privately in a Vancouver hotel room with the expected results."

"You mean you let him fuck you?" exclaimed the horrified Ping Kin in graphic English, too loudly for her comfort.

Hushing him, she objected, "No, that was never the plan, and I had my trusty Mountie detective friend hovering nearby watching remotely to jump in and prevent any real action; just enough to get something on Zhang. I wanted him to know I was not a push over and would resist him successfully.

"He is too powerful to risk open conflict, so the warning had to be just enough to cause him to back off."

She quoted hopefully, "'If you ignore the dragon it will eat you. If you defy the dragon it will overpower you. But if you ride the dragon you can use its power'.

"My Mountie had in fact recorded a full, explicit video of Zhang's naked intention. I will spare you the gruesome details, but it could be a very damning loss of face for him domestically and as it turned out he also ridiculed himself seriously on film."

This second piece of information caused Ping Kin to pause, think carefully and ask what had happened then. She said she later gave Zhang a copy without any direct threat on her part, but trying to appear assertive.

Ping Kin gave her a long appreciative hug still shaking his head at her resolve. "That was a polished performance which left Zhang immediately unthreatened but with reluctant respectful of your tactics.

"Possibly it provides just enough leverage to help persuade him to leave us alone. I respect your attempt but regret you risked your precious relationship with Ron. You acted somewhat desperately and I think you say, were *'Grasping at straws'.*"

He smiled cynically. "Well, after all these celibate, pure years we finally got around to talking about sex!"

AS THIS was most likely to prove Ping Kin's last business visit, they all sat down with their coffee in Ron's now grand office overlooking the harbour, to review the years.

Ping Kin was in a reflective mood. "I will miss our 'a thousand moves in one second' computer program which is old fashioned now. We built that first pre-set untraceable system to move cash deposits through innumerable bank accounts around the world at lightning speed. Only the dumb operators ever get caught.

"What will happen to my 'wiping' team which is one of the best in the business specialising in accessing any programmes and deleting selected contents? Do they get jobs in Shanghai or go back to jail?

"Anyway, my guys are now way ahead of me. They have found a way to get into legitimate company transfer systems, piggy-backing to make capital transfers between countries. Then they take out the money again without detection. Pretty neat, eh?"

His office was now riddled with informers operating check-up systems. The Six also had an independent, private auditing team somewhere, probably in Beijing, which he said turned up from time to time.

"I cannot trust any of my staff, of course and always have to retain sufficient private access codes to keep myself indispensible.

"You have never approved, Ron, but I had to look after myself. I was not able to skim anything off until I could absolutely trust someone, who turned out to be the intelligent student who sidled into my office one day offering demurely to be my girlfriend."

"Best girlfriend I ever had," he kidded Ron, "always out seen holding hands and dining together."

Maisie broke in. "We were the most stylish dancers around, showing off constantly on the casino dance floors. How about our tango? No one doubted our close relationship. You bought my very first swirling long Lane Crawford designer gown."

He smiled. "Like it or not Ron, she obviously loved the intrigue involved and has taken risks over the years. Our method mainly involved unexpected windfall profits or spin-off gains we intercepted from the crooked Six before they could be recorded in their accounting system,

"The fortune, deposited as US dollars in well-established facilities around the world has become significant over the years, and is ours to take. It exists to no one but us. What you do with your share it is entirely up to you."

"Are we ready?" asked Ping Kin. "Whatever might happen to me, our personal funds will now be separated. They will be completely under our individual control. Any personal financial connection with Macau and Zhang will be gone."

She smiled and nodded. He touched the key, completing the process they had designed together to deliver them from The Six and free them from the financial clutches of Black Renminbi.

Chapter 50

Huang: Consulting the Oracle

AH-CY was still puzzled months after the tense dinner in Vancouver. When she explained about this much later to Maisie, she said she could just not let it go.

Back in Beijing she pondered why Zhang had actually been so aggressively able to bend Maisie to his will? Showing his national trusting characteristic, Ronnie did not seem even to entertain a suspicion that anything untoward was going on.

So whatever it was, it was between Zhang and Maisie. But she knew about Leyland's gradual pullout from direct business relations with Zhang's Macau bank, with no continuing problems or pressure remaining there unless it involved Poon. But why Poon?

She realised that also left Wong, who had been tied up with this crowd in Hong Kong, and whom she knew to be Maisie's brother. She had not mentioned him. He had not appeared once, even at social functions while they were in Vancouver which was understandable because he was a crook.

She had decided that was all very strange, so there were lose ends to investigate, but months later she was still no further ahead. Her biggest concern remained Zhang's growing political instability which was an apparent threat to her family.

She decided she could not risk doing this all alone but needed to involve her father.

HE HAD lived unmarried since her mother died, in the quiet luxury of a spacious city penthouse, attended by a bevy of bustling, personally selected and accommodating young women. He was regularly visited by his close colleagues in the establishment who enjoyed his status as one of the few remaining revolutionary heroes.

One of his ever-observant sycophants, instructed to dress modestly for the occasion, smilingly served tea. After reports on his successful grandchildren they got down to business. Ah-Cy just frankly told the entire story, requesting his advice on how to proceed.

He thanked her for her family loyalty, admitting he too had his own experts investigating her husband who was proving too risky. "I am relieved that you can deal with this difficulty so dispassionately. I admit I know a great deal about your life because Lo has been in my pay reporting on the side since the beginning." He grinned again slyly as the significance of Lo as a personal informant brought a concerned frown to her face.

He was amused also that she thought she had silenced the young agent in Vancouver and actually laughed out loud when she angrily called the kid a little bastard. He explained, " Lo was curious about your visit to the Vancouver consulate and later strong-arming a full account of the agent's report from him.

"Lo had observed as part of his duties that your husband had an assignation with Ms Leyland, but did not stay around for the arrival of the cavalry." Again his mouth twitched at his depiction of the Mounties.

He counted off on his bony fingers Zhang's transgressions of which he was aware. The early share purchase scandal, secretly consorting with a woman from a banned sect in Ottawa, the recent strange activity involving the Mounties in Vancouver, several other dubious ventures linked to his man Wong involving risky drug dealing, and showing excessive greed with state funds through his Macau set-up.

"'We have the advantage of detailed knowledge of Zhang's activities which we must keep to ourselves and use to our advantage, '*Long sleeves are an advantage in a dance*'.

"Your job is to find out exactly what Zhang is doing, then to ensure that it never becomes openly revealed. Then we will together decide upon action."

He added apologetically that he was in his 90s, otherwise he would deal with him himself. Her husband too had powerful friends, so she must tread cautiously, he warned her, especially increasing her financial war chest.

Then he surprised her even more by resting his hand on her arm speaking to her personally, as never before in her life.

"I always wanted an assertive boy but I was encouraged when our strong man Lo reported to me that he had reluctantly performed services for your personal pleasure, but only at your explicit instruction."

With a sly smile, apparently normally reserved for comments between men, he added confidentially, "I pay Lo handsomely for his confidential reports mainly concerning Zhang, so feel free to be inventive and work him harder."

His inappropriate suggestion appalled her but perversely she was strangely pleased he had welcomed her into his old boys' club. After those revelations about Zhang, however, sex could not in fact have been further from her mind.

SHE was a little concerned about the active campaign against corruption and she was aware there had been hundreds of imprisonments, but no one too senior had fallen so it appeared to be business as usual at her level. Then again, she thought sarcastically, perhaps they were all now pure. Not on the take anymore?

Her father was clearly still moving in top company but whom

the impulsive Zhang supported was far from clear which made him vulnerable. If he went, she could go too.

She sighed at the realisation her father's closeness may not have quite shown fondness but rather regret at having to tell her she was on her own. His attempts at humour did signify he was trying hard to be personal. Perhaps in his outdated way he was accepting she was a big girl, able to deal with life?

Perhaps after all, there was some affection, she wondered wistfully?

Where should she start, she thought? Her first convenient approach for information seemed to be Lo but she obviously could not trust him so she decided to keep him as a last resort. She knew Dean Poon was the key to the Macau activity but Zhang would have him tightly under surveillance. That left Maisie and she knew exactly how to get her attention.

Maisie's children had heard their mother's stories about Hong Kong from birth. In their early years they grew up with English and her first language Cantonese.

They even had an old nanny who managed their young years cackling away in Cantonese constantly so they were almost fluent but nevertheless they always spoke English. Visitors from China immediately knew they were Canadian although their Eurasian appearance gave a big clue, while their mother insisted they were 'Aseurians'.

Johnnie was finishing a business degree aiming to join Leyland. Cathie had completed a degree in political science which prompted her to set off on the adventure of a Masters Degree in Hong Kong, taking along her own selection of umbrellas for the protests.

Over their happy margaritas back in False Creek, Ah-Cy had skated around the activities taking place in Hong Kong or discussion of its future, because Maisie was so passionately on the side of the demonstrators that their friendship could not have survived a serious discussion.

She did know that Maisie was worried about her daughter parading around the streets in Hong Kong, especially with reports of some violence, so she simply sent Maisie an email suggesting meeting her there for a shopping spree, for which she would make the arrangements.

Chapter 51

Trust: Practical female logic

THEY STAYED luxuriously at the Mandarin Oriental, reassuring Maisie about Cathie's well being by meeting her several times while they shopped extensively in Central and on Nathan Road.

Over all the meals, bottles of wine, and especially their pre-dinner margarita tradition, Ah-Cy, tactfully calling her Maisie, tried gently to probe the subject of business, of her brother Wong and even guardedly of Zhang, without response. She had almost decided upon a direct approach when it unexpectedly came from Maisie.

It had required two margaritas but she opened her new Gucci Stirrup crocodile handbag to slide a flash drive across the table to Ah-Cy, who slowly pushed it back.

"If it contains a record of you with Zhang, I already know all about it and do not need to see it."

Maisie nodded numbly, just dropping the damning evidence back into her silk- lined Gucci.

They went to dinner together overlooking the brilliant lights of Statue Square, pointedly talking about shopping in Hong Kong and anything other than their personal relationships or the troublesome local politics.

THE following day, however, Cathie was not as tactful with her Auntie Arcie.

She pointedly parked her umbrella by the cocktail table and emotionally launched into the protest arguments. "The folks here must be allowed to live by the agreed rule of law, exercise democracy, have a free press and especially be able to demonstrate peacefully. China is purposely eroding the agreement. The rich, well-off people in Hong Kong do not seem to care, so long as their commerce is protected. The young people see no future."

Ah-Cy calmly replied, "I do not see China acting that way. Communism has lifted our people out of poverty while removing our long-time forced kowtowing to the Western world. In general, people in China understand freedom differently. Freedom of expression has to be restrained so that the government can maintain social stability. You cannot let people with far-out individual views spoil it for everybody.

"China is becoming more and more open and free. With good reason young people don't have access to corrupting websites like Google or Twitter, but they have personal safety to move around. They do not have to fear violent crime, so it depends on what you meant by freedom.

"We believed democracy is the same as chaos which cannot be allowed in a highly populated country. The armed police are there to protect the vast majority, not to harass.

"Young kids need to learn from birth what is good for them and that freedom comes with responsibility. Something went wrong with education in Hong Kong. Now they are rioting! If you don't have early education then you have to re-educate. Sometimes we get a little impatient with stubborn people so be careful!"

With difficulty Maisie fought off her urge to comment, respecting her daughter's ability to make her own arguments.

And indeed, Cathie replied angrily, "They are protesting not rioting, but it has no effect! I am in political science and am well aware you are just spouting the official line!

"Yes, you have your much-vaunted Constitutional Article 35 guaranteeing all those freedoms, but they just do not actually exist! People and particularly children must have the right to question that openly.

"China is one of the most brutal, totalitarian states anywhere, denying human rights and now beginning to impose its awful control on free people around the entire world. It is finally dawning on us, even our profiteers, that this must be stopped.

"And talking of profiteers how is it that in a communist country your political leaders and their families, like you, are some of the richest people in the world? Your internet generation in China will one day demand answers and their quest for freedom of expression will then change your system."

She finished with a smirk, speaking Cantonese, *"It is easier to dam a river than silence the voice of the people."*

Ah-Cy was shocked by hearing such heresy spoken so openly but reacted calmly. "Hong Kong only contains seven million people, part of a hundred million in Guangdong. You will obviously not be allowed to confront the entire Chinese system in this way, so why all the fuss? All the wealthy people and big companies are supporting China anyway in the interest of their profits. You have to lose!"

Cathie jumped up, waved her umbrella angrily and retorted, "We shall see!"

They heard her exiting, singing the stirring *'Glory to Hong Kong'* protest song loudly and defiantly.

AH-CY, as a senior Party member in the security service, was observing the events in Hong Kong very closely and decided this sort of behaviour had to be stopped. Rebel-rousing songs like that must be banned and these criminals arrested.

However, now was not the time for those concerns and she turned her bright smile sweetly upon Maisie. "We have more pressing personal problems to discuss. May I be forthright? Man Lok has become a danger to us both so we have to decide how to deal with him. We will have to be totally honest with each other which will entail both of us taking some risk. Do you trust me?"

Maisie replied, "I want to but we have to take it step by step."

Ah-Cy adopting her motherly pose took her hand to admit, "My biggest puzzle as a woman is why you ever become involved with Zhang?" But she nodded with growing appreciation as Maisie haltingly explained the entire saga back from her young life encounter with him in the Wanchai hotel, to his continuing active harassment in Canada.

As the story progressed Ah-Cy added in a few anecdotes in her funny style about him, including the latest she had heard from Lo about the dancing, bell-ringing naked sect maiden, plus his revitalised pursuit of Wong's ageing over-sexed wife on the side again.

By the time Maisie had described the staged event in the hotel room, his startled climax, revealed contrasting white pubic hair and magically disappearing penis, they were doubled up with laughter at their similar experiences, with their mutual trust sealed.

Ah-Cy said sadly, "Your strategy might work in Canada but China is a controlled men's world, and it was probably a futile gesture. I doubt he has any conscience left anyway but he could possibly be concerned at a loss of establishment status for insulting us Huangs."

Seeing Maisie had started to frown, she hurriedly reassured her, "Don't worry, I have a saving solution to offer but first I need to ask about my second puzzle: Wong."

That entire account took even longer and a couple more glasses of wine, but fitted into the intelligence Ah-Cy had collected, while she increased the younger woman's confidence in her by augmenting the facts.

She told her cynically, "Zhang's secret assignation with you was not the only one in Vancouver. He slipped away several times for meetings with Wong including enjoying the hostesses at the nightclubs. The reason was not entirely his considerable appetite for casual philandering. The large-scale drug dealing is proving to be his undoing. But let me start at the beginning."

She started by telling her story way back when she had been lonely and had taken advantage of Zhang's ambition, initially for her first sex but then for stability and her desire for children, as their political joint activities developed together.

She explained about Zhang's subsequent return to the university, the formation of The Six and how Dr Poon came into the picture to manage their 'windfall capital extractions'.

"My intention now is to retain those funds in my family and remove you and Dr Poon completely in the process."

Having spent the entire evening on their revelations they were exhausted and called it a day. As they parted Ah-Cy yawned but said she still had several phone calls to make before proposing tomorrow what they should do next.

HER father listened in silence on the phone and then said he had something to add.

"That young security fellow in Vancouver, the 'little bastard', is in fact very bright. He was not upfront with you only telling you what you needed to know.

"The consulate knew the Mounties kept a close tail on Zhang during his official trips to Canada and were aware of his meetings with the Vancouver drug dealer Wong. That visit to Vancouver just confirmed his connections with Wong to them, with the juicy quickie with the real estate woman thrown in. It was your husband Zhang the 'little bastard' was checking on not the real estate lady.

"The Zhang situation had alarmed the embassy because our policy was to pursue better trade relations with Canada who were understandably very upset that a significant proportion of drugs flowing into their country were coming from China.

"I have a small cocktail party planned tomorrow with some old official friends which is timely although I suspect Zhang's days are done, making it possibly already out of our control.

"Still, there are apparently considerable sums in Zhang's Macau investments which have not been exposed or connected in any way with his drug-related or nightclub activities. Safeguard those assets for my negotiations but particularly for the family if possible."

THE next day, their breakfast together was serious as Ah-Cy outlined her plan. She did not disclose her lifetime of quiet security duties just putting her father forward as the source of all her information.

She explained how Zhang and Wong's relationship expanded in Canada from nightclubs and the importation business, to serious prostitution, money-laundering and drug-dealing, attracting attention from the RCMP but even worse for him, from China.

"Zhang has become too greedy but might expose China in Canada where publicity cannot be suppressed and delicate inter-government arrangements might be compromised.

"His fate is out of our control but we need urgently to meet Dr Poon because the Macau investments have not yet been implicated, might be saved and prove to be a way out."

PURPOSELY, Maisie arranged first to join Ping Kin for dim sum alone in a very public Hong Kong restaurant where the noise level prevented them being taped or overheard. The apparently social meal was intended to mask the serious business content of their discussion.

Maisie said, "I hate her communist politics but in this situation I believe we can trust her personal motives. It is obviously very dangerous for you, so I will go along with what you decide."

He just sat thinking. Then, "I am far from convinced that ruling class Ms Huang can be trusted but I see the practicality of her personal approach. Frankly I am holding few options!"

They all met back in the swept security of Ah-Cy's suite where she confirmed that Zhang was in serious trouble with the establishment, now likely to be removed but not for any actions associated with the Macau operation so far as she knew.

"I intend to keep the Macau operation in business to the benefit of our family, personally replacing Zhang and giving me control. Is that technically possible?"

Ping Kin considered his reply. "I can over-ride controls on about two-thirds of the funds with difficulty but with real risk of personal exposure.

"Zhang has purposely moved the other third out of my reach but in total we are still talking about several billion US dollars all located out of China.

"Zhang has obviously reserved funds for this very eventuality, knowing his fate could one day depend upon his capital worth allowing him to buy his way out of trouble."

Ah-Cy had faith if she could report back to her father that Zhang had a billion or so of his own outside to offer, he would be able to make a deal for him with the money. After all, Zhang was an older man with a record of long service to the country in his favour. The less fuss the better.

She finished by arranging to meet again in a couple of days. "My father will talk to his elder colleagues. Dr Poon, your personal safety and ability to leave the country are part of any arrangement we make but I need to know if you intend to extract funds for yourself which might cause problems with my prospective partners in The Six?"

He replied with a smile, "Mr Zhang has already unknowingly and adequately taken care of that."

"WHAT are you going to tell Ron?" questioned a very serious Ah-Cy when they were again alone that evening, trying to sound concerned for them, although more worried about her own security.

"That kept me awake all night," confessed Maisie, "and I called him first thing this morning."

Ah-Cy tried hard to hide her alarm. It was Maisie's turn to be reassuring.

"He is very sensitive and he obviously realised all along that I had some sort of unfortunate history with Zhang, but he never probes my past. Like all Canadians he is forgiving to a fault. He was obviously aware something dramatic was happening in Vancouver which is why he made such a clear statement about his love for me at your unfortunate Peking duck dinner!"

"Anyway," she continued sombrely, "today I told him only that the powerful Huang family had fallen out with Zhang and he would soon be totally out of our associated companies and all our lives.

"I said I have to stay around for a few days to settle the details with you and Ping Kin but that Macau would be gone. He was clearly pleased but to my relief asked no questions. Ron is sensitive and perceptive. I sense he knows far more than he is saying but trusts me to deal with it."

Totally genuine for once, Ah-Cy just sighed deeply, being unable in her defensive loneliness to admit she envied Maisie's close relationship with Ron. She nodded acceptingly.

THE elders at the venerable Huang's penthouse sipped their rich Ningxia Red and agreed the vines and expertise stolen from France had immeasurably improved the vintage.

They drank carefully from their antique ceramic chalices, while each was being attentively served sweet and savoury canapés by his individual, seductively revealed beauty that Huang always provided to lighten their formal agendas.

In awe his colleagues inspected the priceless collection of porcelain Huang had acquired. He explained, "I was originally interested in the skilful middle periods but lately I am moving to the older Great Yuan Dynasty. This is a modest reward for my lifetime of service to the motherland."

When they had settled down, Huang admitted that he and the family were seriously concerned by the earlier report that his son-in-law, a senior establishment member, caused embarrassment in Canada.

"I concurred with the proposals he must be stripped of all his positions including business appointments. In view of his long service, especially in economic planning, I hope that a lenient punishment might be recommended but you must do what is right."

He signalled for the long-legged female sommelier to recharge their drinks adding, almost as an aside, "I am confident I will soon know the whereabouts of many hundreds of millions of dollars Zhang has hoarded overseas by our next meeting."

Chapter 52

Celebrity: Brings exposure

MAISIE had been back in Vancouver for only a few months when Wong disappeared. Ping Kin confirmed he had not been seen in Hong Kong at the nightclub nor so far as he knew in China and it was also a total mystery on that side of the Pacific.

A few days after Wong went missing Maisie, once again the company confidante had another unexpected quietly sobbing woman approach her for help, this time openly in the office. She was a mature accountant, a very beautiful, blonde and tall person, with innocent, tear-filled gorgeous big blue eyes.

The tale she had to tell about Wong was shocking. "Mr Wong was always coming on to me at the office and then he started sexually abusing me, I was frightened and he made these videos which I found in his desk. I want to sue his company," she said crying hysterically. "You will keep me safe if he comes back, won't you?"

This time it did not involve Leyland. Maisie therefore could formally contact Sergeant Singh to get the poor shivering girl protection. He offered immunity from charges in exchange for the damning business information she had amassed, although mainly concerning activities at The Warehouse.

Pritam just could not believe his lucky break but he faced severe competition from his fellow officers, male and female, who all had valid reasons to interview the woman. She willingly complied and several of them found her a very satisfying witness and made a new friend.

PRITAM caught up to Ronnie on the sidewalk as he was heading to The Club for lunch. He was back to wearing nondescript jeans with a tee shirt and would have blended in except for his jaunty fluorescent pink turban.

"I am now fully in charge of investigating your brother-in-law's disappearance. I have concluded it indeed involves foul play by your Black Renminbians.

"The eminent lawyer Mr Stumpenberg QC is aghast at his disappearance. Wong's alleged criminal activities leave him amazed. Just amazed! He has, of course, offered his entire cooperation in police investigations."

"Stump?" asked Ron sarcastically. "You are surely not suggesting a well-known lawyer might be involved in Wong vanishing?"

"Absolutely not, "replied the sleuth indignantly, "but we had to check him out. We knew from detective work he had met the man as have many business people. But he assured us no connection with him personally appears in any of his records.

"He was very helpful and confidentially allowing me to look through a list of his clients. Wong has never been one and neither incidentally has his son Ivan Wong whom we also questioned. I was looking for you. Ron, to warn you will be pulled in again for formal questioning. We have Mr Wong's electronic devices but they are proving difficult to open so we need your help with his access passwords.

"I am sorry, Ron, but they are on to you and connect you with the whole Black Renminbian gang. I will help you all I can but you must cooperate! How many times do I have to warn you?"

Ron shook his head. "I would love to invite you into The Club for a drink, except you are wearing jeans. Dress code, you know." He bounded up to The Club entrance, trying to appear composed.

He received his traditional, "Good morning Mr Leyland," from the ever-welcoming greeter who knew all the members personally. He left his unidentified companion standing conspicuously alone at the bottom of the crafted stone steps, disconcertingly with very steady eyes, a confident smile and no trace of his nervous head wag.

JOHNNIE Leyland was working part-time in Logger's executive office. He had done well in Commerce and was deciding whether to do a Masters or take Law. Either would work for him to go into one of the family businesses eventually.

He had of course heard about the strange disappearance of his Uncle Wong and called his cousin Sasha in New York to get the scoop.

While they had been at high school the cousins had all been great pals, skiing regularly and partying together, and his sister remained close to Sasha who was finishing her music scholarship at The Juilliard.

She could add nothing. "I hate my father and I am estranged from them all, including my mother, the Botox queen! Last time I was back I came across her and her masseur who is our age for Chrissake, hard at it outside on the patio. She just waved her hand to send me away and carried on.

"Did you hear the scam she has going to pay for her service from him?" She related Olga's whole sorry jeweller money-laundering scam to him, and they ended laughing together at her weird parents.

"Anyway," she closed, "I have a boyfriend here in New York you've got to meet and my music career has taken off, so I will not be back to live. They can screw up their lives as much as they want."

They had all regretfully broken off their relationship with Ivan when his lifestyle became embarrassing so Johnnie was surprised when his mother asked that he contact him.

"I can't get involved personally but something is going down and Ivan must be warned. I have spoken to a contact in the RCMP and Ivan can avoid being charged if he comes forward now with evidence. We have to prevent any family connections if we can."

Ivan too was surprised when his cousin arranged a pub lunch but just laughed at the suggestion he could be in any trouble. "I agreed a lot of undercover things go on in my world but people at my management level are totally insulated from liability. I am very well protected by my own top-level personal lawyer who has all the necessary establishment connections.

"Actually, I have just been promoted to a senior position involving all the country. When did you last hear of a white-collar public personality being busted in Canada?

"All you can afford is a couple of beers and a hamburger at this grubby campus pub while I personally own two of the best restaurants in town, just on the side. Have you seen how I live? Do you think I'm crazy enough to just give all that up?

"Don't worry, Johnnie, nothing can happen to me now!"

MAISIE was nowhere as complacent having found herself reluctantly thrown into the limelight. She had become more and more disenchanted with her money-oriented political friends and had channelled increasing family trust funds towards international and local Canadian human rights activist groups, with Logger's wholehearted support. She was speaking up publically against denial of civil rights, especially in China and Hong Kong.

Her activist approach had been discovered by the Canadian press warranting a small but high profile front-page story. This attracted extensive and expanding social media attention, particularly fascinated by her beauty and social status.

Where they obtained the highly personal and revealing pictures was a mystery but when they were published she had suddenly become a hunted celebrity.

She was identified as a key supporter of Canadian nationals being harassed in the country by overseas agencies attempting to stifle their opinions and threatening retribution in their home countries for non-compliance. Finally the RCMP and CSIS were going public on the subject, naturally when they felt opinion was in their favour!

She knew that, in the case of China it was all an international policy aimed at preventing any form of the dissent anywhere and suspected that her friend, the ardent communist apologist Ah-Cy, with her many Canadian connections, had to be involved. She, of course, actually had no idea how right she was!

"HOW could they get such crystal-clear close-up shots of me to publish, sunning and dancing around our pool in Barbados? Our lodge is so far away and so secluded," she puzzled at a family dinner.

"How did anyone know we had a place there, anyway?" asked Ron."We keep our off-shore dealings pretty quiet."

"Pity we only saw the pictures they could publish," sighed Ron's sister suggestively to her girlfriend. "We all do stuff au natural around your pool there. Good thing no one seems interested in pictures of Ron's bum as well," she giggled, to general laughter.

Ron responded defensively, "Well anyway, it has definitely improved real estate sales. We may need to release more private shots of all of you to keep up the excitement!'

"Tut, tut," murmured his mother Jeanne, mildly of course and as always quietly from the background, just shaking her head in disapproval but secure in her status of teaching philosophy at the university. "You are intent upon changing the world, all on your own!"

"*Une pour tous, tous pour une!*" she suddenly exclaimed, jumping up and coming out of her shell. She liked to demonstrate her origins in Outremont, coming from another part of the Canadian mosaic involving degrees at McGill and her doctorate at La Sorbonne.

Maisie and Ron's sister leaped to join her in their joint family salute, holding up their hands together and showing off their matching Princess Diana blue sapphire rings.

"A unity gift to my ladies," Logger had said. He just sat beaming with pleasure.

He rounded out the amicable discussion by suggesting, "This

sensational nonsense is unfortunately all more salacious and attention grabbing than other people's seriously violated human rights. But it won't keep their attention very long."

This was partly right but then the media had discovered that the highly publicised missing Wong Mai Fu was Maisie's brother it started a renewed media frenzy.

AH-CY'S 'little bastard' security officer in their Vancouver Consulate was gleefully fast off the mark reporting directed to her 'personally and very confidentially' on the whole story, delighted that his suspicions had been confirmed. Complete with the glossy frontal enlargements of course.

It was now clear to him, "Mr Zhang and Ms Leyland must have been up to something very suspicious in that hotel room. I request your approval of further investigation." She decided he had become a loose cannon and arranged for him to be immediately promoted to Beijing where she could keep an eye him.

Maisie's anti-China political views were now public knowledge in Canada and had to be recorded in Ah-Cy's department's official reports. Ah-Cy sighed that she could forget about mentally calling her *Mai Xi* any longer but she was acutely aware they each now depended for their future wellbeing upon mutual trust and silence.

She held the greater leverage if needed and thought ominously that at least that mouthy daughter was still in Hong Kong, within easy reach.

Now being a senior in State Security, she had her own powerful connections and obviously could have fixed the Zhang problem herself but she had painstakingly planned with Ping Kin that the only possible evidence from the Macau money led back to her father. She had no personal risk of exposure whatsoever.

That is why she had involved the venerable Huang at all.

The more immediately worry, thanks to the 'little bastard', was that their security system was drawing links between Zhang, Maisie's business relationship with him, the disappeared criminal Wong and herself. She was being asked passing questions but there was as yet no direct connection to her.

She mused with a wry smile whether she had over-reacted to Maisie's futile intimate gesture with Zhang which was unintentionally succeeding through her intervention. Had her Macau plan become too dangerous to continue? Perhaps she should abort it.

Chapter 53

Proverb: *'Salvation follows the Renminbi'*

IT WAS shaping up as just another day in the Macau office for Ping Kin when the doors burst open. Without notice their entire operation was taken over by a swarm of earnest professionals in business attire. They offered no resistance considering the intruders were backed by armed security officers.

He was simply told it was an audit. No one would be able to leave the premises until it was completed when they would be dismissed. Ping Kin was courteously handed the authorisation which required him to provide access to all computer passwords, which he did, only as necessary for an audit.

It was a long day with meals brought in. Finally, in the early evening the deadly serious manager of the audit team advised their work was complete, assembled the entire staff to thank them for their cooperation, and marched out as uniformly as they had arrived.

The security group however told Ping Kin to remain, having produced instructions for him to accompany them to a further meeting. When they took him to a rooftop suite at one of the luxury casino hotels, he was not entirely surprised to see Mr Zhang sitting awaiting him.Pointedly he left him standing.

"I had business in Hong Kong which I decided to follow up with a little fun gambling in Macau. Are you a gambler?" he asked, a little too sharply for Ping Kin's liking.

"While I was here I decided on a spot audit which gives us a reason to chat. As you know the exhaustive examination could only reveal that all funds are in place, confirming everything is well, as always."

Swirling his brandy thoughtfully he continued, "So the audit is clean but I have a strange feeling something is going on. As a fellow financier I recognise we can be the best financial fraudsters, so I worry.

"I was told much of your recent computer activity has concentrated somewhere in Canada. Why? I am guessing it involves the beautiful *Mai Xi*, with whom I have to admit I am a little obsessed. But you are gay.

"I assume you know about the immature action she tried on to influence me? If she had asked her good friend my wife, she would have known we long ago gave up on personal fidelity. So her physical posturing was futile, although I do admire her civilised tactics.

"The two of you have certainly given me a problem. But the financial affairs are in order and you have always previously presented yourself honourably."

After thinking for a couple of minutes he waved his snifter dismissively and said that he was free to go.

Ping Kin bowed submissively and departed quietly, sardonically nodding to the silent thugs by the door. He nonchalantly strolled out, his heart thumping. How much did the unreadable Zhang know of their plans and what did 'free to go' mean?

SO OFTEN alone in his difficult decisions, Zhang silently finished his brandy. Poon knew way too much. No one can be trusted in this world requiring he should be silenced. All it would take would be a nod to his security officers.

On the other hand, he mused, he did instinctively like the stylish fellow who would probably just happily disappear off into his gay world. Surely the disappearance of the woman's brother was warning enough?

Then a darker mood took him. His thoughts moved to the image of *Mai Xi* posing in defiance of him and his failure to take her. His warped mind jumped back to the memory of his first nightclub meeting with Poon, applauding the spread-eagled stripper, who in his feverish imagination now became the turncoat *Mai Xi*, grovelling in submission at his feet.

He would enjoy *Mai Xi* later but Poon, who was also a turncoat, had to be dealt with immediately. He made his decision.

He signalled to Lo, standing quietly by the door. He barked that Poon must be silenced; he knew far too much. He ordered Lo to look after it.

WHEN he slunk away from the casino penthouse, Ping Kin decided the time had come to flee. He must take his chances but he knew that he must act normally. Everything was in place to put Ms Huang's plan into operation and she was fully informed. But Zhang still appeared very much in command and he was losing his nerve.

He booked a regular business trip the next day to New York, where much of their legitimate business took place, then nervously waited for something to happen.

In the morning he set off just pulling his expected carry-on and briefcase, like all the travellers around him, headed into the business class lounge. He tensed when he saw Zhang's well-suited goon Lo approaching with his usual support. He knew running was pointless.

Lo stretched a tired smile and advised politely, "I was instructed from Beijing to watch over you the last few days to ensure your safety. We will wait until you have boarded and departed."

His companion fetched them coffee which they sat calmly sipping without uttering a word until his flight was called. They both nodded civilly as he boarded and left him sweating in relief.

Ping Kin had purposely selected a foreign carrier but only when it was heading out of Chinese airspace did he sigh in relief and reach gratefully for the complimentary champagne.

Reluctantly, he watched his motherland's coastline finally fade away in the haze for the very last time. He raised his glass in a sad salute.

LO, self-assured as ever, had returned downtown to find that Zhang had already been picked up by State Security as Ms Huang had advised would happen and quietly spirited the few miles over the border into nearby Guangdong.

He received her instructions, as his new boss, to return immediately to her personally in Beijing. He knew well what that entailed and wondered what physical contortions of stamina she would demand of him this time, flexing his impressive but ageing muscles in anticipation.

He knew that he was getting a bit old for all this physical nonsense and she was considering his suggestion that he become an occasional personal consultant to her, on semi-retirement.

He had proposed an ambitious, impressively endowed young guard in her security attachment whom he knew she already had her eye on to replace him. As instruction, he had reserved him for a tryout with them this session.

A wry smile softened his usually hard face, as he realised he was loudly humming a stirring revolutionary marching song.

Chapter 54

Denouement: Just deserts?

'URGENT you come to meet in Barbados," was the brief message Ping Kin left them a few afternoons later. If Ron and Maisie were indeed suspected in Wong's disappearance no one had informed the airport security since their usual flight out of Canada and through New York was without incident, with Nexus security uncaring.

They had bought their waterfront vacation villa on the Barbados south coast many years previously and Ping Kin used it on visits and to moor his large yacht, which they borrowed. He was once again their guest as they enjoyed a late afternoon drink on their extensive patio. Leone would join them later.

To entertain their guests, Maisie had selected a reasonably modest, but flowing and diaphanous Elie Saab poolside blue creation, which she snapped up at a fashion show in Milan earlier that year because it set off her Princess Diana sapphire ring so well. She quickly poured their rum, being anxious to hear what Ping Kin had to say.

"After we met in Hong Kong with Ms Huang, I set up a highly encrypted and temporary personal contact with her, which we have now totally destroyed. That was to arrange the ownership switch at the bank, outing Zhang and benefitting the hidden Huang family through her father.

"But before anything was committed, Zhang turned up in Macau for an unannounced audit and in a threatening mood. I panicked and fled. When I arrived in New York, however, I got a reassuring message from Ms Huang that Zhang had already been arrested in Macau and instructing me to complete all the transactions online.

"I had it all set up and passed full control of their funds over to the new manager we had selected. Her last message to me before we self-destructed was to pass on her thanks to you, Maisie, to say she would be in touch as soon as prudent and specifically, *Ganbei*. She said you would know what that meant. So here I am."

"What a story," Ron gulped. "What happens now?"

Ping Kin smiled. "Well, I have left China irrevocably! Zhang has of course lost all his positions in state companies, so he is no longer involved in any of your business arrangements with China. He is gone from the scene.

Maisie knows well how to access her private funds which are just sitting around in secure US currency. You have no overseas income to declare, nothing traceable to you, so what to do about revealing it in the future is all up to your consciences."

She had a self-righteous grin on her face. "We researched our complicated Canadian situation with our lawyer George Oikawa. It took a little time but George has found a way, with Leone's help, to set it up as an international charitable offshore trust we will control but not profit from personally.

"We are going to launch a crusade you wouldn't believe, to protect and promote human rights around the world!"

"With regard offshore funds generally," Ron added, "it is inevitable there will be a declared amnesty to bring home the billions upon billions presently hidden by citizens overseas. An amnesty only makes sense, with the government rake-off in penalties proving irresistible. As usual money will win the day.

We already report all our considerable financial affairs in Canada plus regular stuff overseas, so we seem to be in the clear on all that."

"We are still worried about the money-laundering situation," Maisie sternly accused Ping Kin, "because we mostly haven't a clue where all your Chinese Renminbi came from over the years or how it was earned.

"Of course, neither do all the Canadian authorities but they seem to be getting more serious. Fortunately they know bugger all about the subject either. They are just learning."

Ron added, "But, in our case they have got Wong's and perhaps our historic electronic records. Sooner or later they will find a way to access them making life difficult for us."

"I have that all covered too, as part of the arrangements with Ms Huang," reported the super-relaxed computer technician, Ping Kin. "Just let's enjoy this beautiful early sunset. Maisie, how about making us another rum punch?"

LEONE joined them at sundown, exclaiming, "Well, I'm ready to go."

"What's the plan?" Maisie asked.

"We wouldn't exactly say we have a plan. Neither of us feels any obligation to our restricting countries and we will not again reside in a tax-paying territory. Just maintain medical plans in Florida, of course, and sail around!

"We have enormous wealth between us and can buy everything we need. That is the ultimate freedom. We will essentially just disappear together. The yacht is packed and we will just sail away!"

Stirring the jug of punch, Maisie agreed, "It sounds tempting but philosophically we had always been basically in different camps. We got involved together but now our ways are parting. Canada is slowly learning how to defend itself in this generally lawless, thieving world.

"Our family is voting for the Canadian way of life and values; whatever they are precisely."

PRITAM wagged his head in disbelief. Amazed, he had heard his tech guys cheering and quickly learned they had unexpectedly broken into

Wong's computer records and remarkably found all the evidence they had hoped for neatly set out for them.

But now he stared blinking in amazement at his own screen where blanks had replaced a lot of his information. He knew immediately they appeared to have been wiped, although he had been told their system was uncrackable.

Many of his previous records of the Leyland case were gone. He scrambled in panic to search through his backup but found it also decimated. Most financial records covertly taken from Ron's company records concerning the Macau set-up over the years had totally disappeared.

None of their other Mountie case records had been compromised nor tampered with but there was no evidence Leyland or the family members had been involved in any activity they were investigating. Indeed, they were not implicated at all.

Pritam saw this was a curious but a definite turn-up for his friends. Even their surveillance tapes were not backed up by facial recognition data.

"Report!" he barked at their staff meeting sounding a little anxious.

The usually pushy, guardedly insubordinate, female corporal in his team spoke up in awe.

"Wong's records are a treasure trove, Sarge. They don't solve his disappearance but they set out in detail all the crooked dealings he and Zhang have been involved in since they came to Canada.

"They identify all the related parties, internationally and in China. Particularly, they reveal their base in Guangdong and how their financial and legal dealings are conducted.

"You were right first time, sir. They are indeed Black Renminbians!"

Excitedly Pritam emailed his mentor, now Assistant Commissioner Jackman. "I request an immediate personal meeting with you, honoured sir. We have finally got your bastards!"

He informed his team, rather formally, that he would ensure that they received commendations for their excellent work. So that afternoon, confused but pleased, they quit early for the day to celebrate, adjourning to their local bar, publically and noisily planning their long-denied raid on The Warehouse and nightclubs.

ON RECEIVING his personal report and analysing the clear evidence, the Assistant Commissioner immediately promoted Pritam to Inspector, with an appointment to his personal staff in Ottawa.

He would later be summoned to Rideau Hall to have a medal pinned on his proud chest by the Governor General, a real decoration with a ribbon and a gong, to display on his red serge dress uniform. He was supported by his beaming wife and their now seven proud young Canadians.

Chapter 55

Choice: Honey-Do

RON'S mother Jeanne, obviously the philosopher in the family, maintained that like it or not, they all had a greater power to which they answered. "Maybe," Maisie joked with her, "but at least some of us have a choice."

"Not Ronnie," Maisie laughed. "My Honey-Do lists I prepare regularly for him have all those characteristics because they come from a decidedly greater power but he can choose whether to comply; well at least in theory!

Seriously though, too many folk in this world are controlled by dictatorial powers and do not have that choice of decision or even of holding an opinion."

"Ah," observed the observant Jeanne, "you are worried about your friend Ah-Cy in China. I think you have both come up against an impossible Gordian knot."

EARLY in the winter of 2019 Maisie got an unexpected local call from Ah-Cy who explained she was passing through and asked to meet at their usual margarita bar.

They embraced fondly and Ah-Cy indicated her new handsome young protector sitting at a separate table with a suggestive wiggle of her eyebrows. She explained her long-term relationship with Lo and the recent introduction to train his replacement. Her hilarious graphic account set them both giggling uncontrollably.

Maisie related the meetings with Ping Kin and Ron in Barbados confirming that her message had been delivered. "Thanks for staying committed and making all that happen. The two fellows were like kids, setting out on their yacht for a new life together.

"Ron and I waved goodbye from our dock until their sail disappeared into the haze of the sun."

Ah-Cy pulled a long face and said, "My seaside jaunt was much less fun, completing the Zhang money transfer to my father."

She explained, "I met the old boys or at least their survivors recently at the seaside town of Beidaihe, near Beijing. We hold family events there for visiting senior political friends. It brings the country's top Party echelon together for highly confidential but personally stressful vacations. My Dad has always been a celebrity there.

"The Six are actually down to The Three and we invited them to my father's beachfront lodge to sip the horrible Baijiu liquor which he favours.

"He announced with a chuckle that a deal had been made regarding Zhang whereby he had disclosed and handed over sufficient of his own holdings to allow him to leave the country, never to return.

"He said Zhang is already living comfortably in a Toronto Rosedale mansion with a new identity having taken advantage of the still existing easy Quebec immigrant investor programme. My old Dad found it amusing that it had only cost him around a million for a quite legal, pay-off to Quebec to get rid of him.

He does not even have to live in that province as he promised. He will have to learn more English but he is no doubt already back in business and is reportedly enjoying your missing brother Wong's wife.

With no extradition, he is now Canada's problem so China will never see him again. And neither will I. Dad patted me on the knee, confirming that he had also secured my divorce, suggesting lewdly that I was free to enjoy my leisure activities. Which believe me, I am!"

She rolled her eyes in the direction of her much younger companion, who was looking away and studiously not paying attention to their hilarity.

When they had calmed down, she continued, "He then mentioned that I had taken on senior political duties but that I would also confidentially assume my previous husband's role managing the investments of The Six. So now they were back to Four, he told them cheerfully.

"They obediently assembled for a meeting in a back room, still astonished at having a female chair. I told them that their funds had been fully audited, that Dr Poon had valid personal reasons to disappear and they accepted my opinion they could let him go.

"I told them all past records are being erased and the process has begun to finally divide up and dissolve the partnership. My colleagues of course nodded thankfully in agreement, just quietly sipping their obviously much-needed Bourbon. I then put on a Zhang-like serious face and said gruffly, '*Prod her enough and any dragon will rise up on her tail!*' You should have seen their faces!

"So it's all done."

THEY relaxed, happy together and savouring the moment they knew could not last.

Ah-Cy joked, "My seaside holidays are obviously totally dull compared to yours judging by the glamorous pictures I have seen of you cavorting in Barbados."

"Oh no!" Maisie exclaimed. "How did you see those so far away in Beijing?"

She had the good grace to blush, causing Ah-Cy to giggle even more at her discomfort and ask, without thinking, "How could you allow that? I would die if anyone saw frontal nude pictures of me like that. Mind you, we would never allow them to be published and the reporters would have been sent straight to lockup for a long time!"

She saw Maisie frown and hastily changed the subject. "I would love to stay longer but I have been recalled to Wuhan to help deal with a containment problem connected with a new strange viral outbreak. It sounds alarmingly like SARS."

"I never took you for much of a medical scientist," Maisie laughed.

"No, silly," she replied, "my specialty is public relations containment for the Party."

Seeing Maisie's change of expression she immediately wished she could take that back, realising that she had just made things worse.

They sat in silence for a few minutes and Maisie said, "This is not going to work, is it?"

They managed to go on with a strained conversation recalling the good times they had together but the discussion moved to a serious level when Maisie raised her many concerns at China's terrible human rights record and their apparent political incursions into Canada.

"Are you part of the '*Fox Hunt*' " she asked directly and Ah-Cy nodded numbly. "We believe in loyalty to our motherland."

For the first time, in a moment of honesty and in a strange way to expiate the guilt she felt for her personal deception, Ah-Cy tried to justify the various programs in which she had been involved in Canada. They sadly agreed that this all provided an impossible obstacle to their continued friendship.

Suddenly angry and accusatorial Maisie snapped, "When are you going to free our Michaels that you kidnapped almost a year ago? And come to that, all the other lost souls oppressed in your dreadful communist system. I have been trying desperately to think of you personally as different but now I have to admit to myself that you are just one of them." Ah-Cy saw the tears brimming in her eyes and started to respond but just ended with a sigh.

They sat in silence again while a fresh round of margaritas was delivered. Then Ah-Cy said decisively, "You have your system of government and I have mine. What choice do we have?"

Maisie raised her glass and suggested wistfully, "Perhaps one day? Anyway, Cheers!"

Ah-Cy replied, with a final sad flash of her brilliant white teeth, "Yes, let's keep up hope. Perhaps one day. Ganbei!"

She chugged her cocktail and emotionally gripped Maisie's hand one final time.

Then she got quickly to her feet and left the restaurant with just one brief, eye catching backward glance. Her tall young attendant nodded in salute to Maisie across the room and followed swiftly.

MAISIE later enjoyed a cosy dinner with Ron in their enclosed winter patio overlooking the sea. The trees were already bare and the incessant rain had started drumming on the glass roof. Their drinks matched the mood of the English Bay outside; Dark and Stormy.

Maisie was snuggled up to Ron, warm and comfortable in her fluffy pink Lululemon lounging outfit. "Will we be having Ah-Cy over for dinner?" Ron asked.

Maisie shook her head. "She has to rush back to China. Some minor viral outbreak problem in Wuhan. But I don't think anyway she'll be dropping in again soon." Ron looked at her quizzically but refrained from commenting.

WHEN they dozed off in their big comfortable bed, Ron put an assuring arm around Maisie as always. Ever since their wonderful first lobster thermidor night together, so long ago in Macau, they had never again seen the point of nightclothes, continuing each night in a warm intimate embrace.

It was also her daily opportunity to review her Honey-Do list while he had no escape.

Sleepily he reported that, as she had instructed, he had met with their lawyers and accountants to comply with the new beneficial ownership disclosure laws imposed as part of the search for laundered money.

"Well, will they find any Black Renminbians?" she chuckled, poking him.

Trying to sleep, he muttered, "Owners are now politely asked to register their names. They won't enquire how they made their money. Honest Canadians will comply. Must weed out the bad guys together. Yesterday's Black Renminbi long gone. Let's get it right next time."

Then silence.

Not giving up, she chatted on, "You guys just shrug off what goes on in China but you will react differently one day when they start enforcing how you must think. You need allies to defeat a bully."

"Whatever," murmured Ron in her ear, "but there are lots of trading partners out there other than China and we do value our complicated freedom, *'Democracy is the worst form of government except for all the others'*."

"That's not a Chinese proverb, silly, it's your old Churchill chestnut," she laughed. "He also said, *'Muddling through is simply a sign of our skill at dealing with the inevitable'*, which is really what is happening."

Such thoughtful stuff," she murmured, snuggling purposefully closer. "Good thing we have distractions."

Later as they drifted off to sleep she heard him breathe, "I love you Maisie."

THE sun was sparkling on the sea at Phuket, the notorious seaside resort, infamous for its internationally popular, if ultra-sleazy, entertainment. The gate to an exclusive beachside villa burst open to release the excitedly barking Wanchow, heading for his daily swim in the warm, turquoise ocean.

Notes

FIRST and foremost I would like to thank our friend Kevin McDonald, the veteran Australian Editor who volunteered to undertake the Production Editing of the book during their Covid isolation in Noosa. He kindly stepped in to review and edit the manuscript and put it into shape for publication. I have worked before with Kevin on a much more complicated rugby book and appreciate his perseverance and skills.

This is all obviously intended as a cynical and symbolic tongue in cheek, dig at Canada's perceived naivety in dealing with the nasty world around us, apparently allowing the bad guys to win. Unfortunately its conclusion seems to be that self interest will always prevail over theoretical principles.

It is absolutely not based upon real people or any actual individual or experienced situations and is solely from my imagination, although obviously related to international history and similar events that undoubtedly happened.

The research filled many hours of the virus-lost 2020 in West Vancouver and the book became a fun venture. It started quite seriously out of frustration at continuing government bleats at all levels and their ineffectual Inquiries. These proved to be based upon opinion, providing few hard facts and with no teeth; then being followed by lack of action because no one is really concerned enough to get to grips, starting at the top, with the complicated subject.

The recently written material and journalism on the featured subjects, display a great deal of increasing concern. They encourage action, are far reaching and ever expanding.

This book owes its existence to research of the subject by those who have influenced and continue to educate us : Jonathan Manthorpe, Tsur Somerville, Ian Mulgrew, Frank Ching, Jonny Wakefield, Ian Young, Richard Zussman, Gordon Hoekstra, Francis Schwartzkopff, Douglas Todd, Arthur Cockfield, Jason Kirby, Keith Fraser, Tiffany Crawford, Alexandra Posadzki, Matthew Campbell, Natalie Pearson, Michael Forsythe, Jason Lee, Jane Cai, Paul Mozur, Rita Trichur, Nathan VanderKlippe, Steven Chase and

Robert Fife, to name just a few earlier writers, as journalistic interest widens. Thank you all.

They would discern the labours of their work in these pages if they should happen to read them and hopefully appreciate an indirect attempt to further promote their convincing conclusions. I have however worked on the basis that nowadays 'news' is news ....once it has been reviewed a half a dozen times more, even if you are going to believe it as background to a novel which is all made up and fiction anyway.

My encouraging wife Lane has been a much appreciated sounding board and captive critic/proof reader during virus seclusion. Our son, Bob offered his thoughtful criticism and help in many ways as always. I cannot speak for the opinions various characters have in the novel but only I am responsible for any social or political conclusions that may be drawn.

The striking cover design was started by Alexa Love and completed by Jaz Welch; such wonderful names and talented personalities.

Chris Labonte dutifully waded through the manuscript several times suggesting structural changes which resulted in many re-writes and a much more readable novel.

Canadians just want to be loved and I have tried to illustrate how unprepared Canada is to deal with the real world from my own observation. Canada has several rocky, evolving relationships to guard against, especially with the currently seriously intruding and aggressive communist China.

The vast majority of people in the non-democratic nations live daily under extensive corruption with no rule of law as protection but we expect them to deal with us here in Canada in our mostly open and enlightened, trusting terms.

Adding to everyone's problem is Canada's general confusion on money laundering itself and many social subjects, due to easy over-acceptance, prejudices, misinformation, fake news, political expediency, social media and out of control technology. Sorry; as we say far too automatically!

You may get the correct impression from the book that I am not a fan of communism but I must admit to a growing concern with problems in our own democratic/capitalist system which I've also tried to illustrate. This actually started out as a serious work but as the ludicrousness of the situation emerged it became apparent it had to be a farce.

It turned out, hopefully as an easy read, getting across a technical message with humour and with a rather unlikely, lightly intimate side suggesting symbolically of course, that life is not all about money.

John D'Eathe, West Vancouver, 2021

Manufactured by Amazon.ca
Bolton, ON

27246190R00175